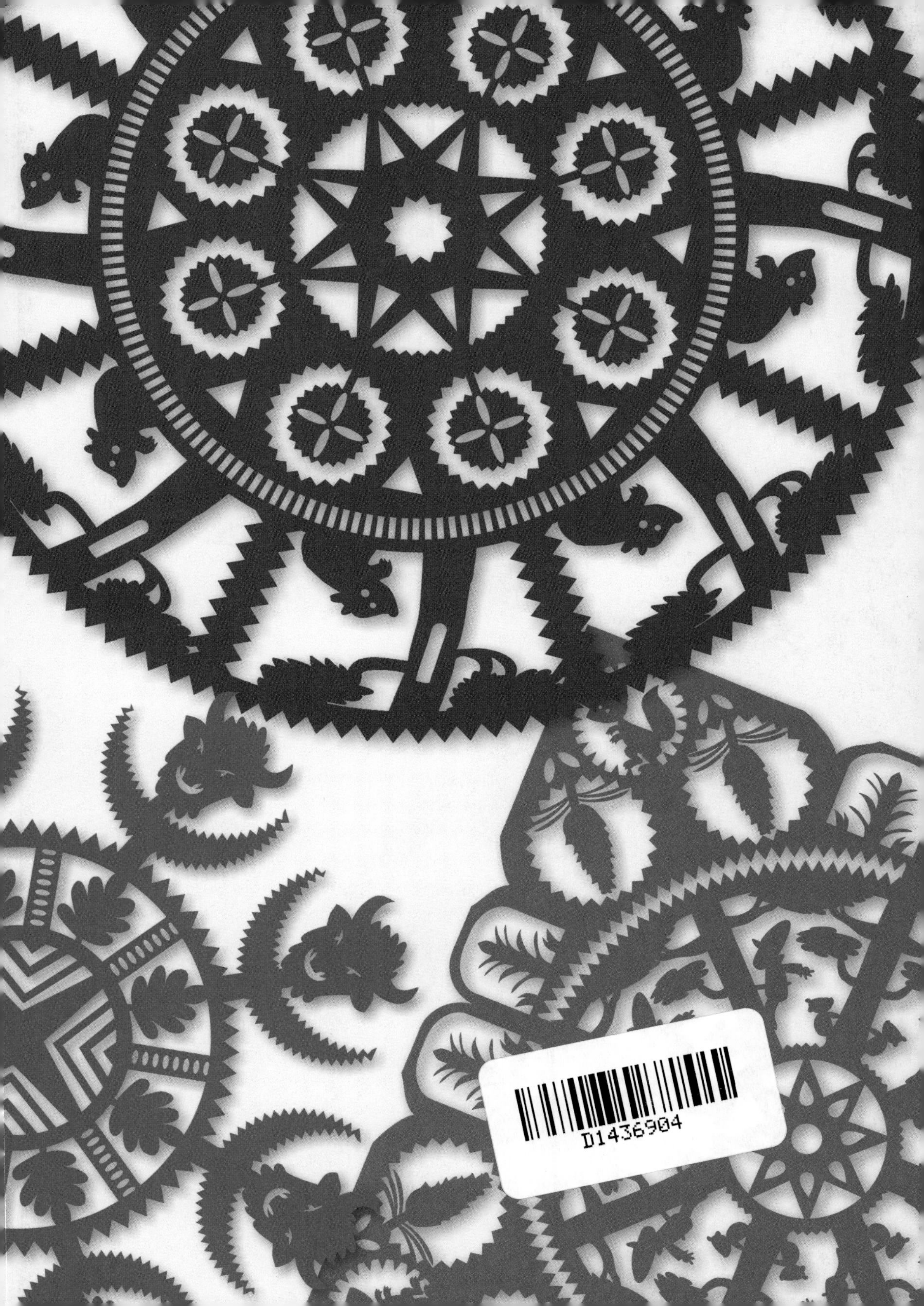

Tomasz Samojlik

Forest beekeeper
and the
treasure of pushcha

London 2014

centrala
Central Europe Comics Art

Forest beekeeper and the treasure of pushcha

First published in Great Britain 2014
by Centrala Ltd.
27B Khama Road
London SW17 OEN
www.centrala.org.uk

Written and Illustrated by Tomasz Samojlik

Editorial and Publishing Director: Michał Słomka

Forest beekeeper and the treasure of pushcha was originally published in Poland as Bartnik Ignat i skarb puszczy by CENTRALA - mądre komiksy, Fredry 7/3, 61-701 Poznań, in 2013.

A CIP record for this book is available from the British Library

Printed and bound in Poland

Order from www.centrala.org.uk

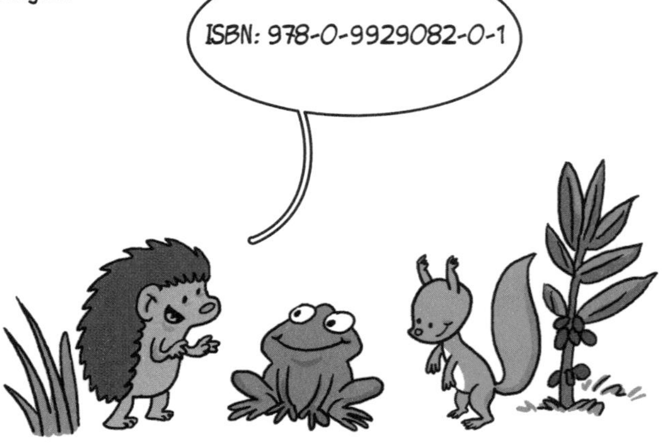
ISBN: 978-0-9929082-0-1

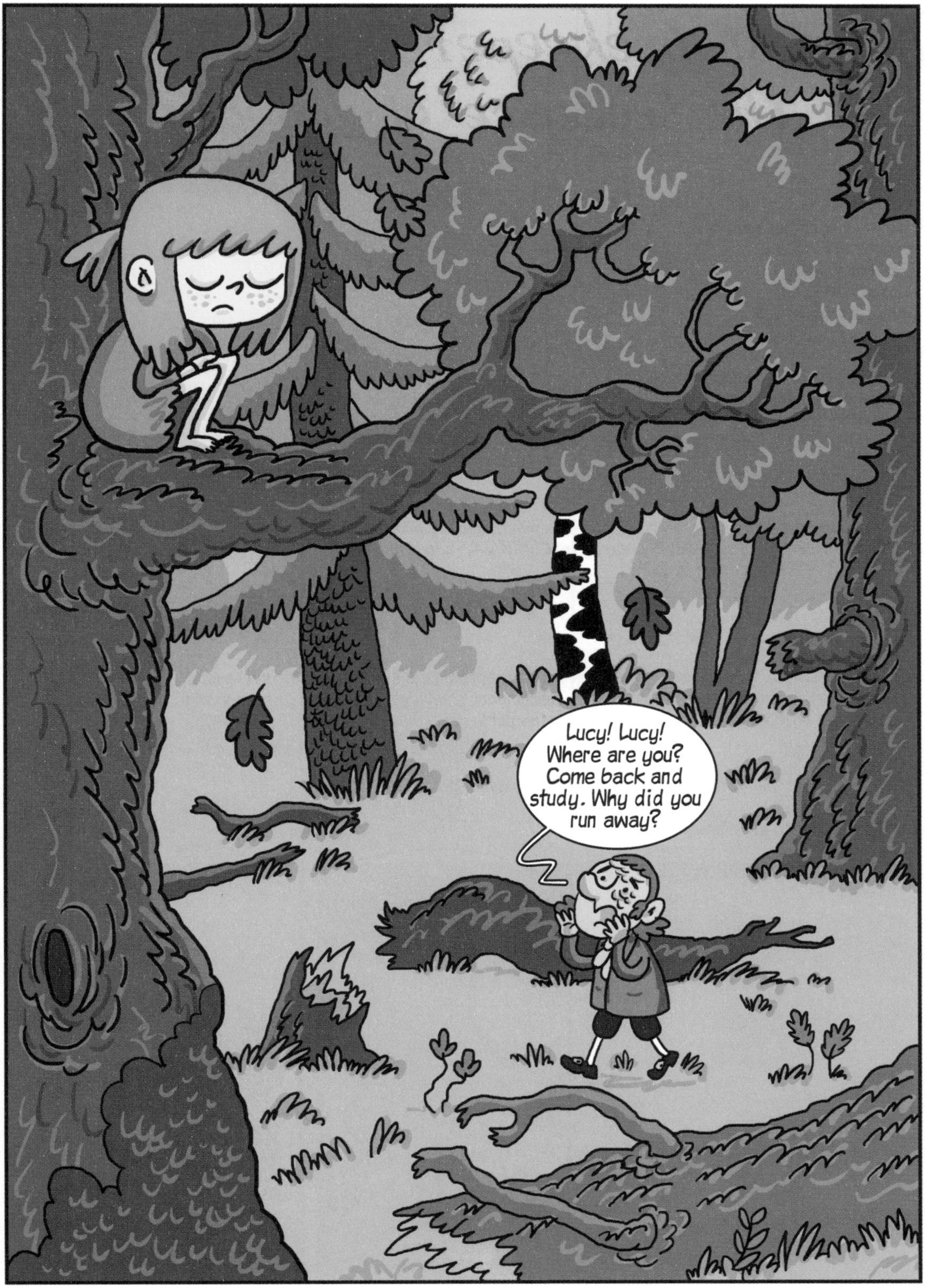
Lucy! Lucy! Where are you? Come back and study. Why did you run away?

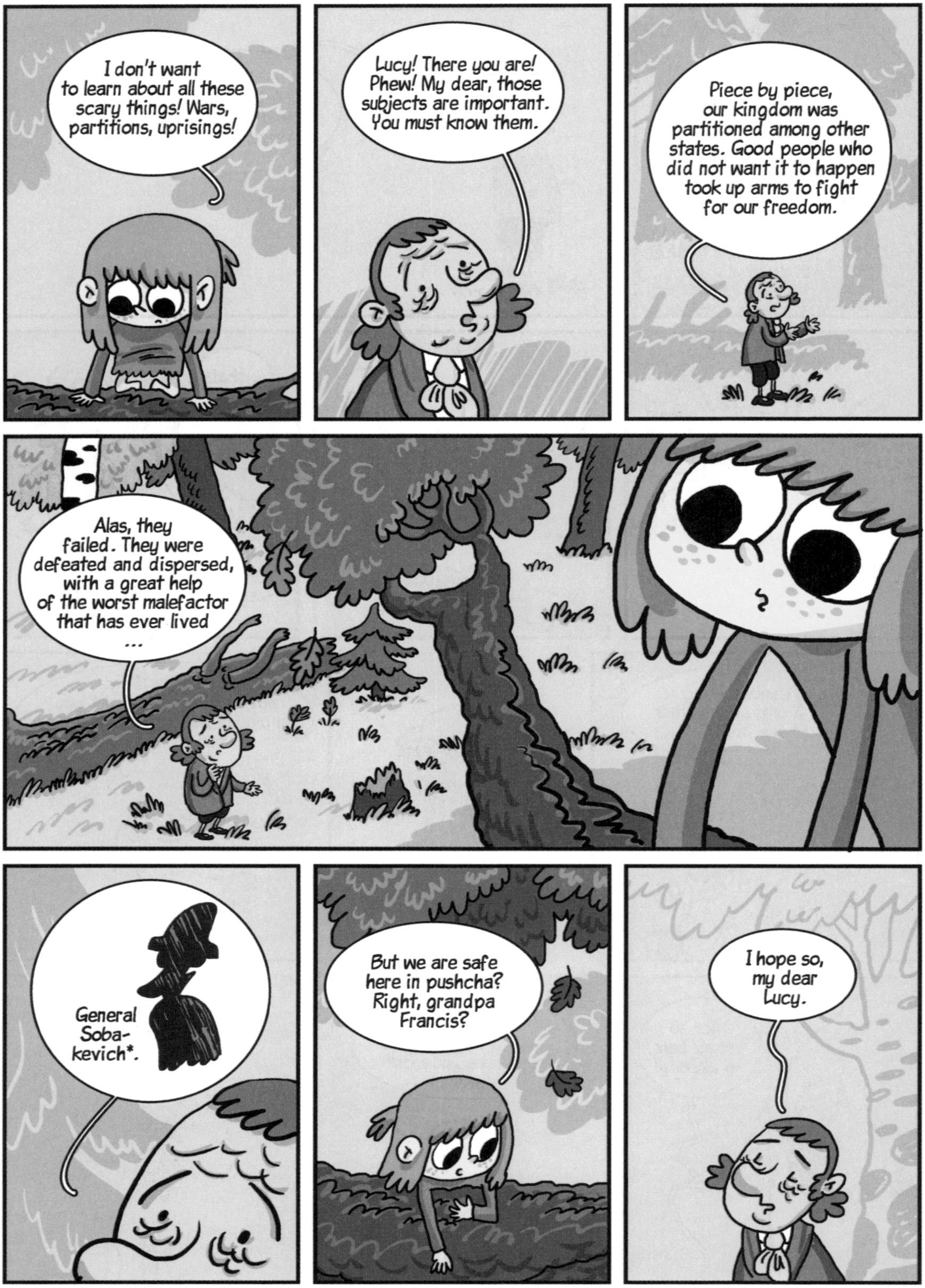
I don't want to learn about all these scary things! Wars, partitions, uprisings!
Lucy! There you are! Phew! My dear, those subjects are important. You must know them.
Piece by piece, our kingdom was partitioned among other states. Good people who did not want it to happen took up arms to fight for our freedom.
Alas, they failed. They were defeated and dispersed, with a great help of the worst malefactor that has ever lived ...
General Soba-kevich*.
But we are safe here in pushcha? Right, grandpa Francis?
I hope so, my dear Lucy.

* Please see the endnote on page 110.

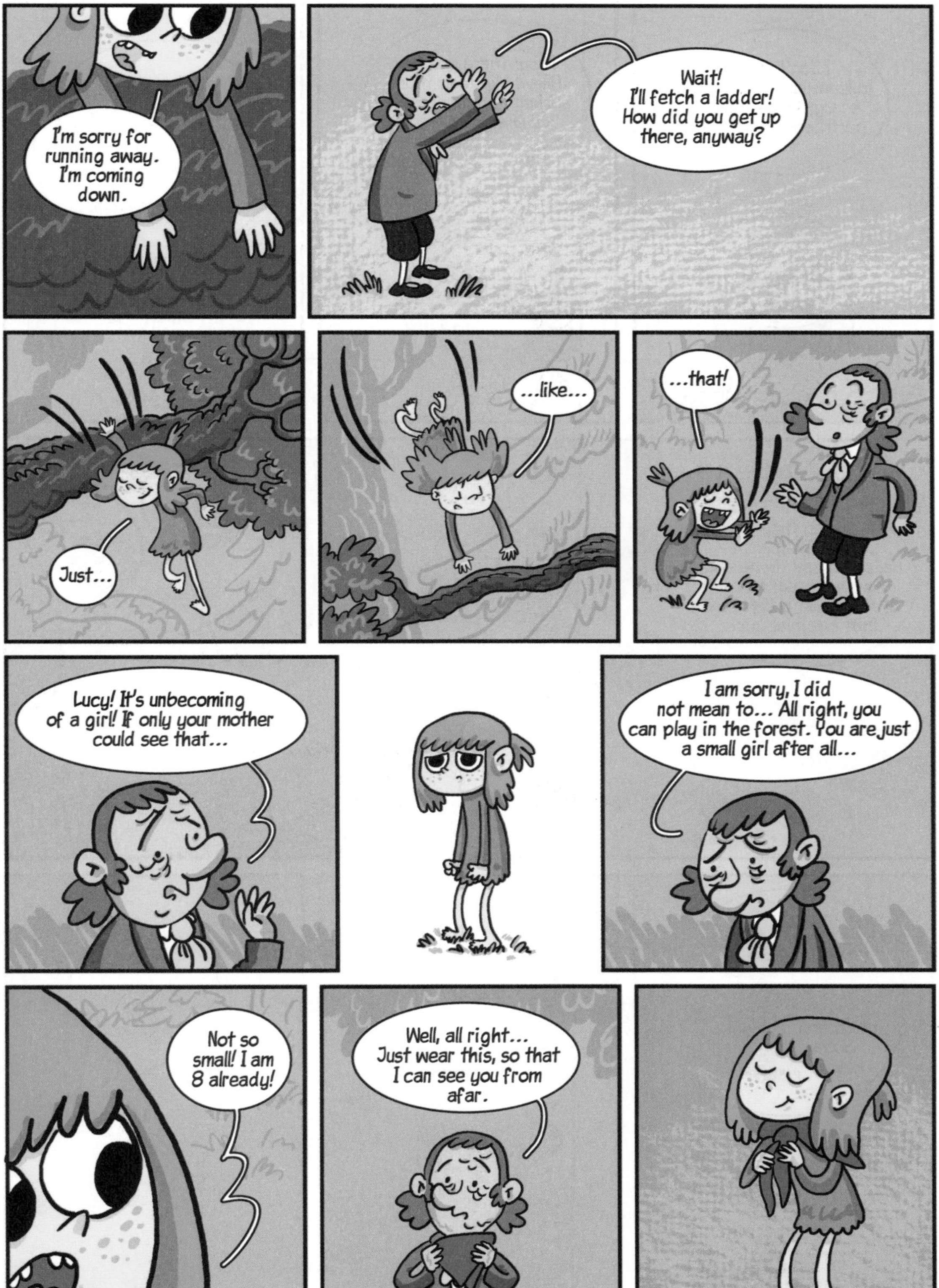
I'm sorry for running away. I'm coming down.
Wait! I'll fetch a ladder! How did you get up there, anyway?
Just...
...like...
...that!
Lucy! It's unbecoming of a girl! If only your mother could see that...
I am sorry, I did not mean to... All right, you can play in the forest. You are just a small girl after all...
Not so small! I am 8 already!
Well, all right... Just wear this, so that I can see you from afar.

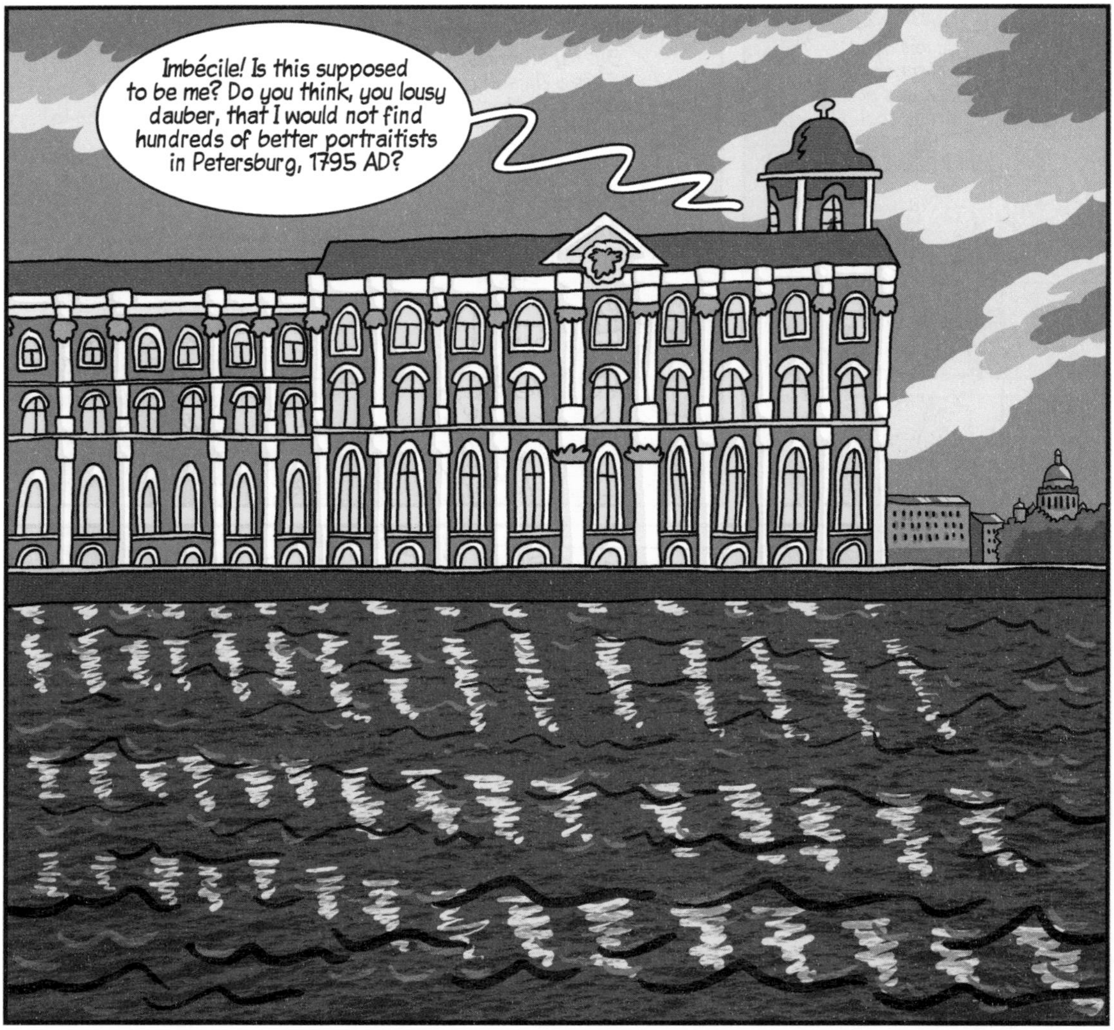
Imbécile! Is this supposed to be me? Do you think, you lousy dauber, that I would not find hundreds of better portraitists in Petersburg, 1795 AD?

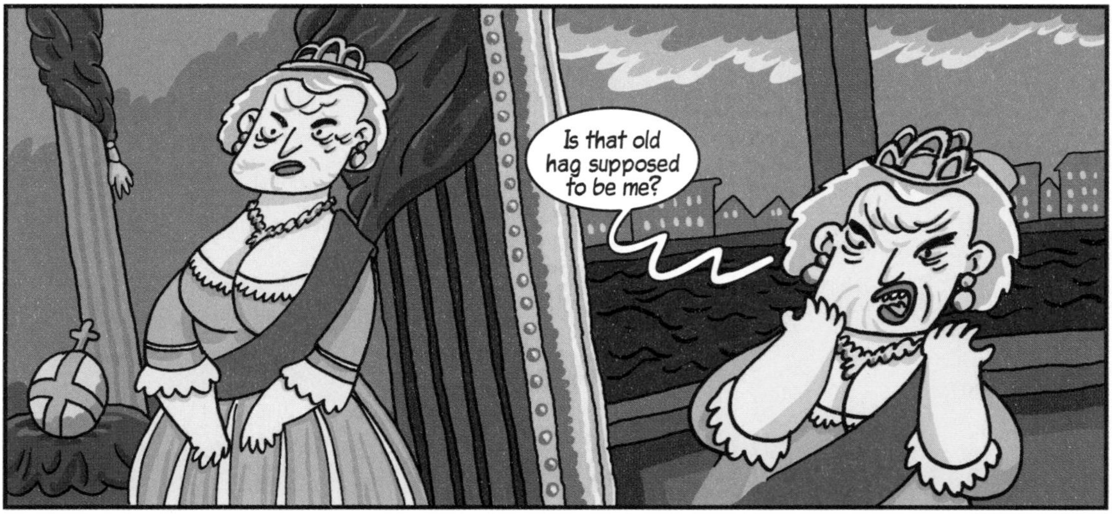
Is that old hag supposed to be me?

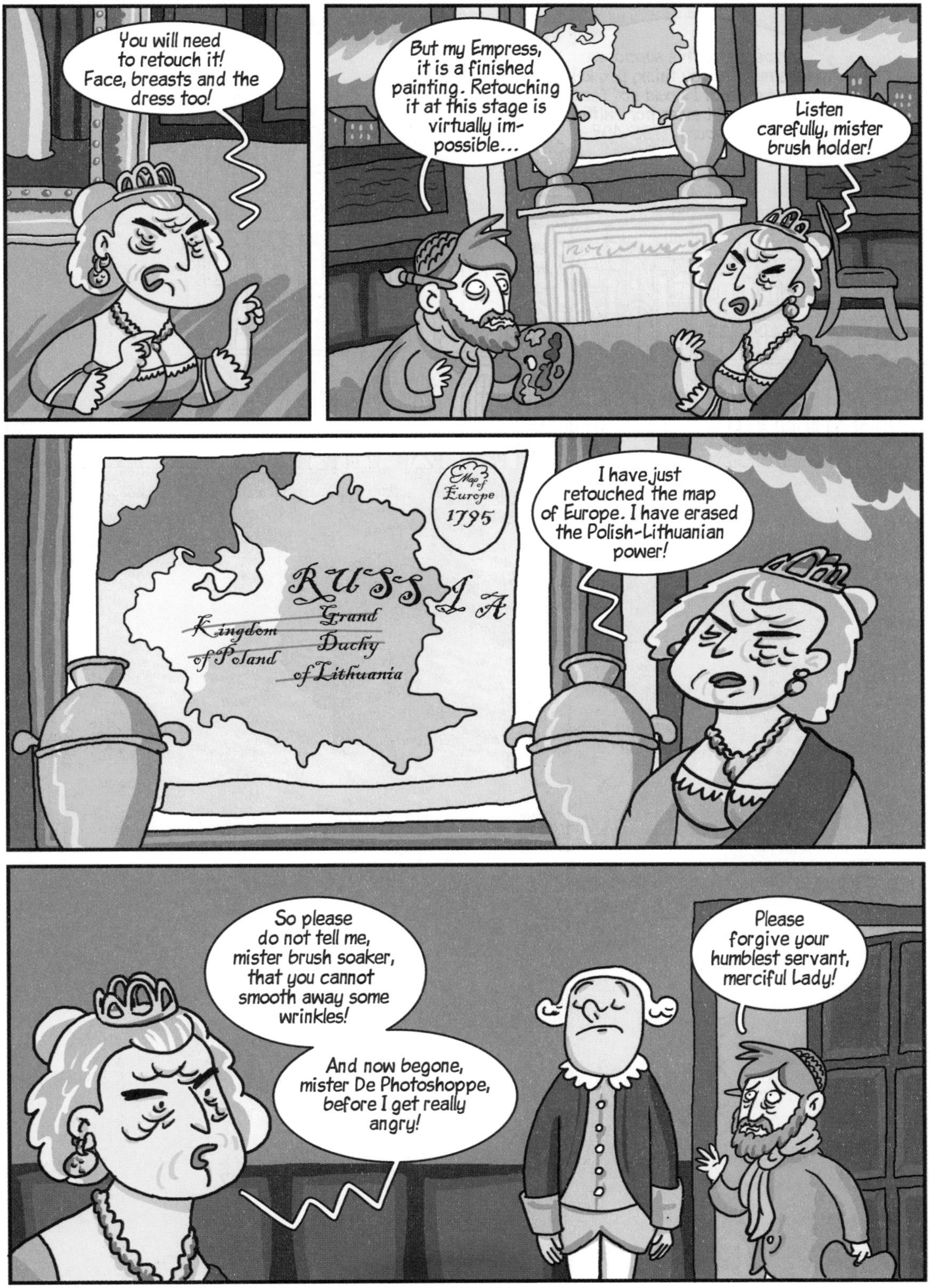
You will need to retouch it! Face, breasts and the dress too!
But my Empress, it is a finished painting. Retouching it at this stage is virtually impossible...
Listen carefully, mister brush holder!
Map of Europe 1795
RUSSIA
Kingdom of Poland
Grand Duchy of Lithuania
I have just retouched the map of Europe. I have erased the Polish-Lithuanian power!
So please do not tell me, mister brush soaker, that you cannot smooth away some wrinkles!
And now begone, mister De Photoshoppe, before I get really angry!
Please forgive your humblest servant, merciful Lady!

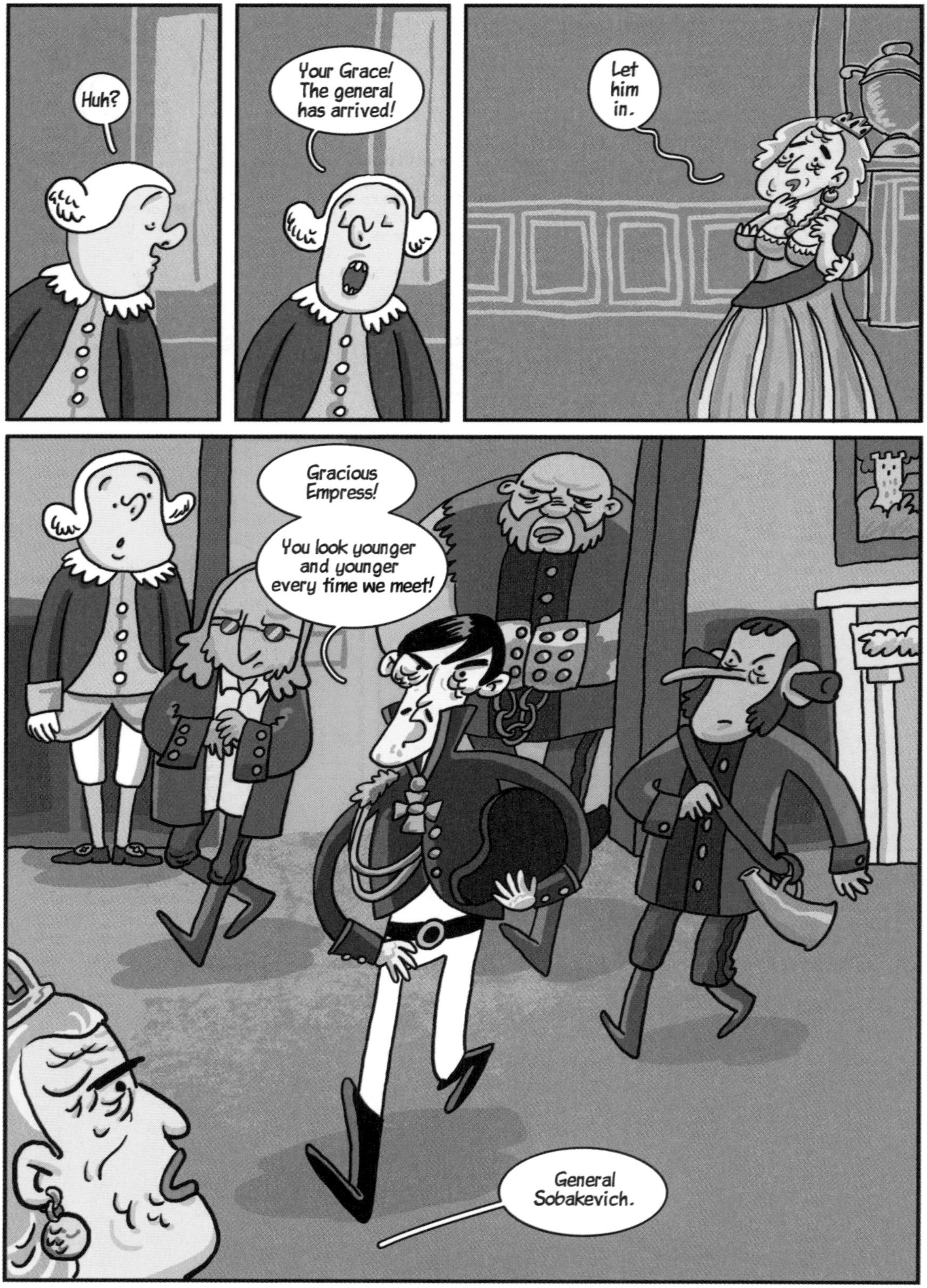
Huh?
Your Grace! The general has arrived!
Let him in.
Gracious Empress!
You look younger and younger every time we meet!
General Sobakevich.

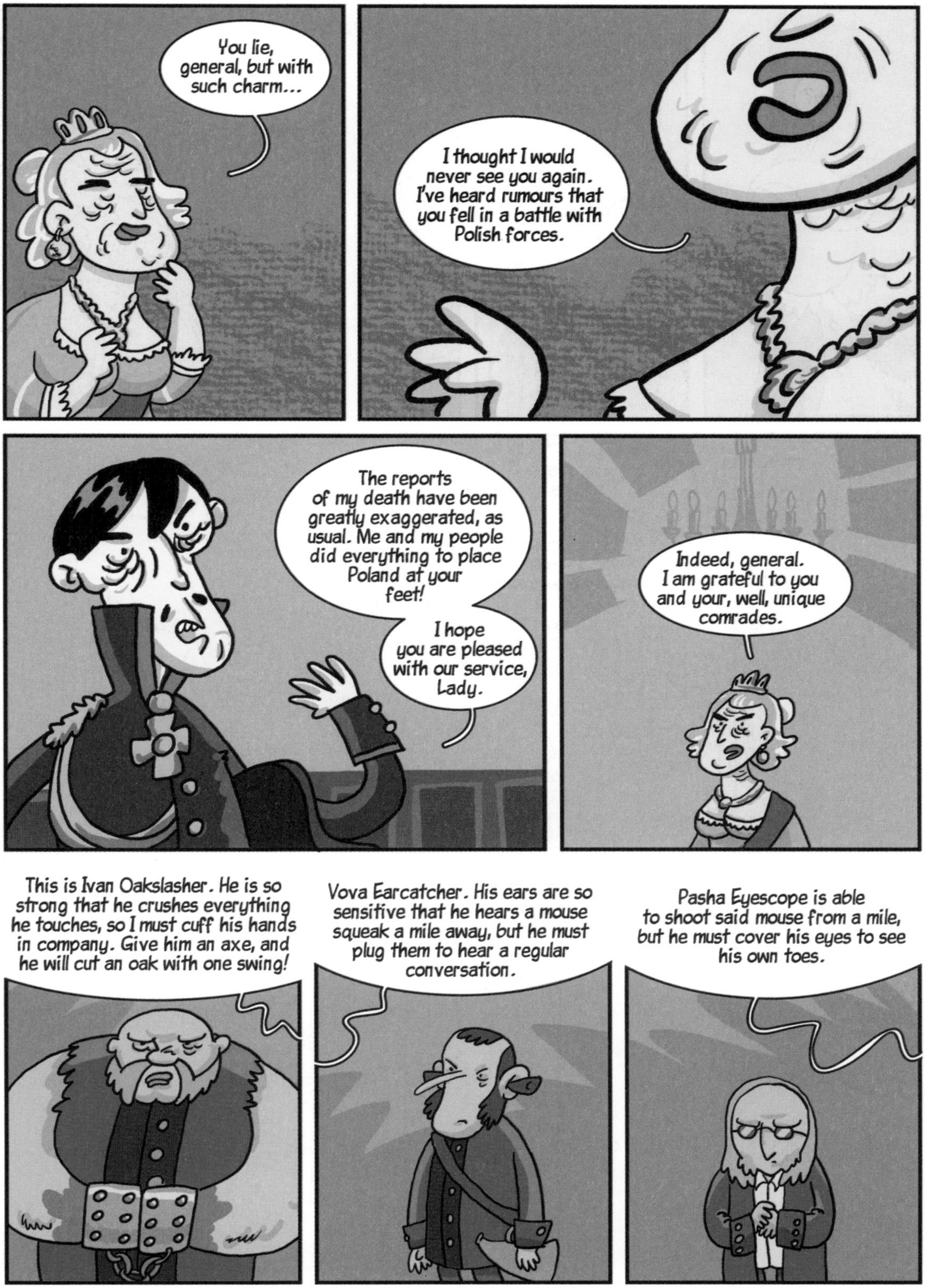

You lie, general, but with such charm...
I thought I would never see you again. I've heard rumours that you fell in a battle with Polish forces.
The reports of my death have been greatly exaggerated, as usual. Me and my people did everything to place Poland at your feet!
I hope you are pleased with our service, Lady.
Indeed, general. I am grateful to you and your, well, unique comrades.
This is Ivan Oakslasher. He is so strong that he crushes everything he touches, so I must cuff his hands in company. Give him an axe, and he will cut an oak with one swing!
Vova Earcatcher. His ears are so sensitive that he hears a mouse squeak a mile away, but he must plug them to hear a regular conversation.
Pasha Eyescope is able to shoot said mouse from a mile, but he must cover his eyes to see his own toes.

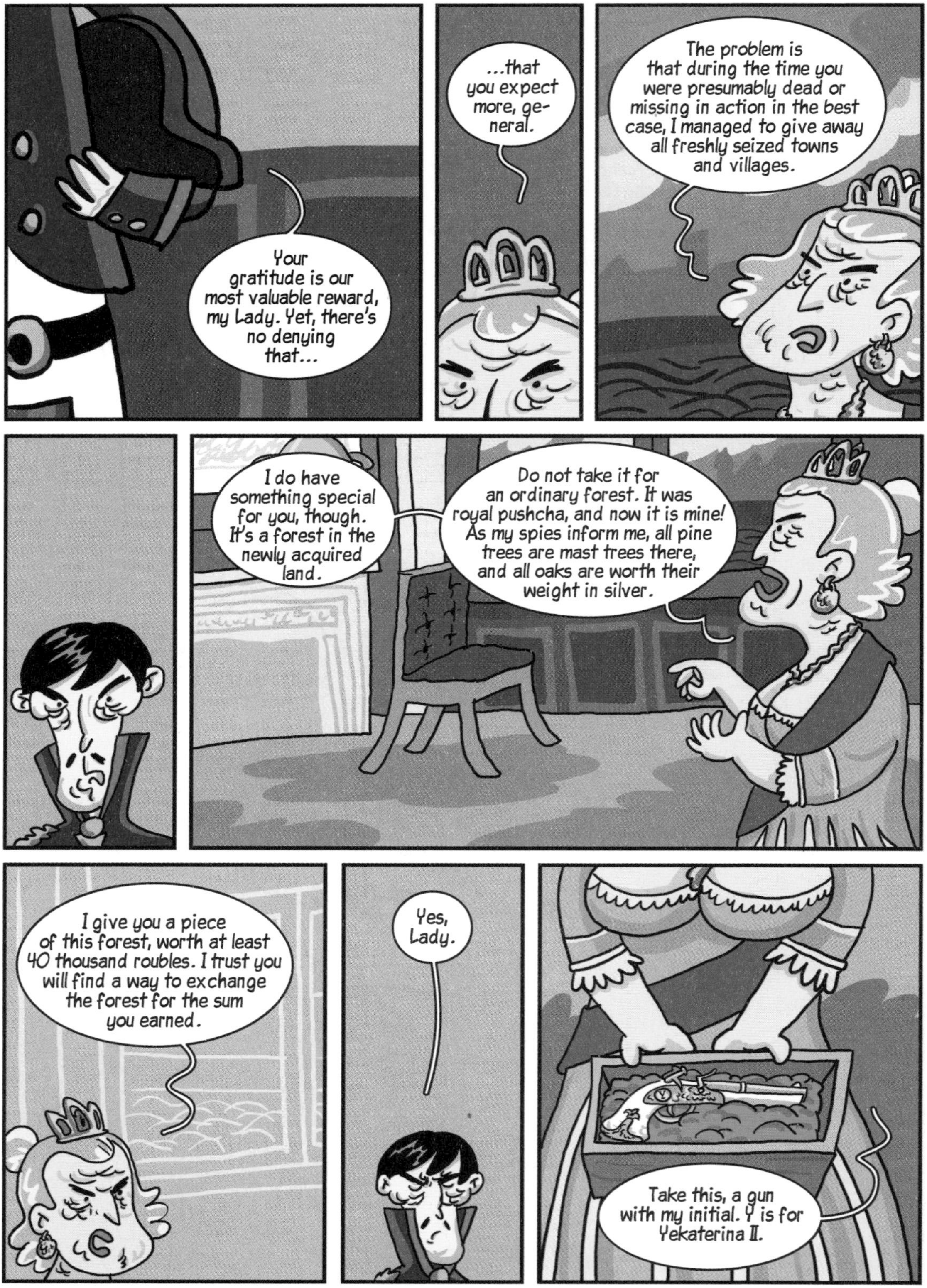
Your gratitude is our most valuable reward, my Lady. Yet, there's no denying that...
...that you expect more, general.
The problem is that during the time you were presumably dead or missing in action in the best case, I managed to give away all freshly seized towns and villages.
I do have something special for you, though. It's a forest in the newly acquired land.
Do not take it for an ordinary forest. It was royal pushcha, and now it is mine! As my spies inform me, all pine trees are mast trees there, and all oaks are worth their weight in silver.
I give you a piece of this forest, worth at least 40 thousand roubles. I trust you will find a way to exchange the forest for the sum you earned.
Yes, Lady.
Take this, a gun with my initial. Y is for Yekaterina II.

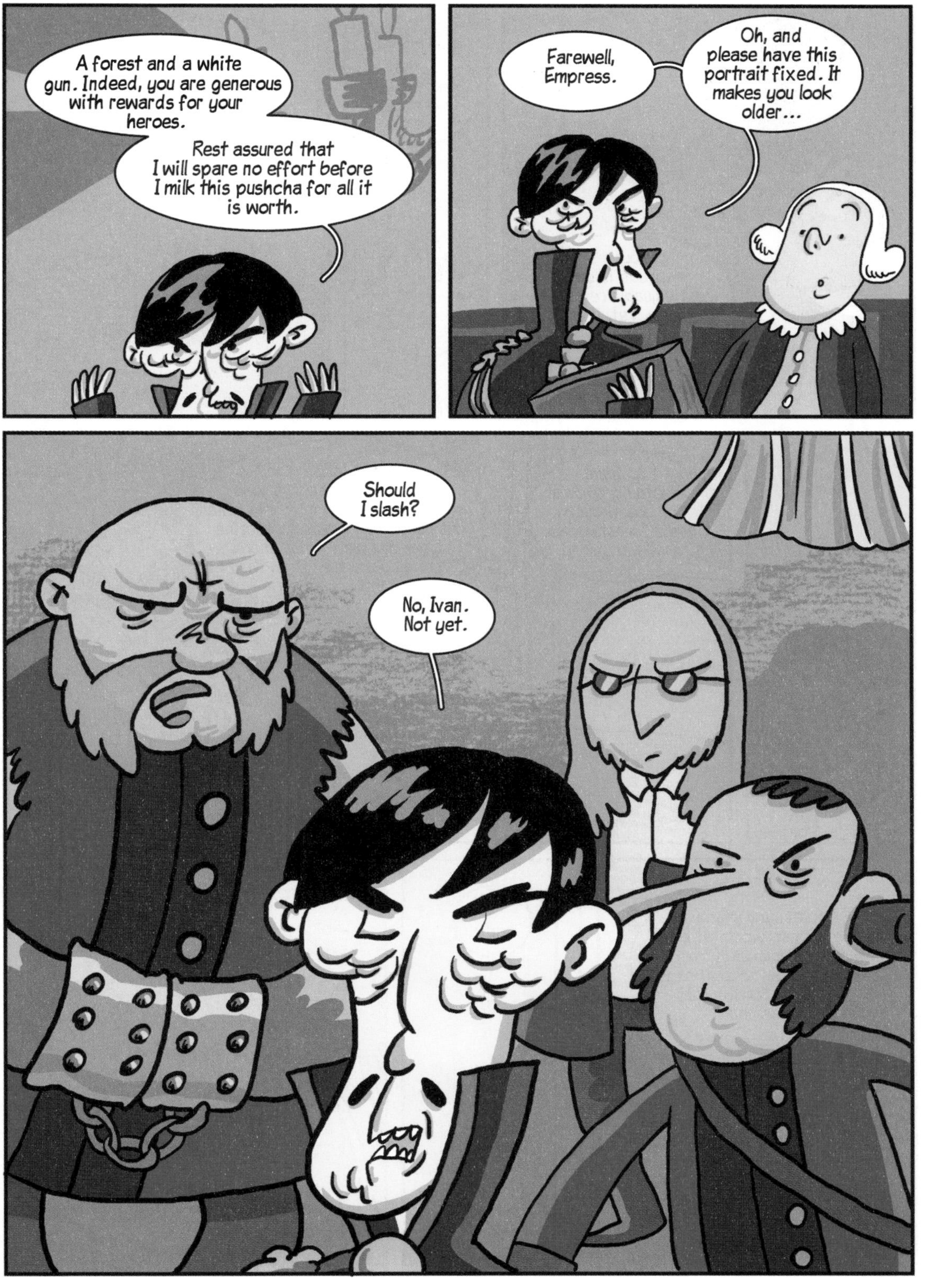
A forest and a white gun. Indeed, you are generous with rewards for your heroes.
Rest assured that I will spare no effort before I milk this pushcha for all it is worth.
Farewell, Empress.
Oh, and please have this portrait fixed. It makes you look older...
Should I slash?
No, Ivan. Not yet.

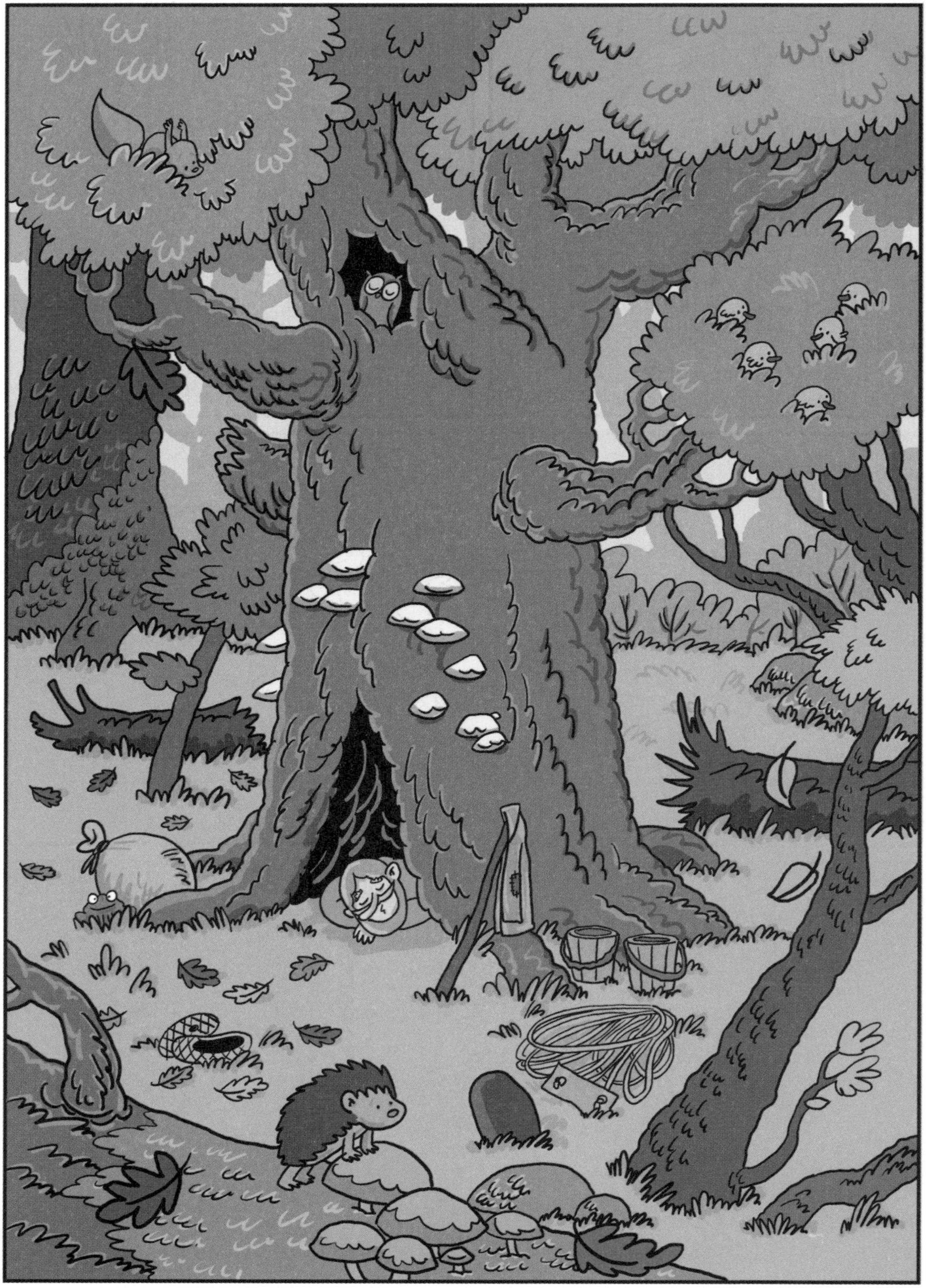

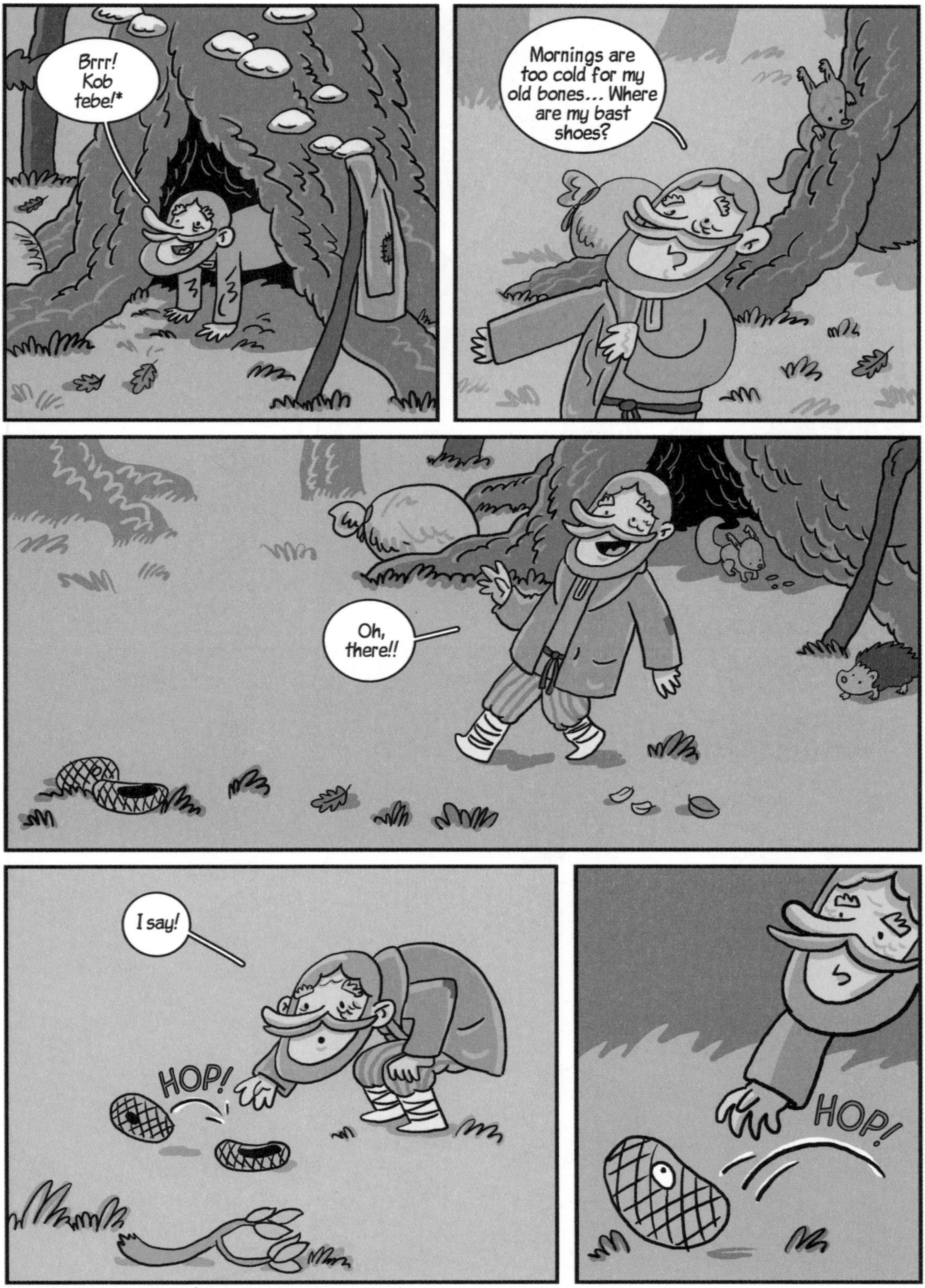
Brrr! Kob tebe!*
Mornings are too cold for my old bones... Where are my bast shoes?
Oh, there!!
I say!
HOP!
HOP!

* What language is Ignat using? Check the endnote on page 110.

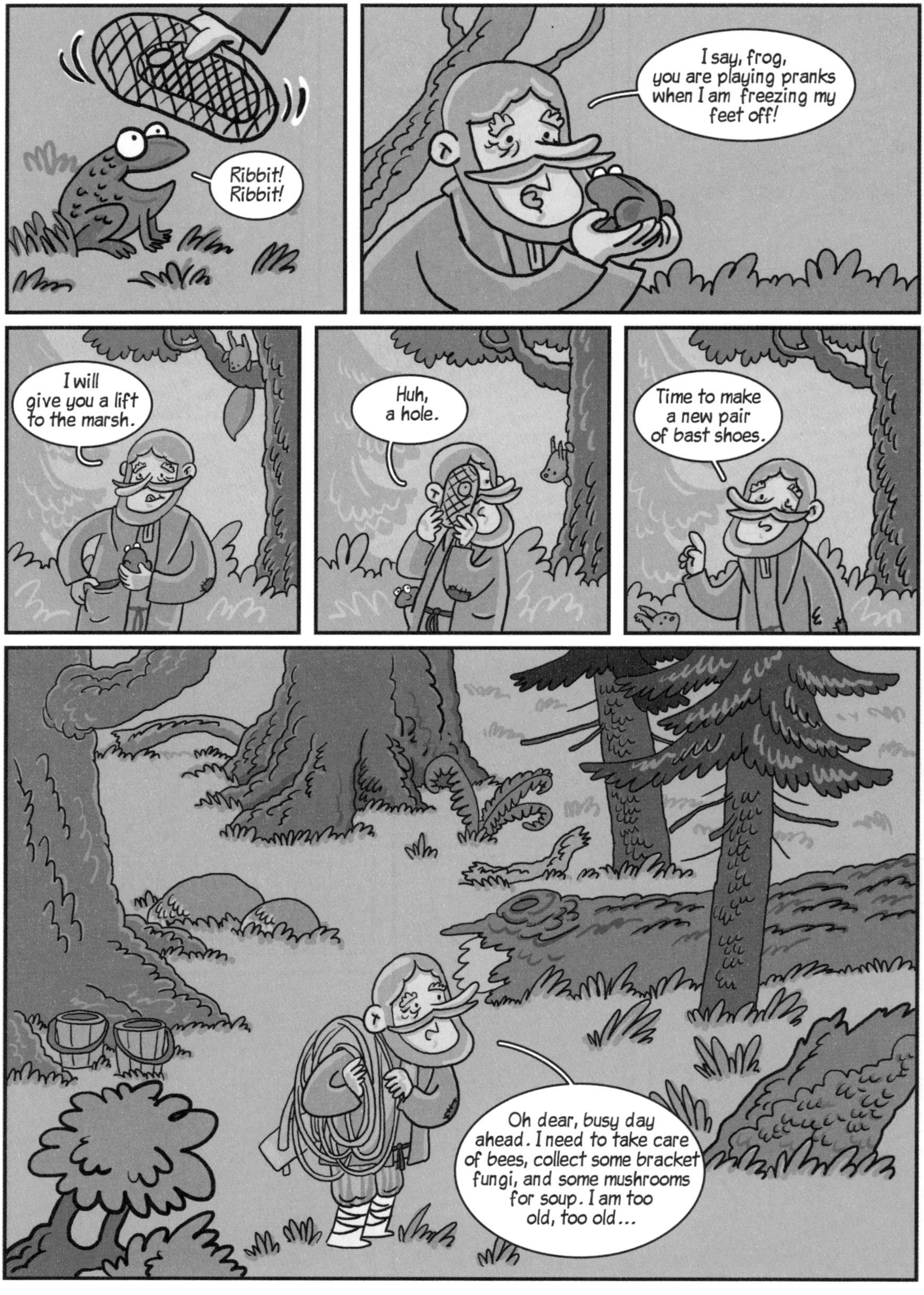
Ribbit! Ribbit!
I say, frog, you are playing pranks when I am freezing my feet off!
I will give you a lift to the marsh.
Huh, a hole.
Time to make a new pair of bast shoes.
Oh dear, busy day ahead. I need to take care of bees, collect some bracket fungi, and some mushrooms for soup. I am too old, too old...

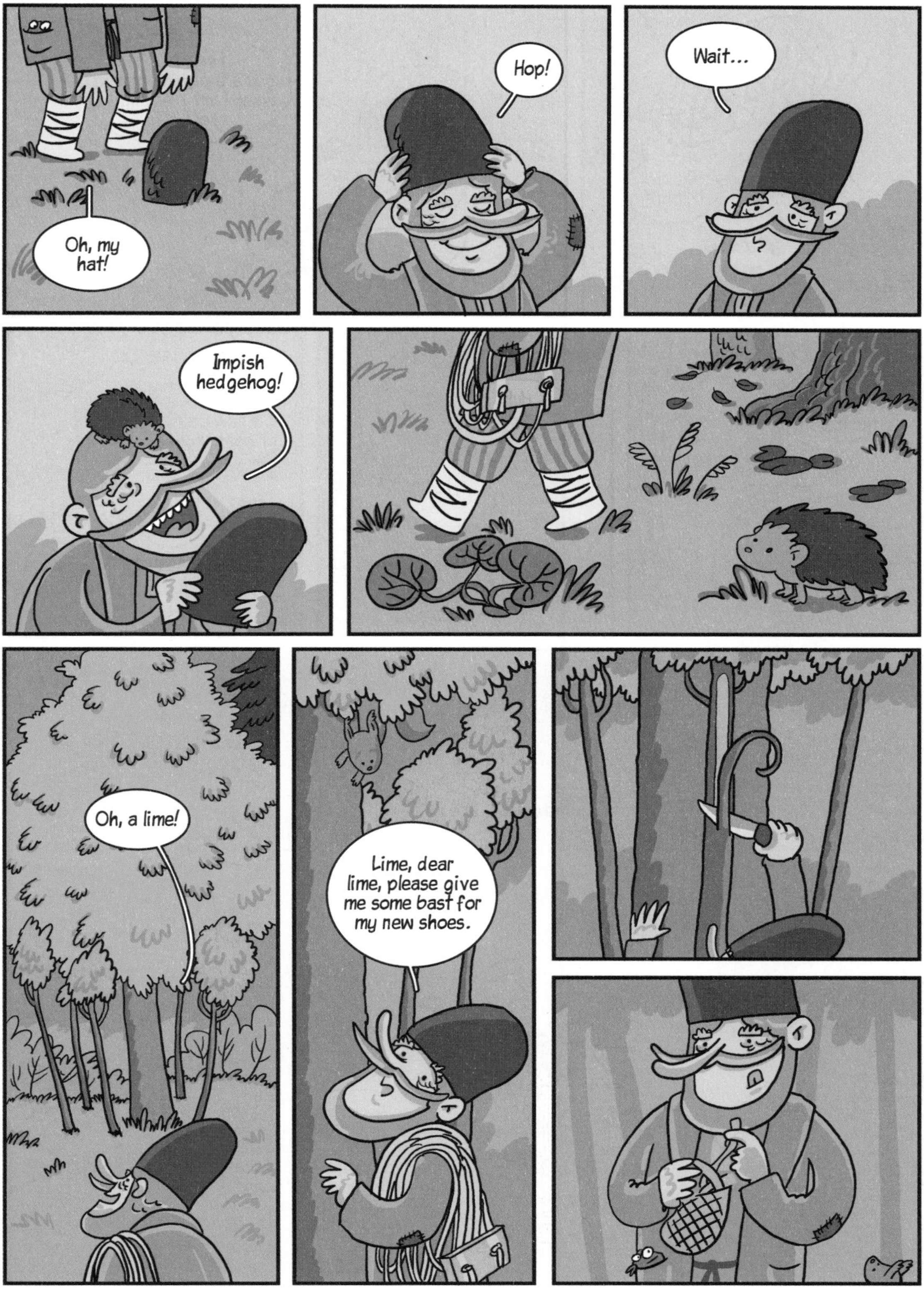
Oh, my hat!
Hop!
Wait...
Impish hedgehog!
Oh, a lime!
Lime, dear lime, please give me some bast for my new shoes.

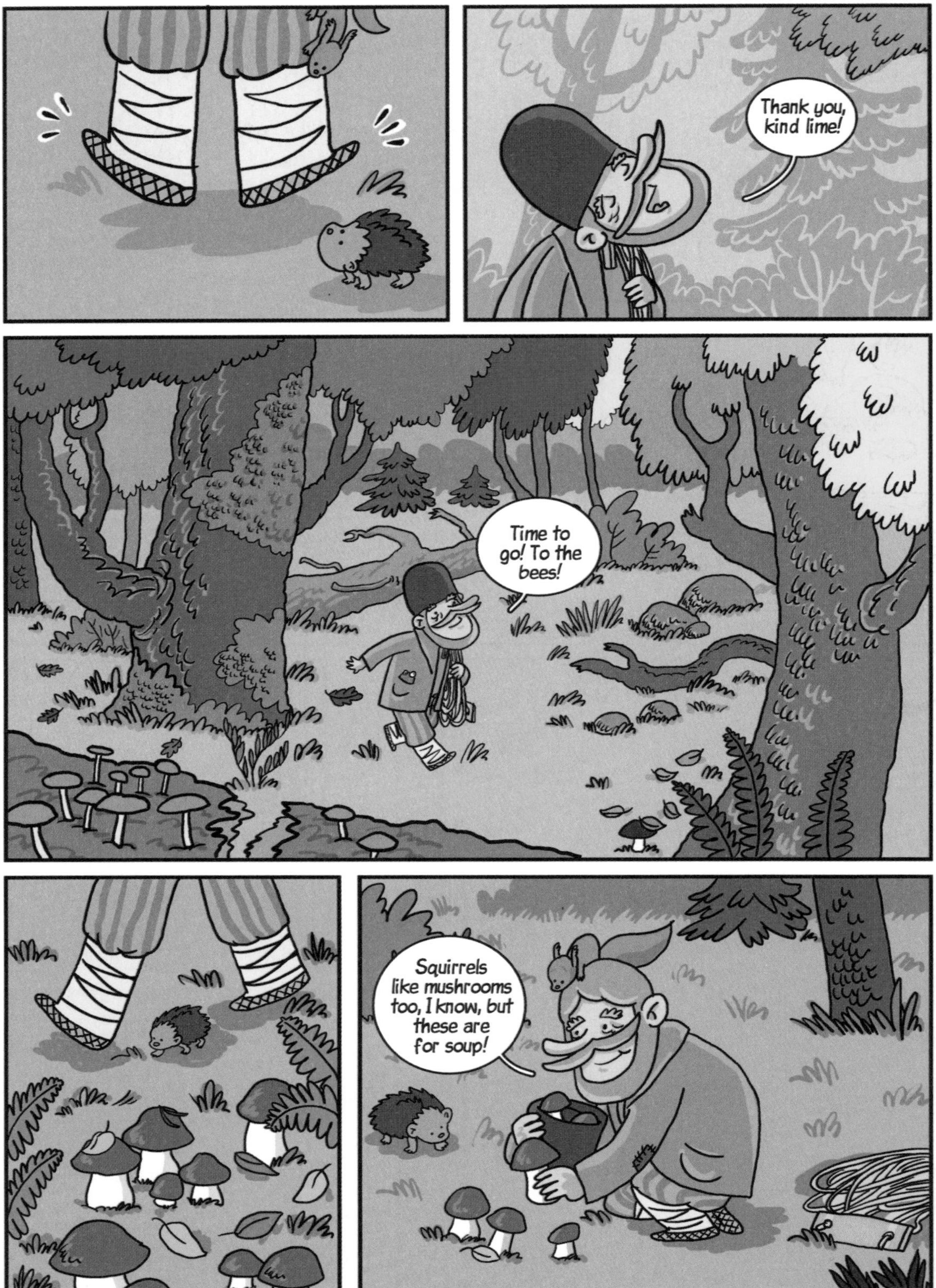
Thank you, kind lime!
Time to go! To the bees!
Squirrels like mushrooms too, I know, but these are for soup!

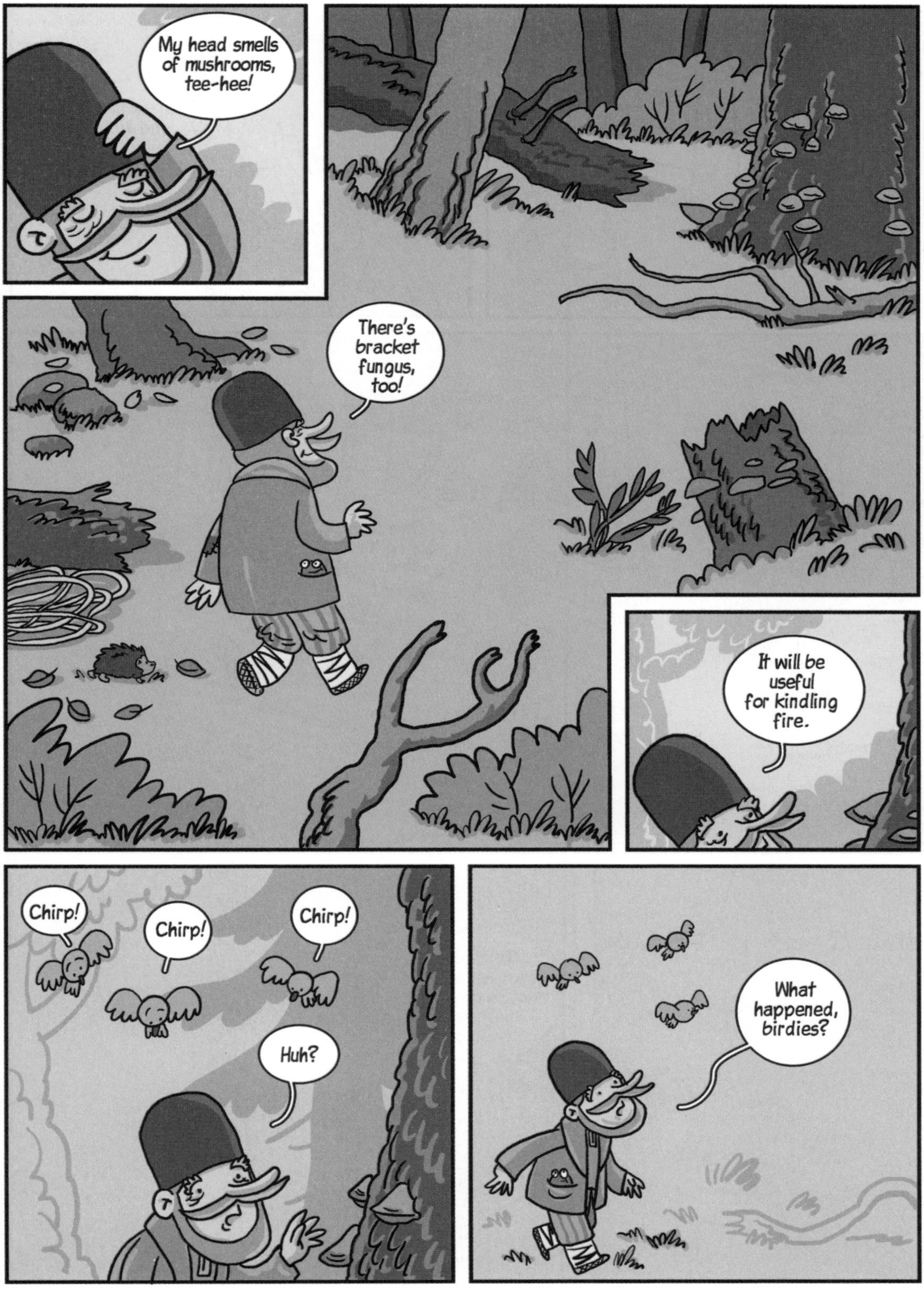
My head smells of mushrooms, tee-hee!
There's bracket fungus, too!
It will be useful for kindling fire.
Chirp!
Chirp!
Chirp!
Huh?
What happened, birdies?

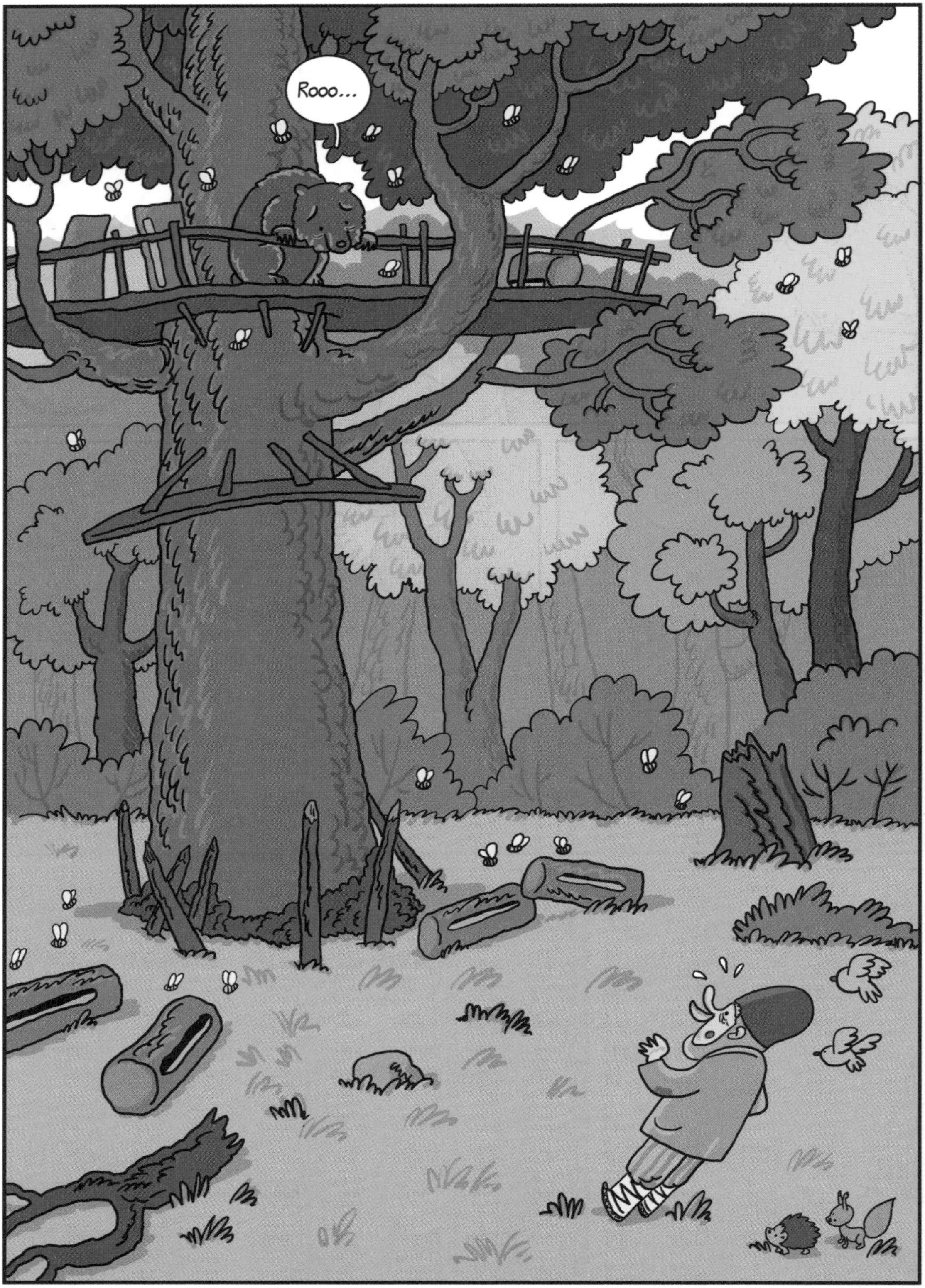
Rooo...

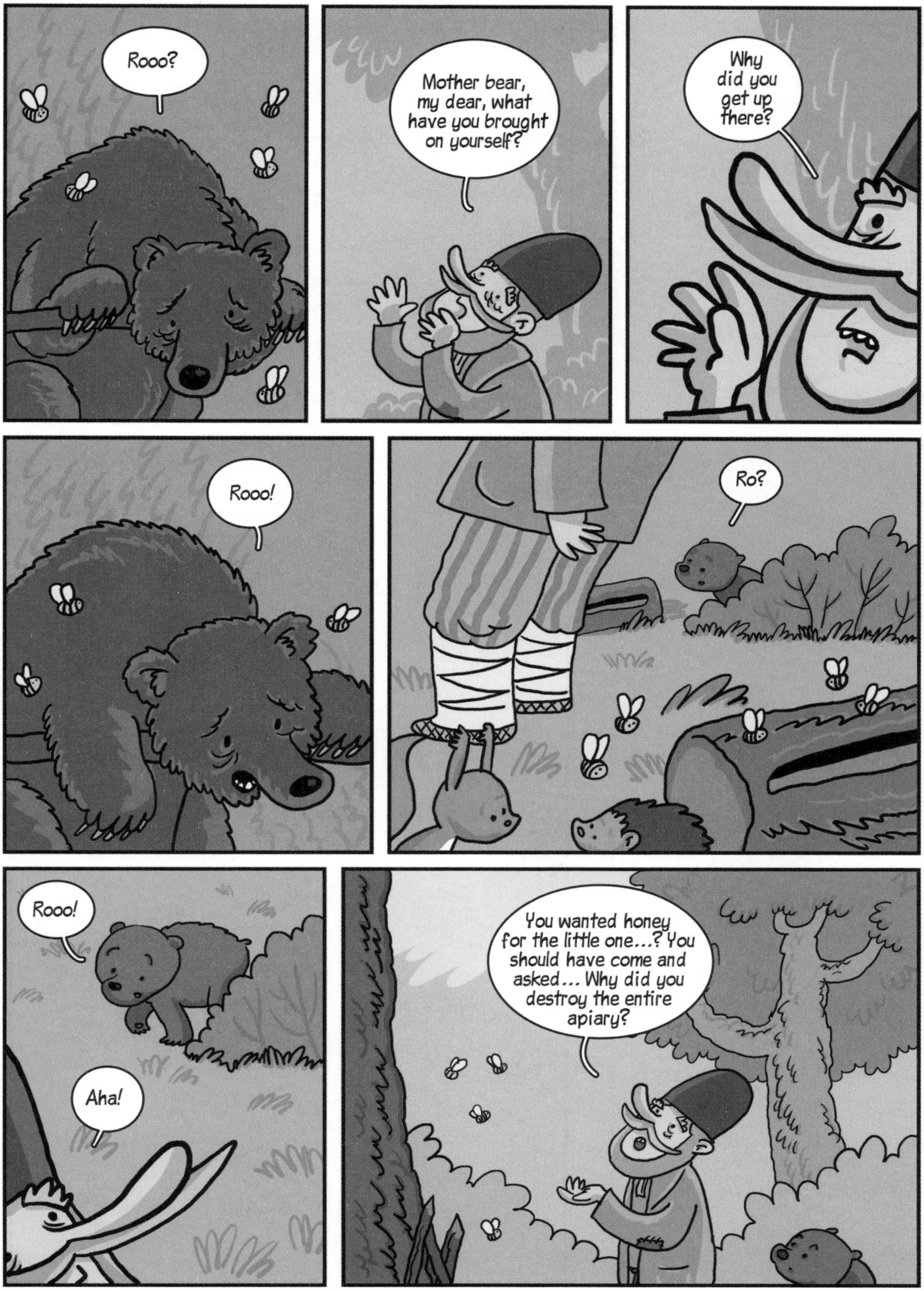
Rooo?
Mother bear, my dear, what have you brought on yourself?
Why did you get up there?
Rooo!
Ro?
Rooo!
Aha!
You wanted honey for the little one...? You should have come and asked... Why did you destroy the entire apiary?

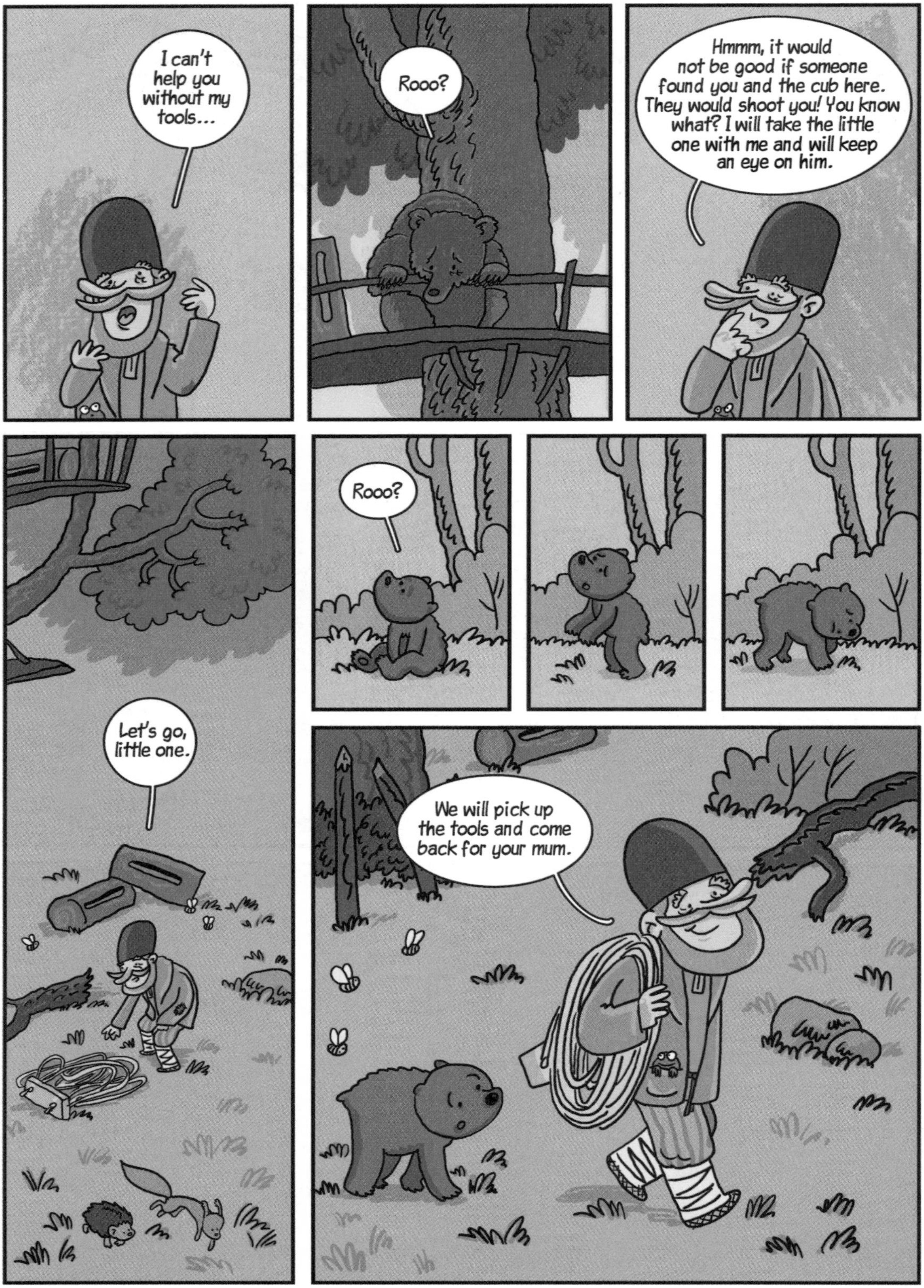
I can't help you without my tools...
Rooo?
Hmmm, it would not be good if someone found you and the cub here. They would shoot you! You know what? I will take the little one with me and will keep an eye on him.
Let's go, little one.
Rooo?
We will pick up the tools and come back for your mum.

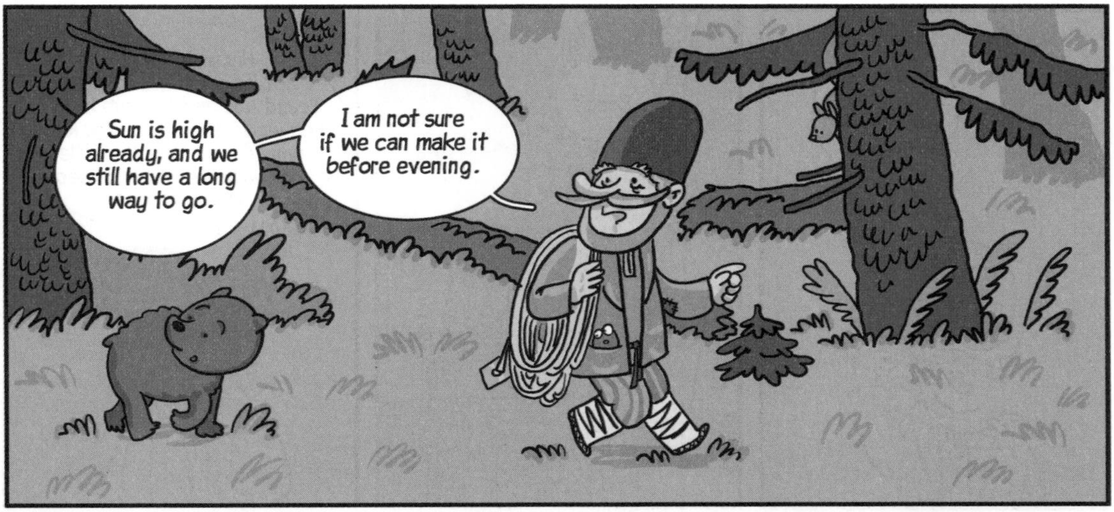

Sun is high already, and we still have a long way to go.
I am not sure if we can make it before evening.

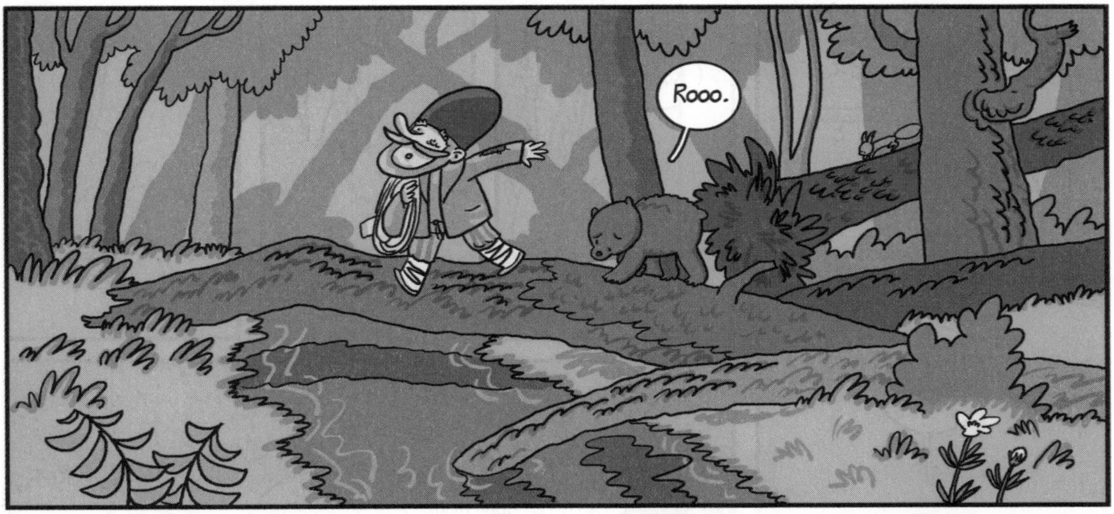

Rooo.

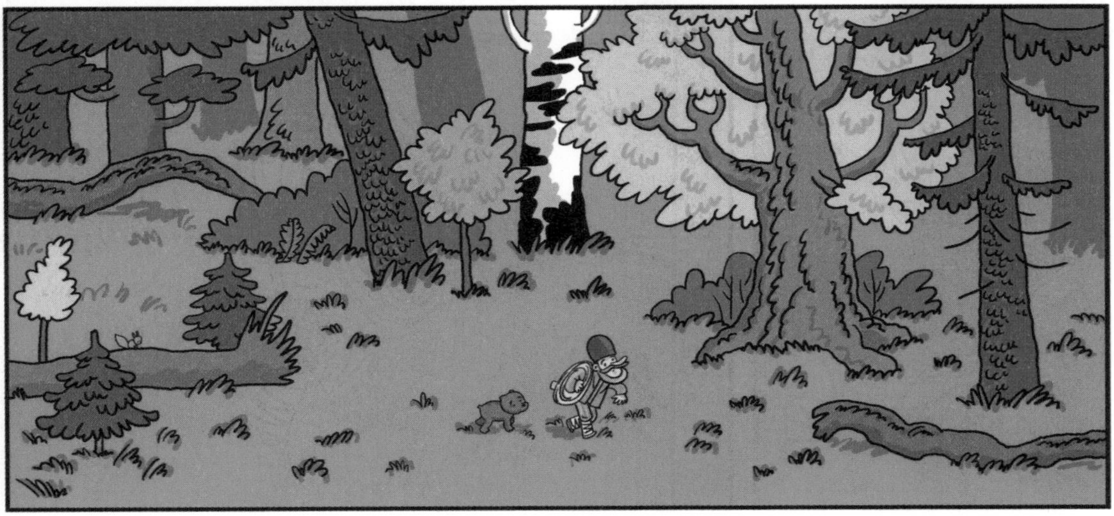

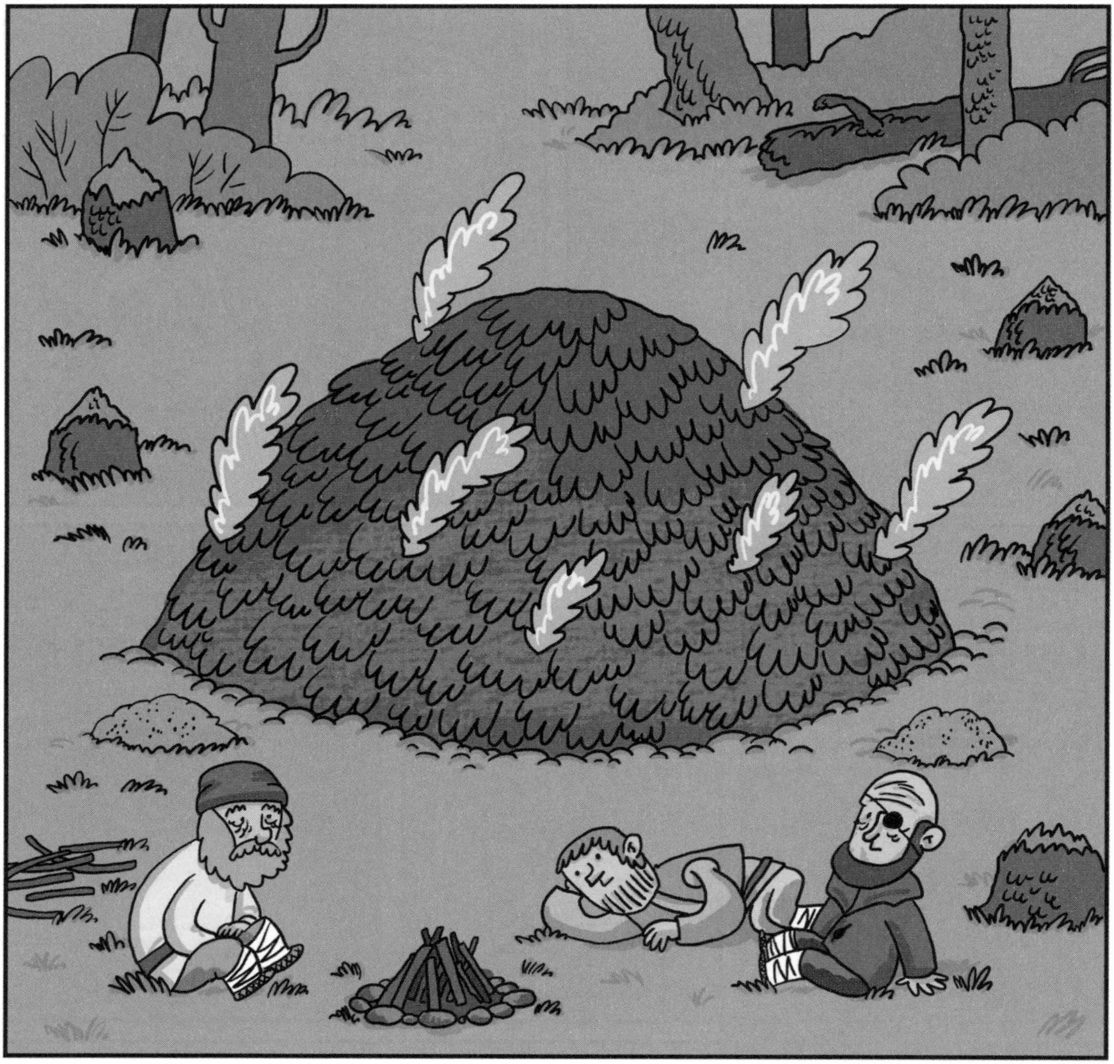

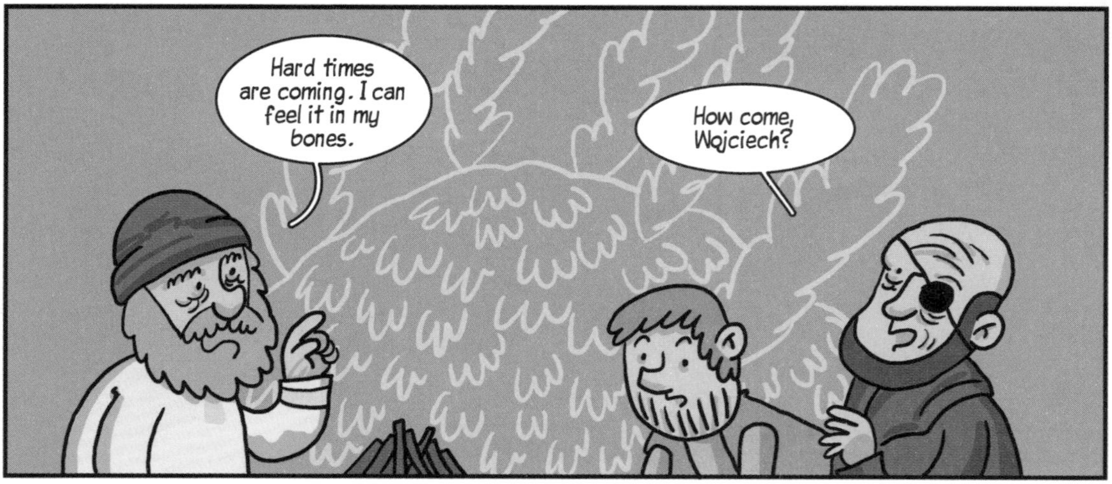
Hard times are coming. I can feel it in my bones.
How come, Wojciech?

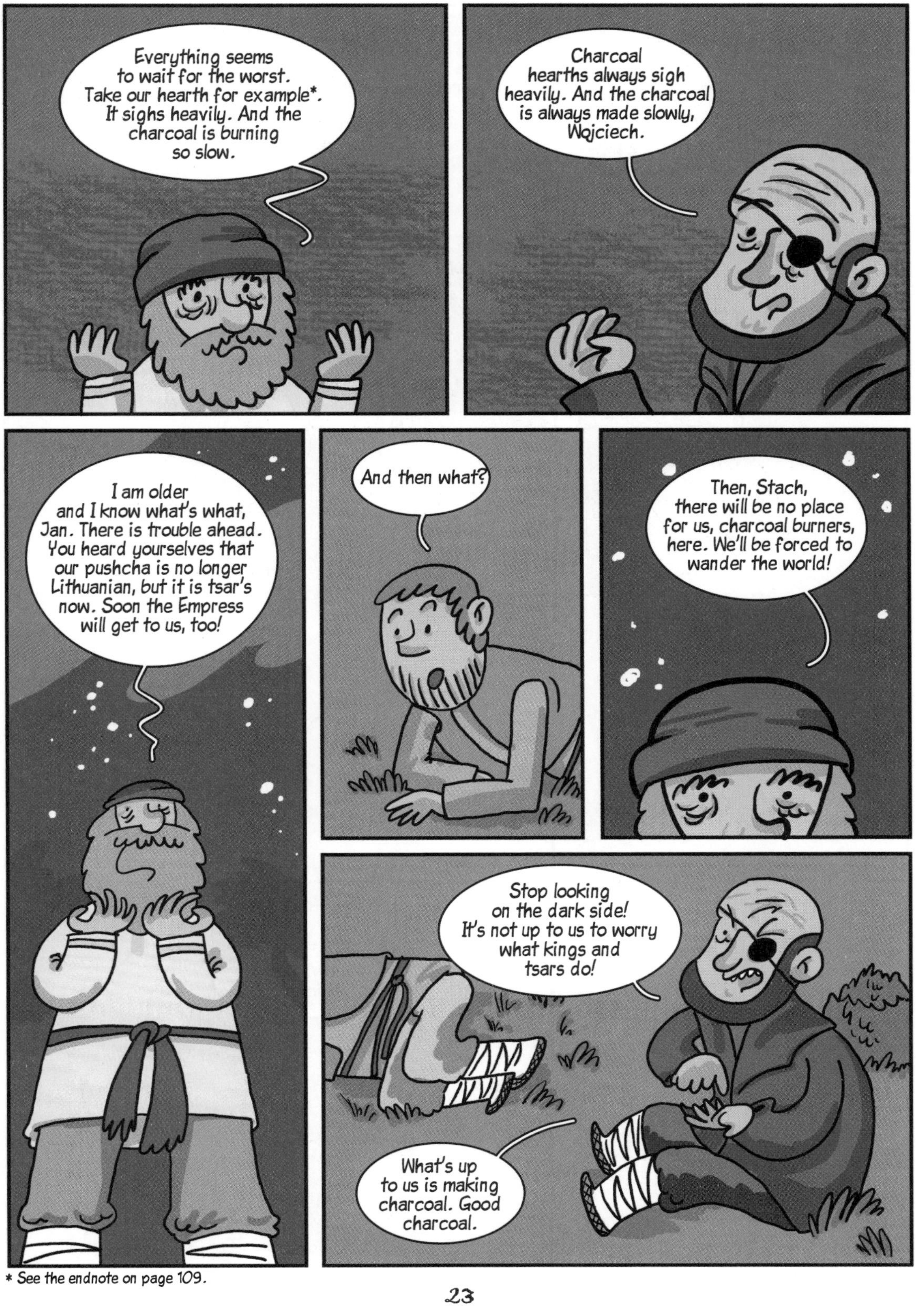
Everything seems to wait for the worst. Take our hearth for example*. It sighs heavily. And the charcoal is burning so slow.
Charcoal hearths always sigh heavily. And the charcoal is always made slowly, Wojciech.
I am older and I know what's what, Jan. There is trouble ahead. You heard yourselves that our pushcha is no longer Lithuanian, but it is tsar's now. Soon the Empress will get to us, too!
And then what?
Then, Stach, there will be no place for us, charcoal burners, here. We'll be forced to wander the world!
Stop looking on the dark side! It's not up to us to worry what kings and tsars do!
What's up to us is making charcoal. Good charcoal.

* See the endnote on page 109.

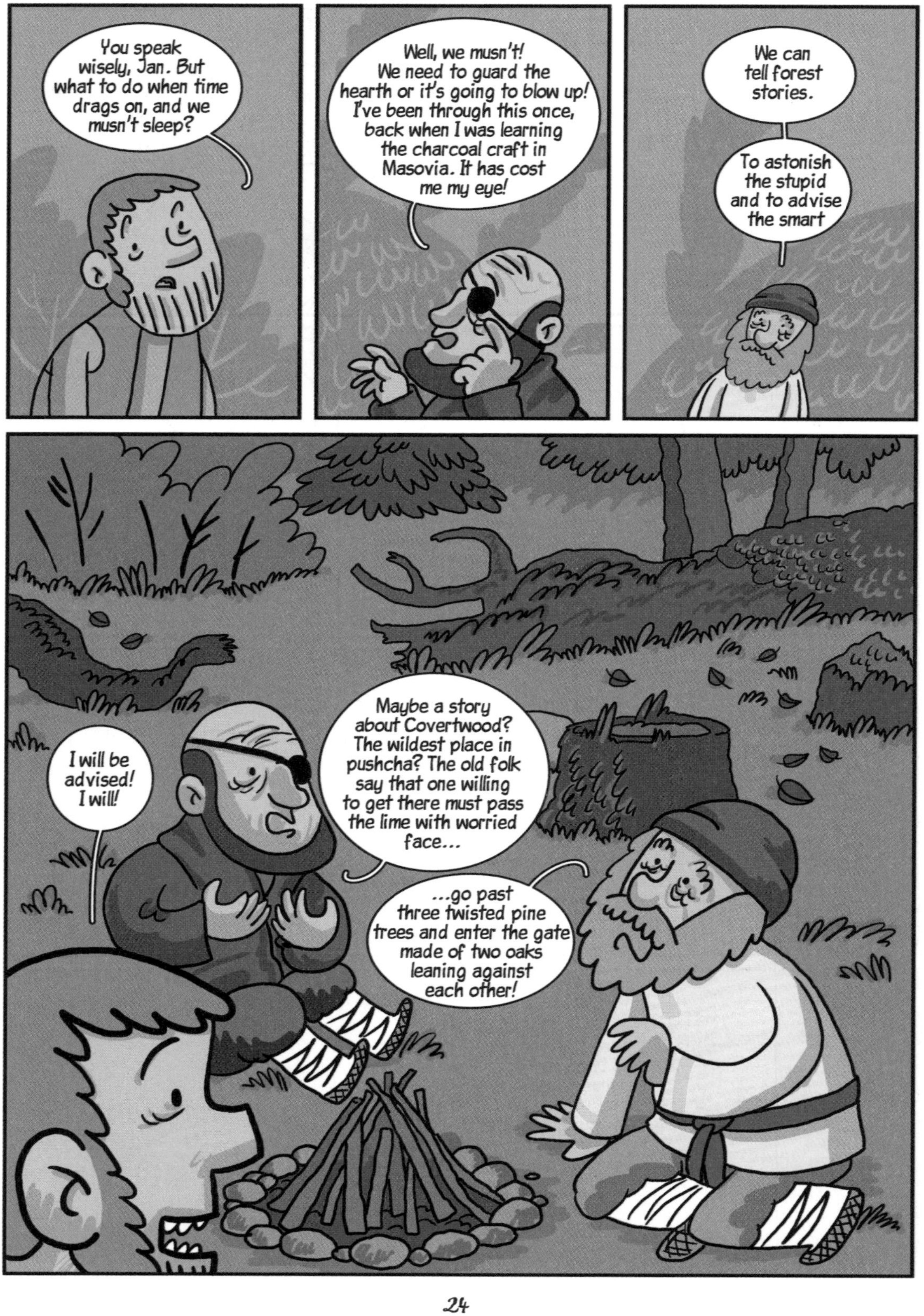
You speak wisely, Jan. But what to do when time drags on, and we musn't sleep?
Well, we musn't! We need to guard the hearth or it's going to blow up! I've been through this once, back when I was learning the charcoal craft in Masovia. It has cost me my eye!
We can tell forest stories.
To astonish the stupid and to advise the smart
I will be advised! I will!
Maybe a story about Covertwood? The wildest place in pushcha? The old folk say that one willing to get there must pass the lime with worried face...
...go past three twisted pine trees and enter the gate made of two oaks leaning against each other!

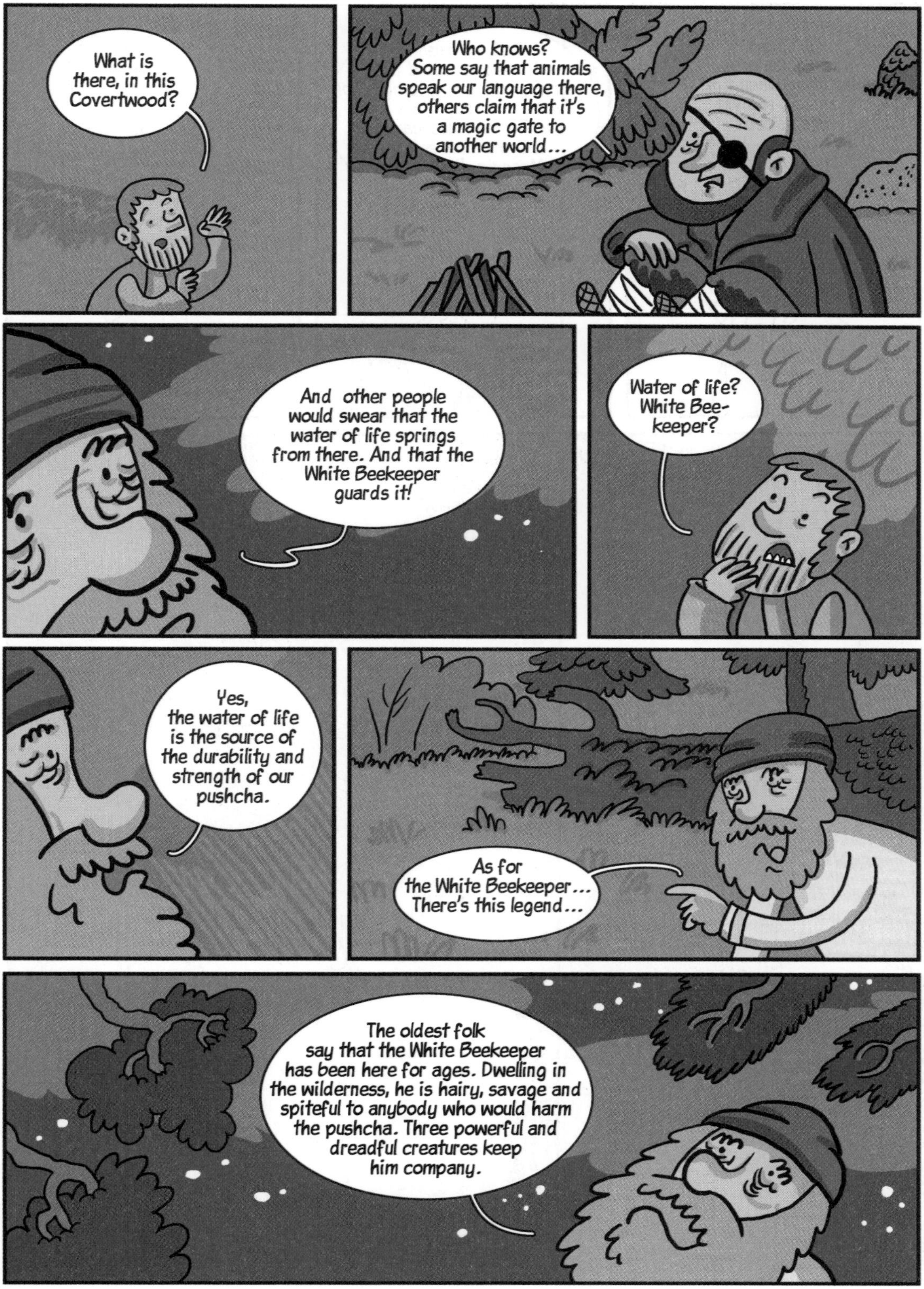
What is there, in this Covertwood?
Who knows? Some say that animals speak our language there, others claim that it's a magic gate to another world...
And other people would swear that the water of life springs from there. And that the White Beekeeper guards it!
Water of life? White Bee-keeper?
Yes, the water of life is the source of the durability and strength of our pushcha.
As for the White Beekeeper... There's this legend...
The oldest folk say that the White Beekeeper has been here for ages. Dwelling in the wilderness, he is hairy, savage and spiteful to anybody who would harm the pushcha. Three powerful and dreadful creatures keep him company.

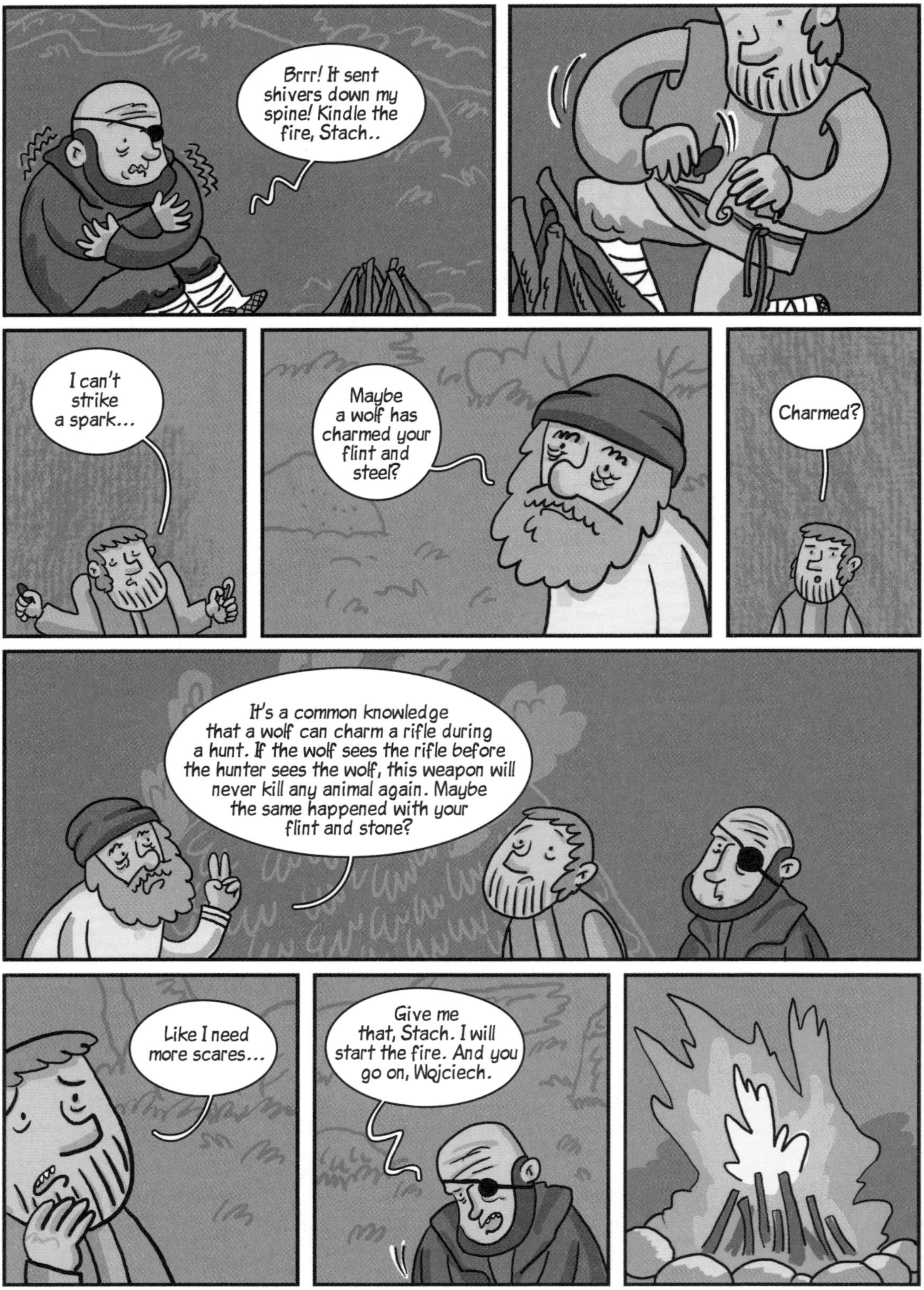

Brrr! It sent shivers down my spine! Kindle the fire, Stach..
I can't strike a spark...
Maybe a wolf has charmed your flint and steel?
Charmed?
It's a common knowledge that a wolf can charm a rifle during a hunt. If the wolf sees the rifle before the hunter sees the wolf, this weapon will never kill any animal again. Maybe the same happened with your flint and stone?
Like I need more scares...
Give me that, Stach. I will start the fire. And you go on, Wojciech.

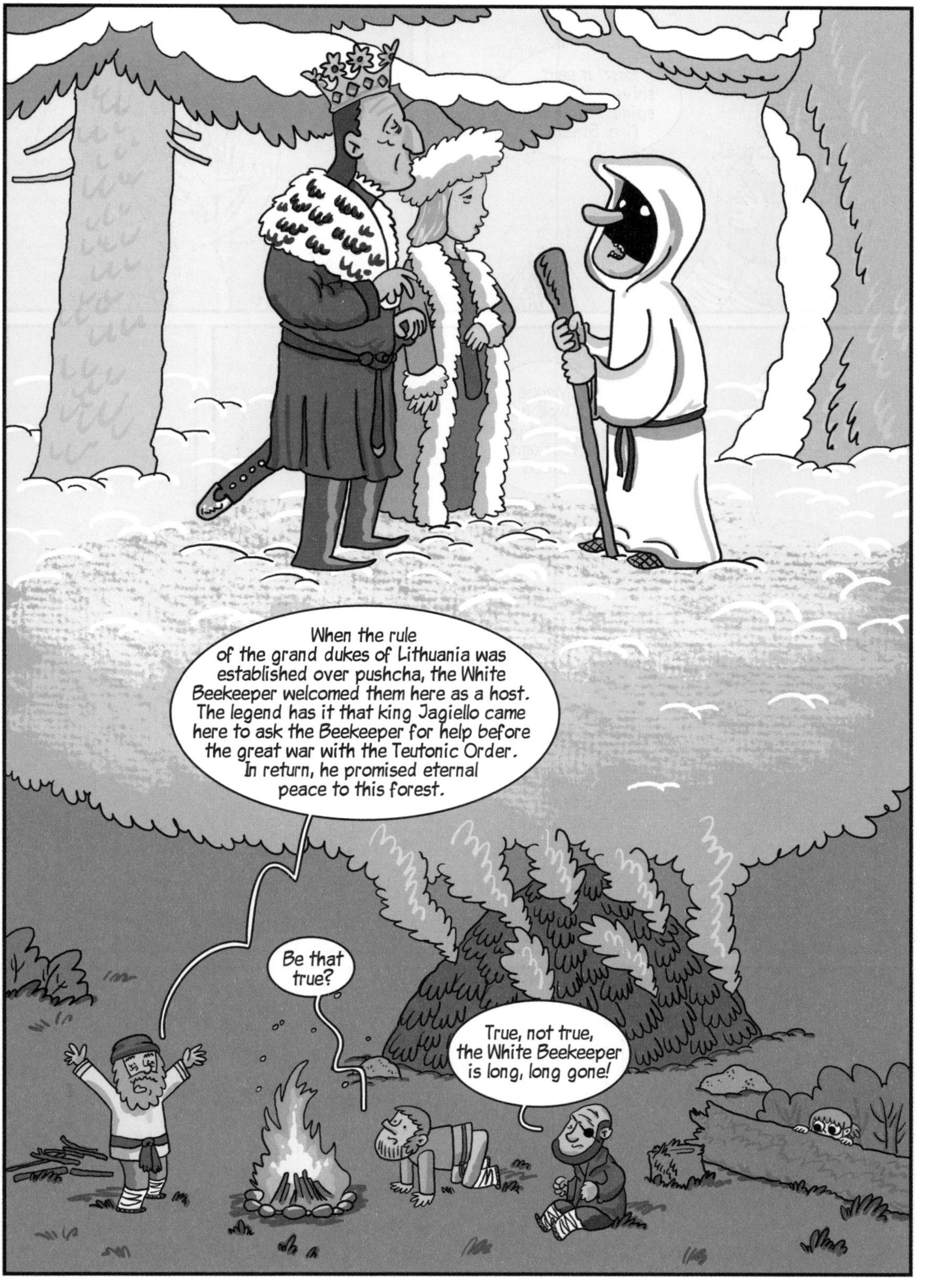
When the rule of the grand dukes of Lithuania was established over pushcha, the White Beekeeper welcomed them here as a host. The legend has it that king Jagiello came here to ask the Beekeeper for help before the great war with the Teutonic Order. In return, he promised eternal peace to this forest.
Be that true?
True, not true, the White Beekeeper is long, long gone!

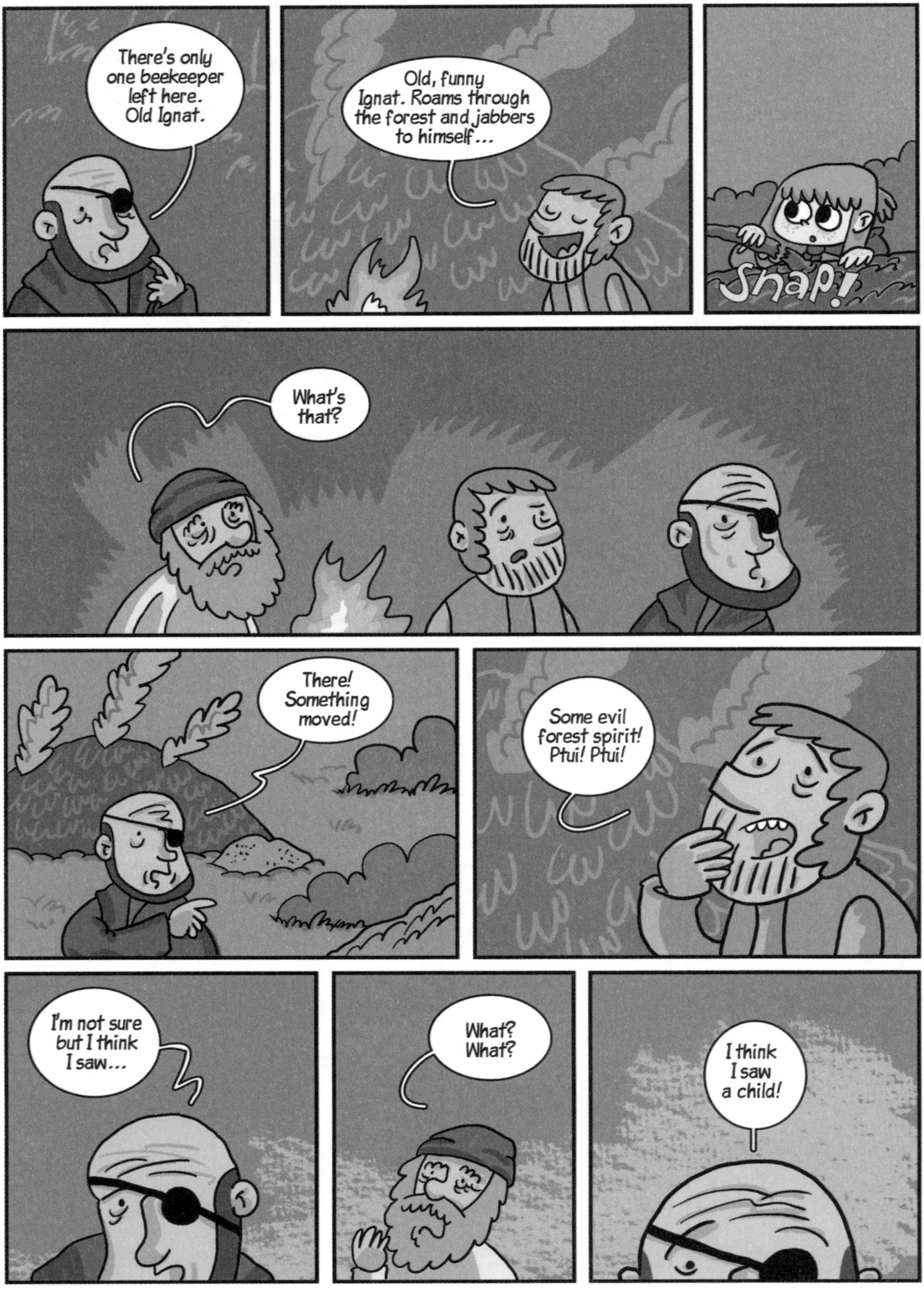
There's only one beekeeper left here. Old Ignat.
Old, funny Ignat. Roams through the forest and jabbers to himself...
Snap!
What's that?
There! Something moved!
Some evil forest spirit! Ptui! Ptui!
I'm not sure but I think I saw...
What? What?
I think I saw a child!

Mother bear, we are back with the tools! We'll free you in no time!

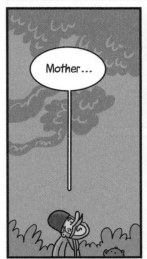

Mother...

She must've found her way down.

Now, little one, you must go and find your mum.

You'll be fine!

Ro?

All right, all right! You can stick with me in the meantime.

29

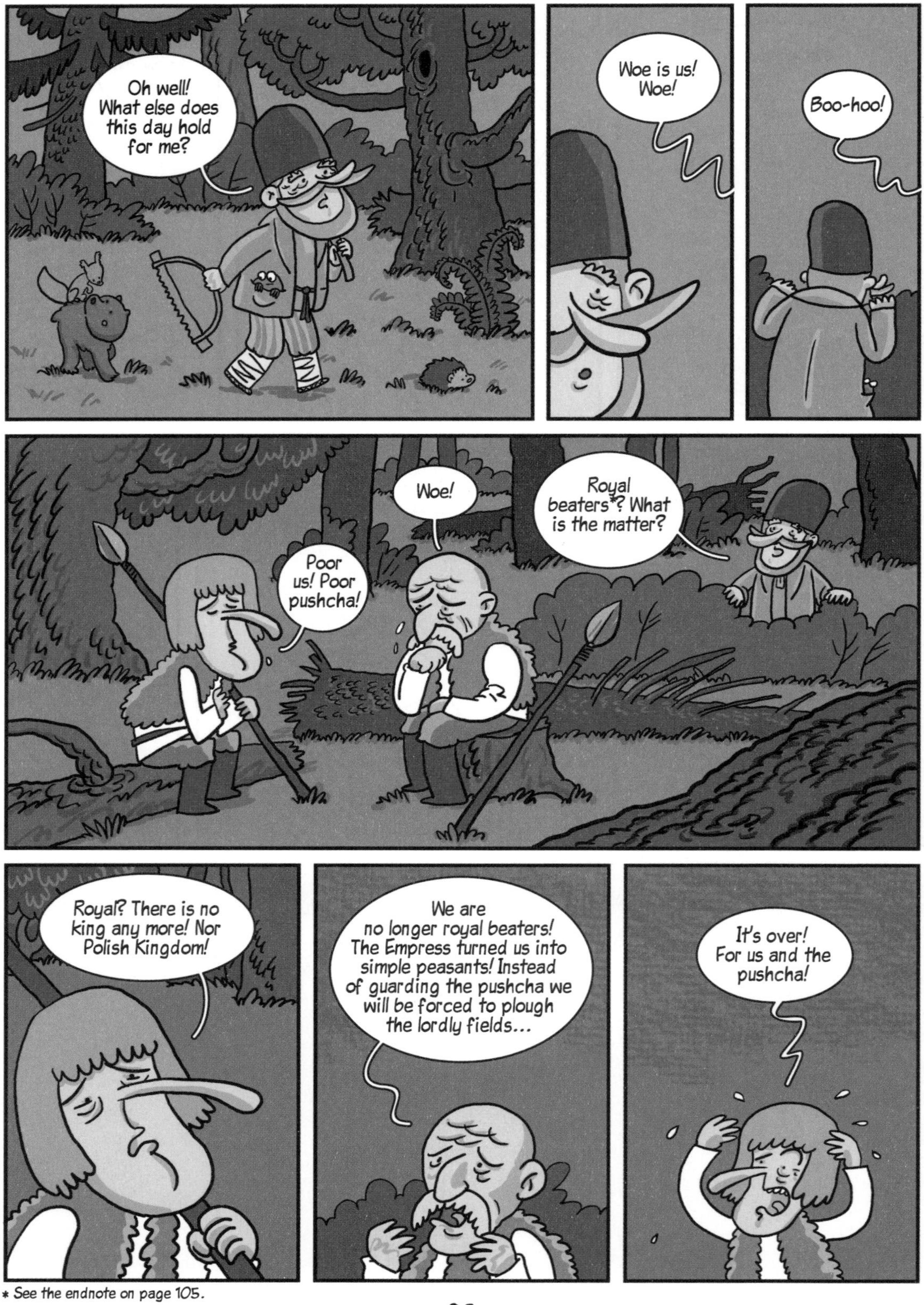
Oh well! What else does this day hold for me?
Woe is us! Woe!
Boo-hoo!
Woe!
Royal beaters*? What is the matter?
Poor us! Poor pushcha!
Royal? There is no king any more! Nor Polish Kingdom!
We are no longer royal beaters! The Empress turned us into simple peasants! Instead of guarding the pushcha we will be forced to plough the lordly fields...
It's over! For us and the pushcha!

* See the endnote on page 105.

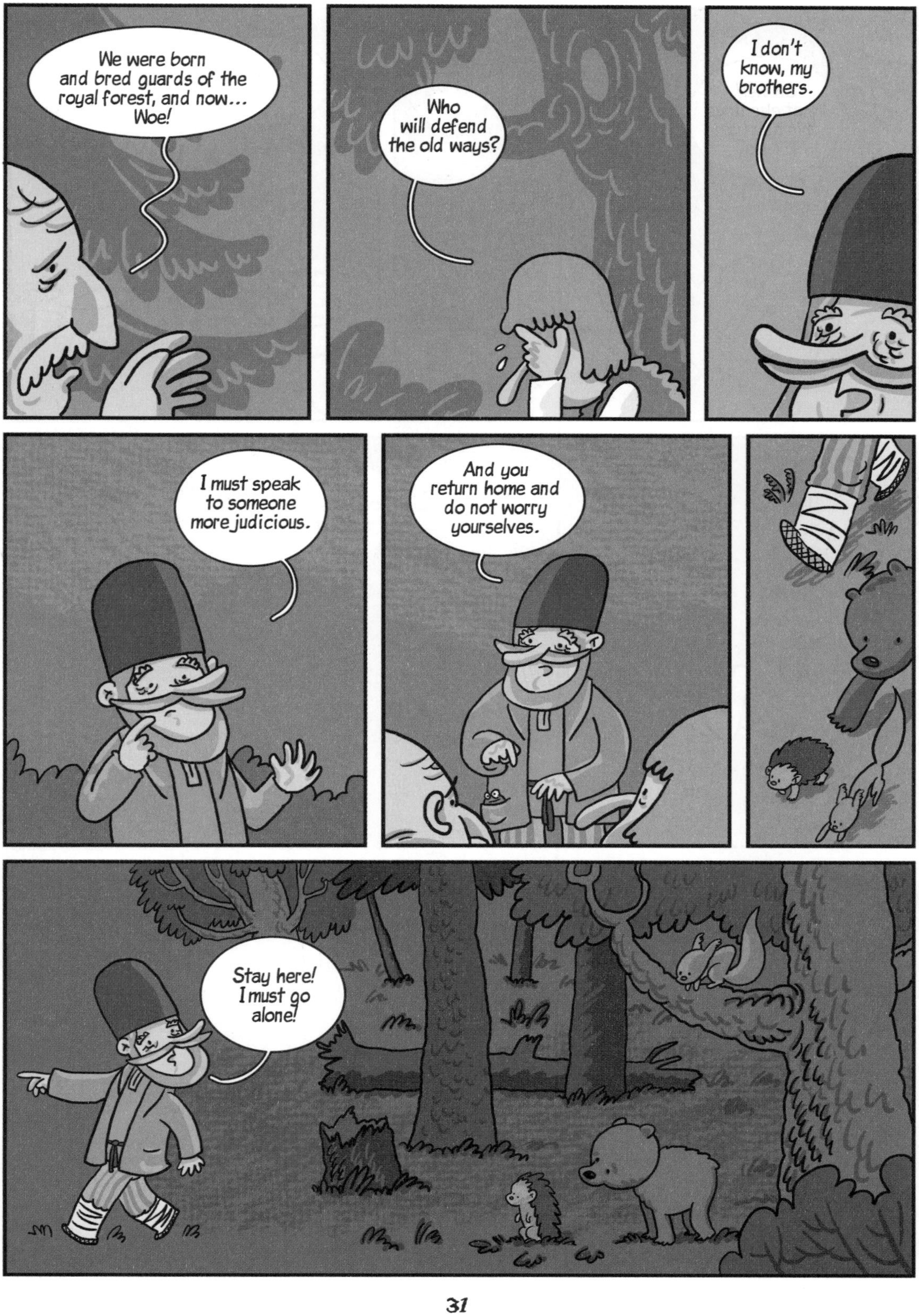
We were born and bred guards of the royal forest, and now... Woe!
Who will defend the old ways?
I don't know, my brothers.
I must speak to someone more judicious.
And you return home and do not worry yourselves.
Stay here! I must go alone!

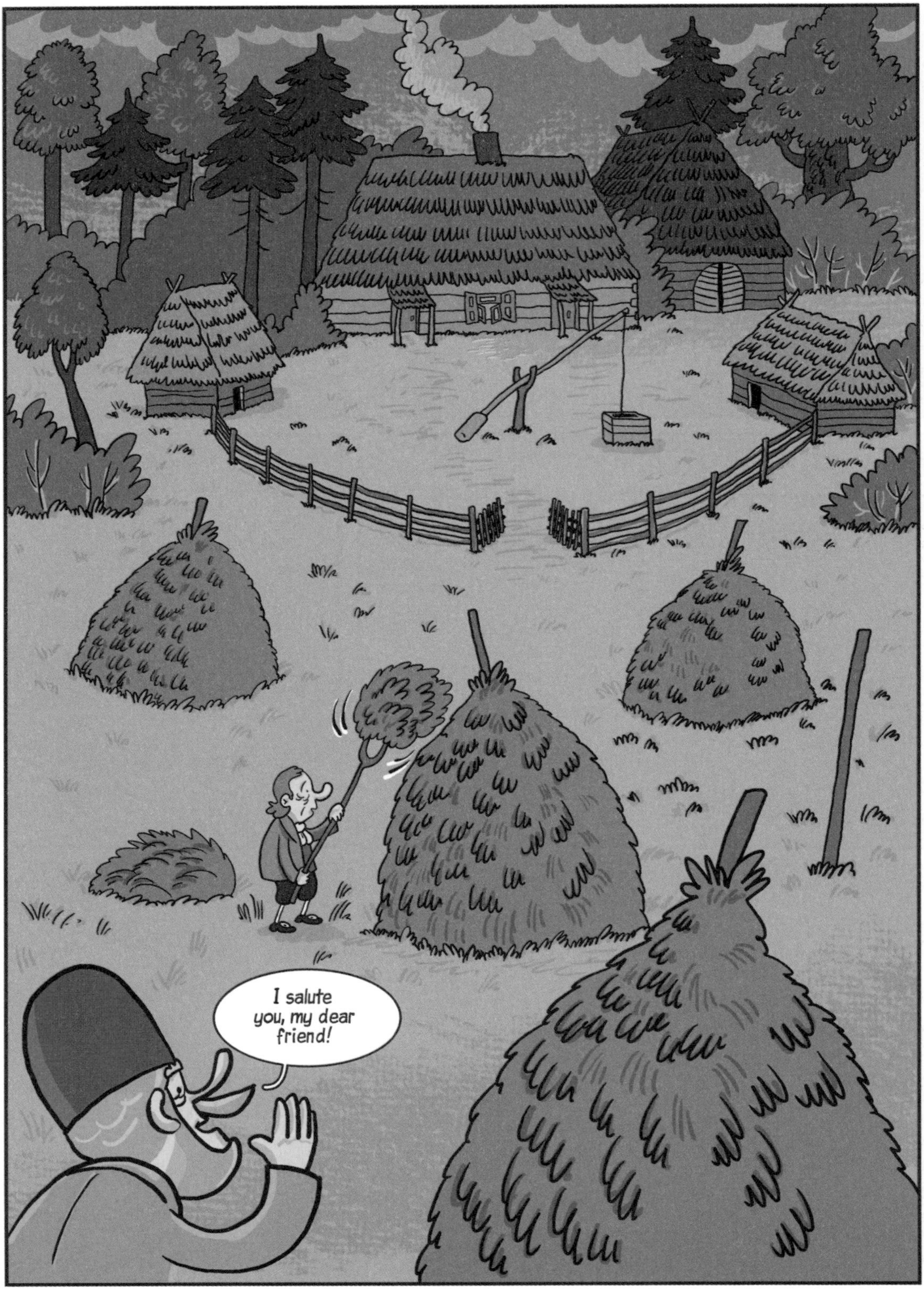
I salute you, my dear friend!

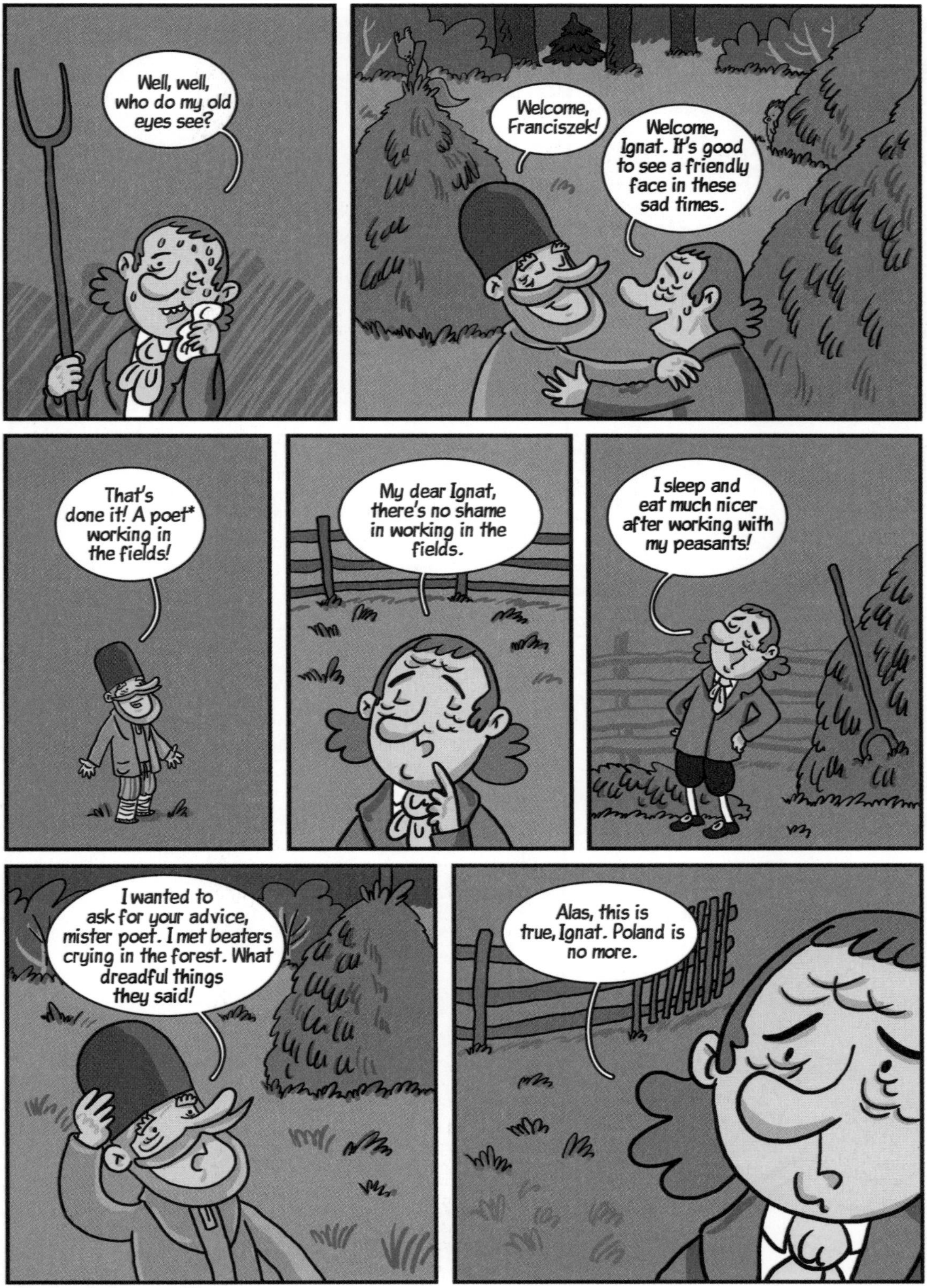
Well, well, who do my old eyes see?
Welcome, Franciszek!
Welcome, Ignat. It's good to see a friendly face in these sad times.
That's done it! A poet* working in the fields!
My dear Ignat, there's no shame in working in the fields.
I sleep and eat much nicer after working with my peasants!
I wanted to ask for your advice, mister poet. I met beaters crying in the forest. What dreadful things they said!
Alas, this is true, Ignat. Poland is no more.

* See the endnote on page 111.

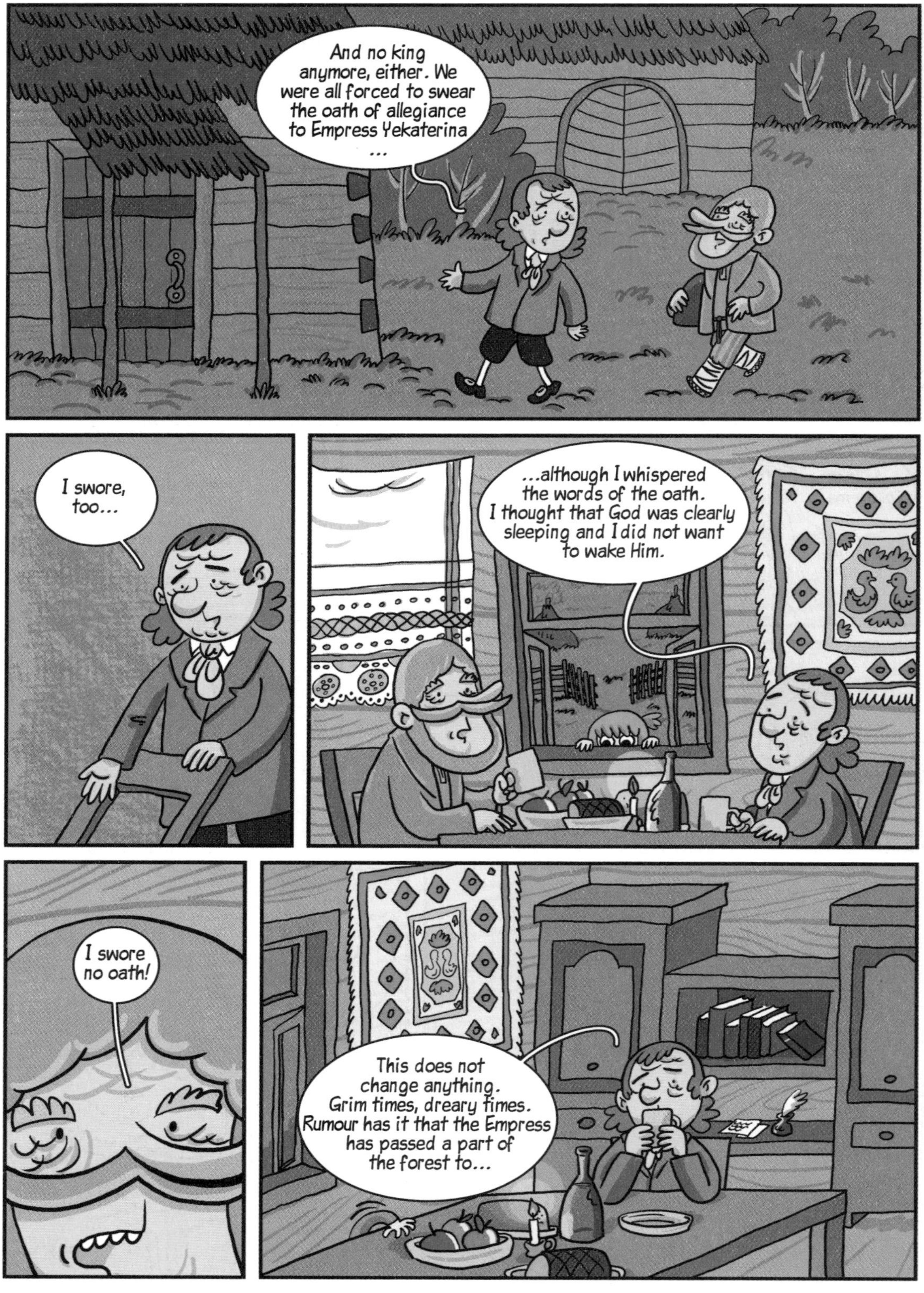
And no king anymore, either. We were all forced to swear the oath of allegiance to Empress Yekaterina ...
I swore, too...
...although I whispered the words of the oath. I thought that God was clearly sleeping and I did not want to wake Him.
I swore no oath!
This does not change anything. Grim times, dreary times. Rumour has it that the Empress has passed a part of the forest to...

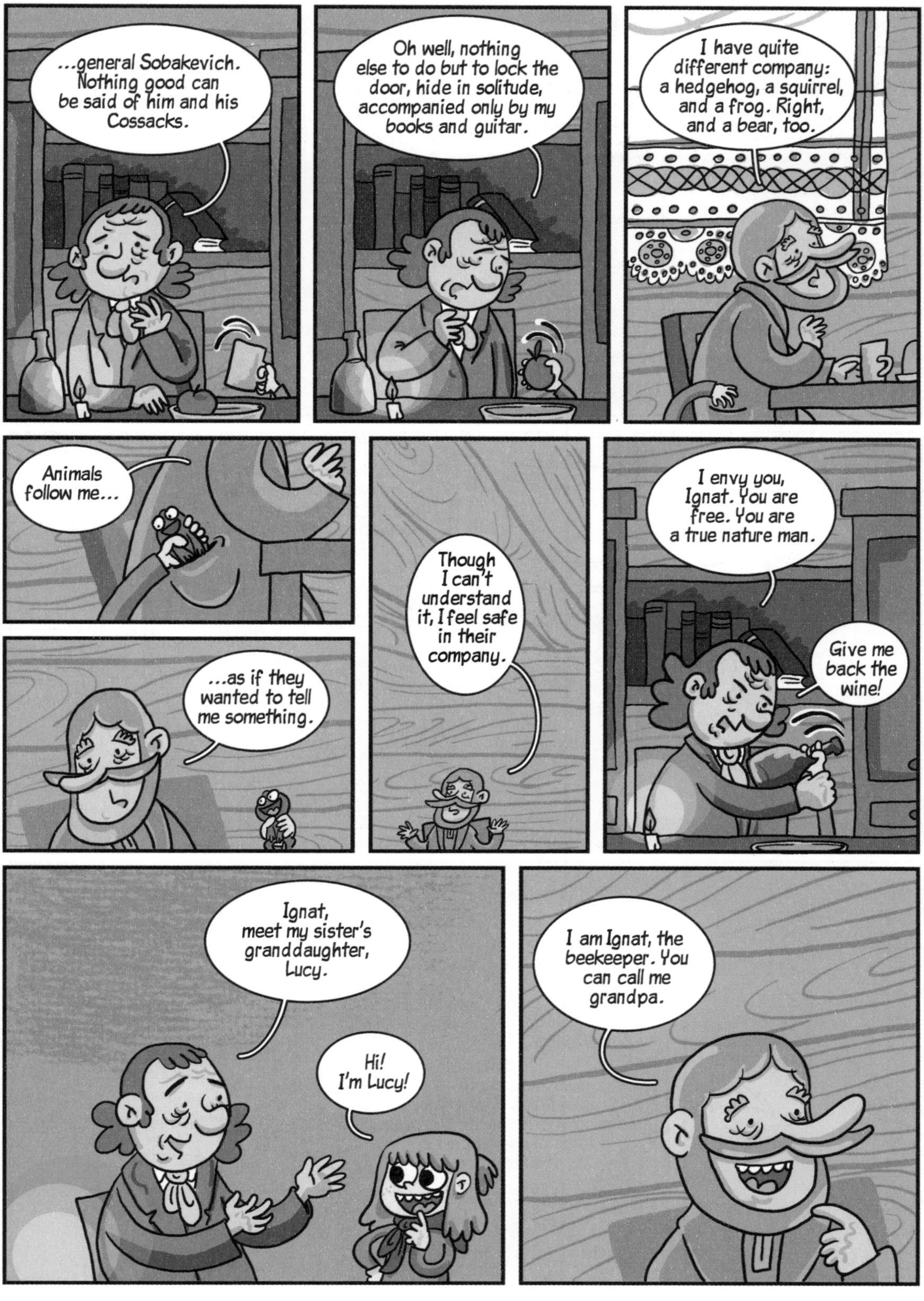
...general Sobakevich. Nothing good can be said of him and his Cossacks.
Oh well, nothing else to do but to lock the door, hide in solitude, accompanied only by my books and guitar.
I have quite different company: a hedgehog, a squirrel, and a frog. Right, and a bear, too.
Animals follow me...
...as if they wanted to tell me something.
Though I can't understand it, I feel safe in their company.
I envy you, Ignat. You are free. You are a true nature man.
Give me back the wine!
Ignat, meet my sister's granddaughter, Lucy.
Hi! I'm Lucy!
I am Ignat, the beekeeper. You can call me grandpa.

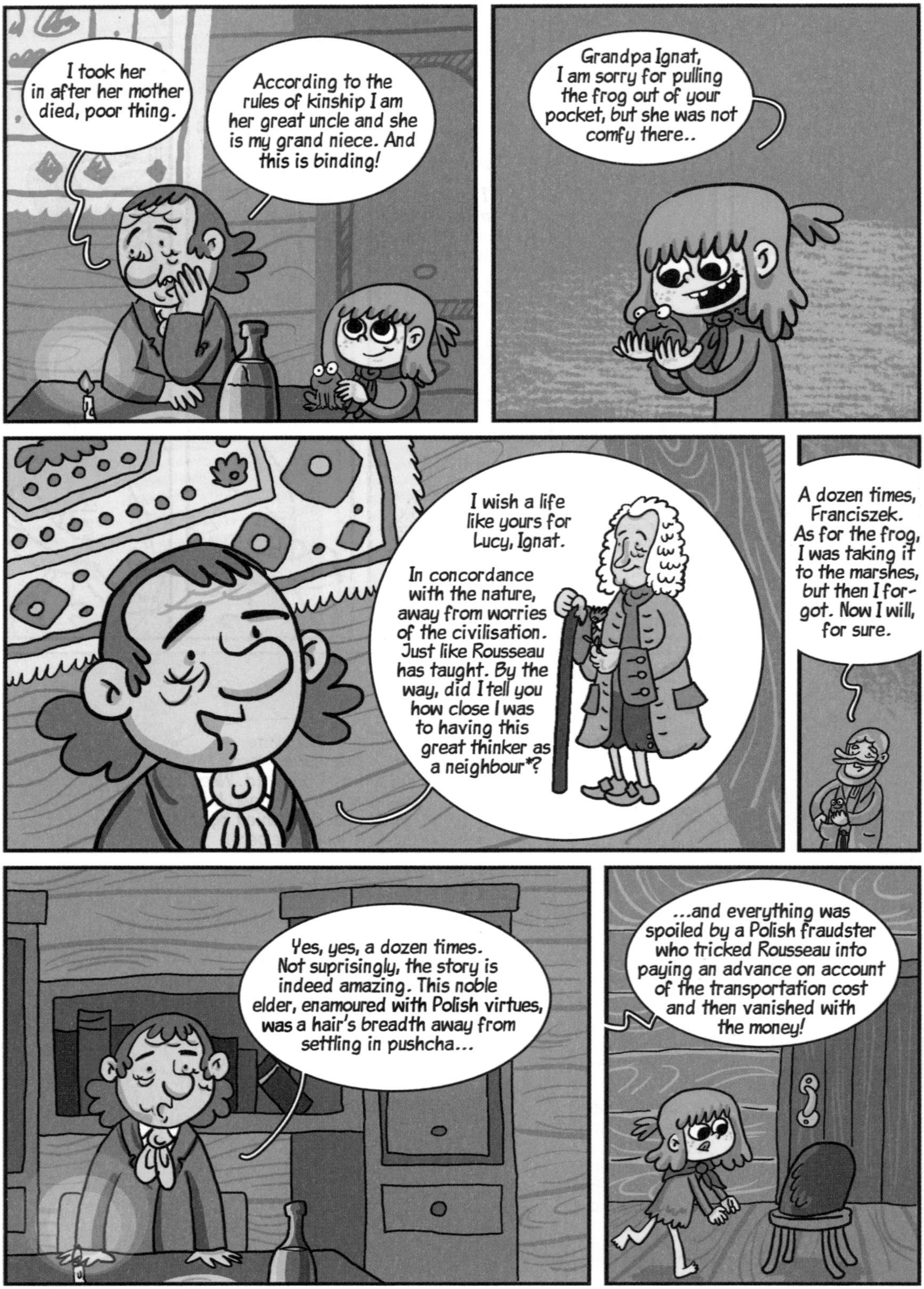

I took her in after her mother died, poor thing.
According to the rules of kinship I am her great uncle and she is my grand niece. And this is binding!
Grandpa Ignat, I am sorry for pulling the frog out of your pocket, but she was not comfy there..
I wish a life like yours for Lucy, Ignat.
In concordance with the nature, away from worries of the civilisation. Just like Rousseau has taught. By the way, did I tell you how close I was to having this great thinker as a neighbour*?
A dozen times, Franciszek. As for the frog, I was taking it to the marshes, but then I for-got. Now I will, for sure.
Yes, yes, a dozen times. Not suprisingly, the story is indeed amazing. This noble elder, enamoured with Polish virtues, was a hair's breadth away from settling in pushcha...
...and everything was spoiled by a Polish fraudster who tricked Rousseau into paying an advance on account of the transportation cost and then vanished with the money!

* See the endnote on page 111.

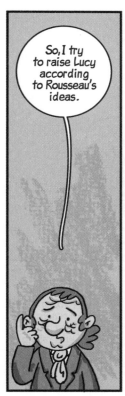

So, I try to raise Lucy according to Rousseau's ideas.

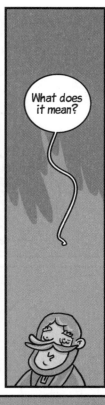

What does it mean?

I let her roam the forest and learn the world as it is.

But you, Franciszek, are not keen on going there!

BAM!

Huh?

I don't have the time, Ignat. All my free time is devoted to writing a poem about a hero from local legends.

The White Beekeeper, ancient defender of this land. Whenever pushcha was in danger, he would appear, accompanied by three animal helpers.

Legend has it that he was guarding the Covertwood, pushcha's most secret place. But what was there? Nobody knows.

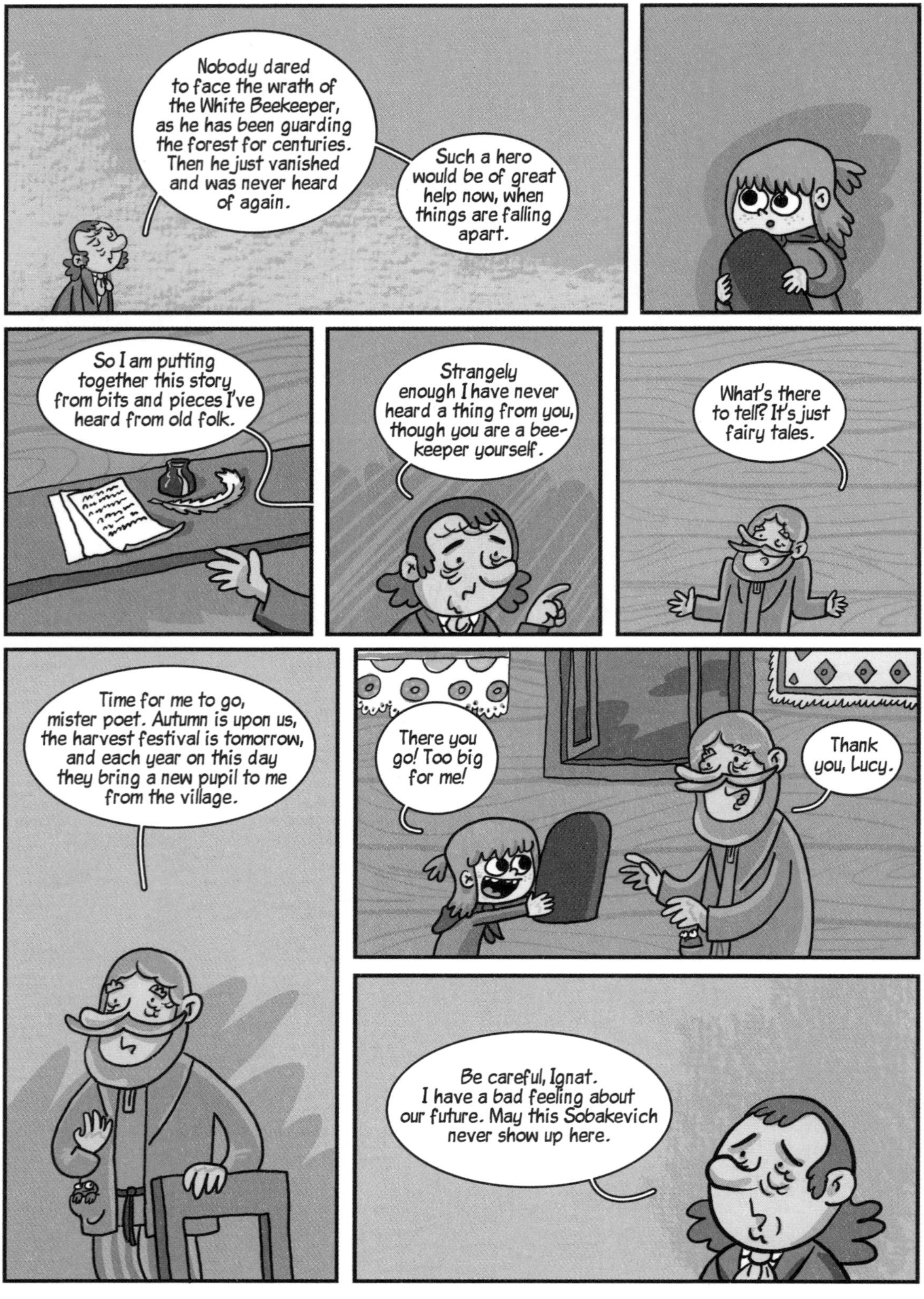
Nobody dared to face the wrath of the White Beekeeper, as he has been guarding the forest for centuries. Then he just vanished and was never heard of again.
Such a hero would be of great help now, when things are falling apart.
So I am putting together this story from bits and pieces I've heard from old folk.
Strangely enough I have never heard a thing from you, though you are a bee-keeper yourself.
What's there to tell? It's just fairy tales.
Time for me to go, mister poet. Autumn is upon us, the harvest festival is tomorrow, and each year on this day they bring a new pupil to me from the village.
There you go! Too big for me!
Thank you, Lucy.
Be careful, Ignat. I have a bad feeling about our future. May this Sobakevich never show up here.

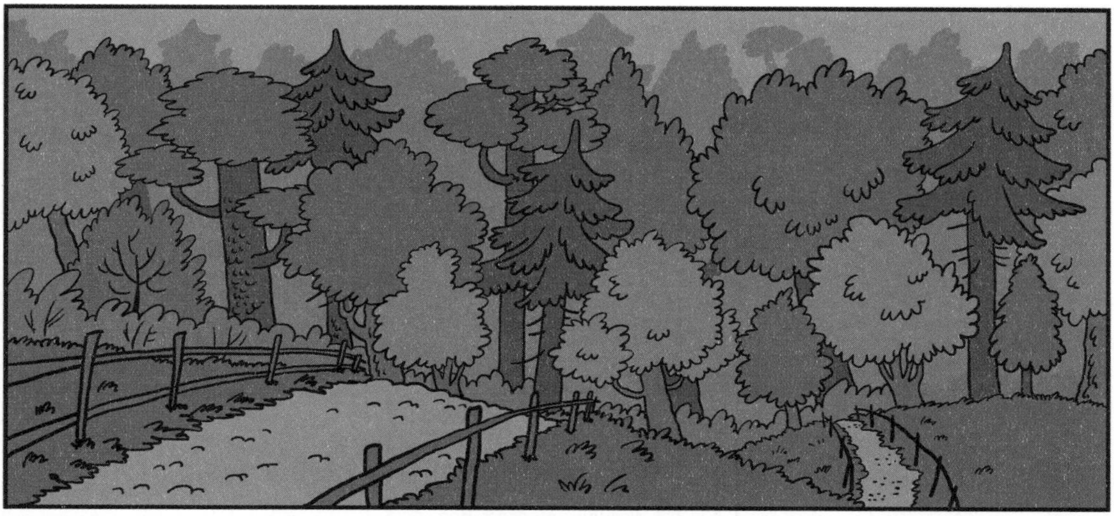

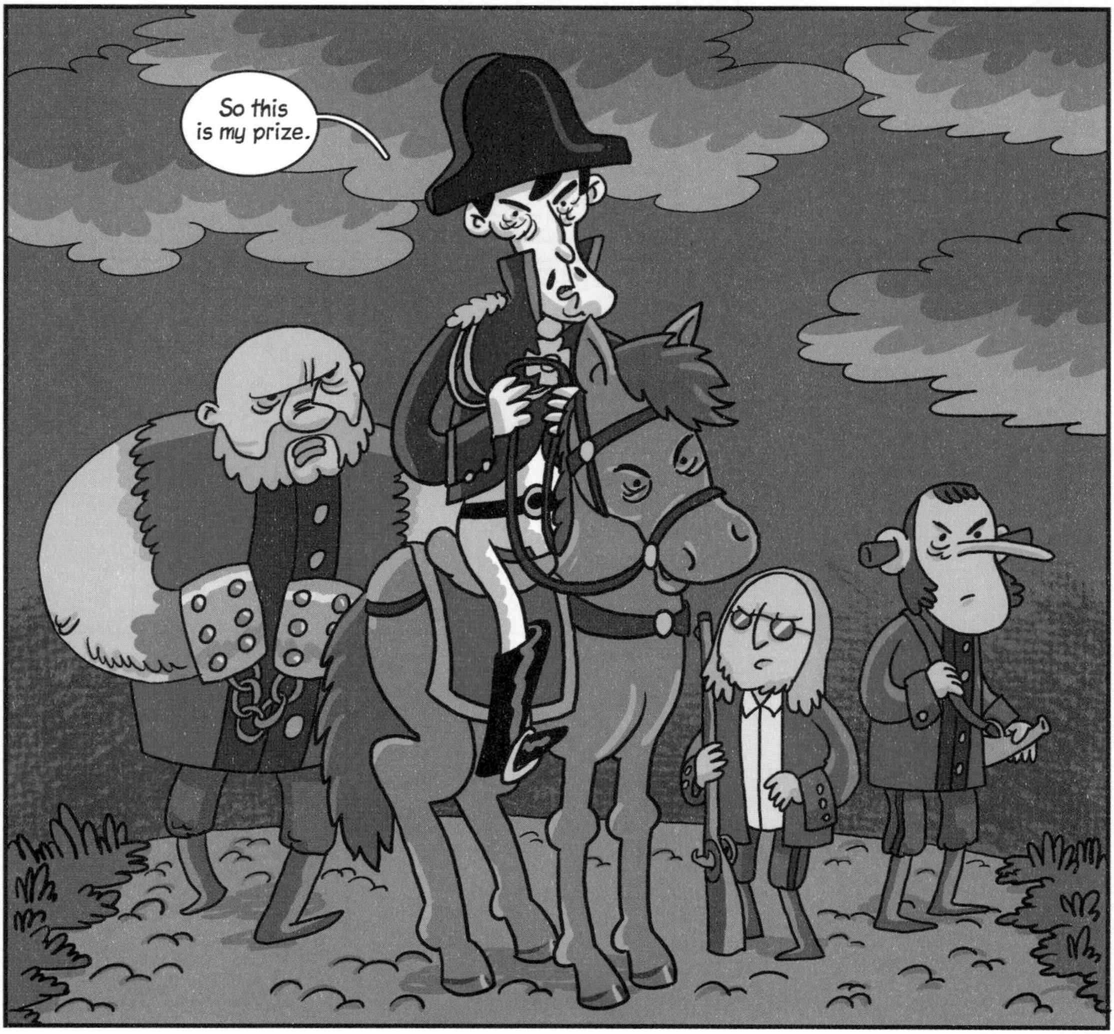
So this is my prize.

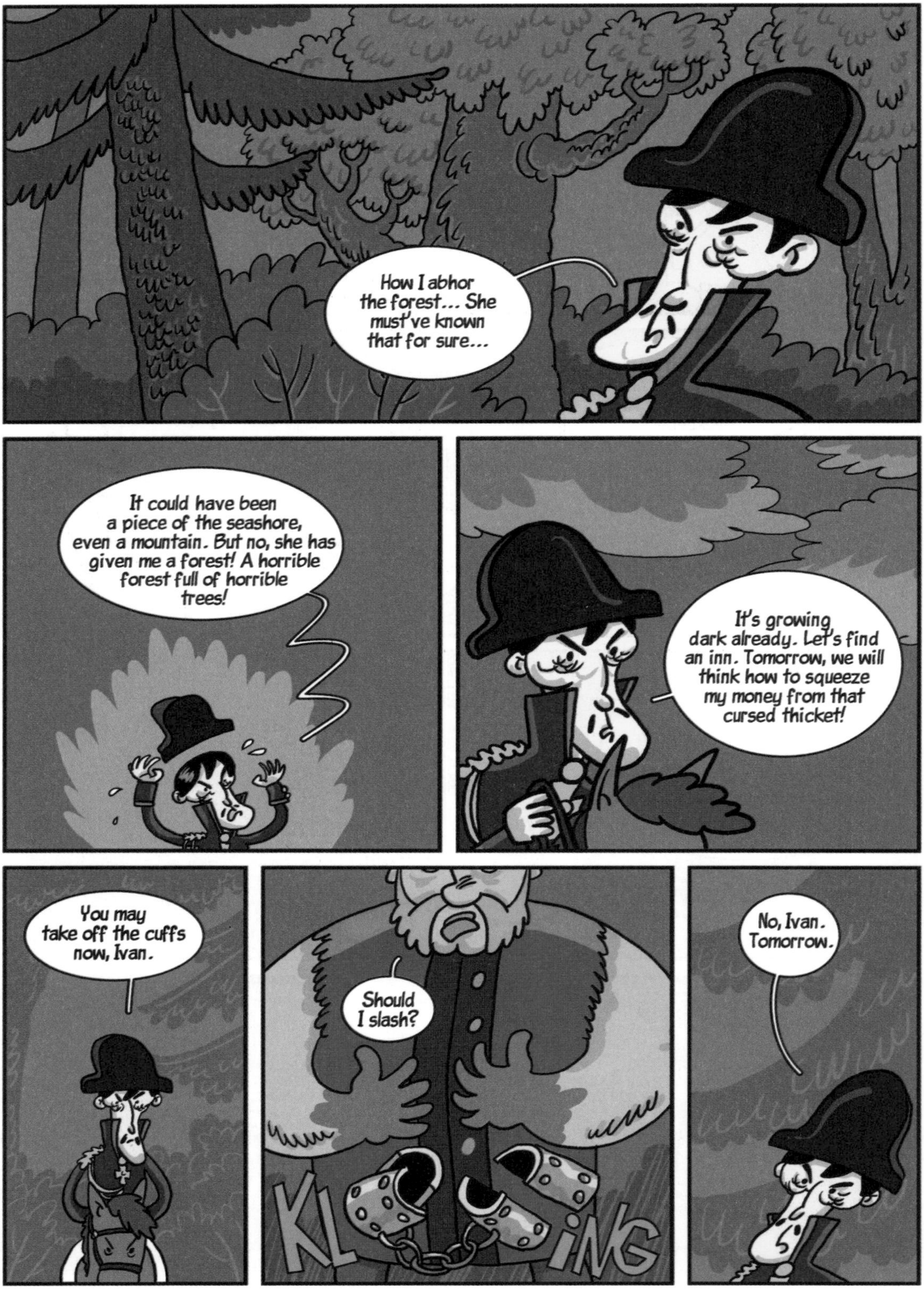
How I abhor the forest... She must've known that for sure...
It could have been a piece of the seashore, even a mountain. But no, she has given me a forest! A horrible forest full of horrible trees!
It's growing dark already. Let's find an inn. Tomorrow, we will think how to squeeze my money from that cursed thicket!
You may take off the cuffs now, Ivan.
Should I slash?
KL
iNG
No, Ivan. Tomorrow.

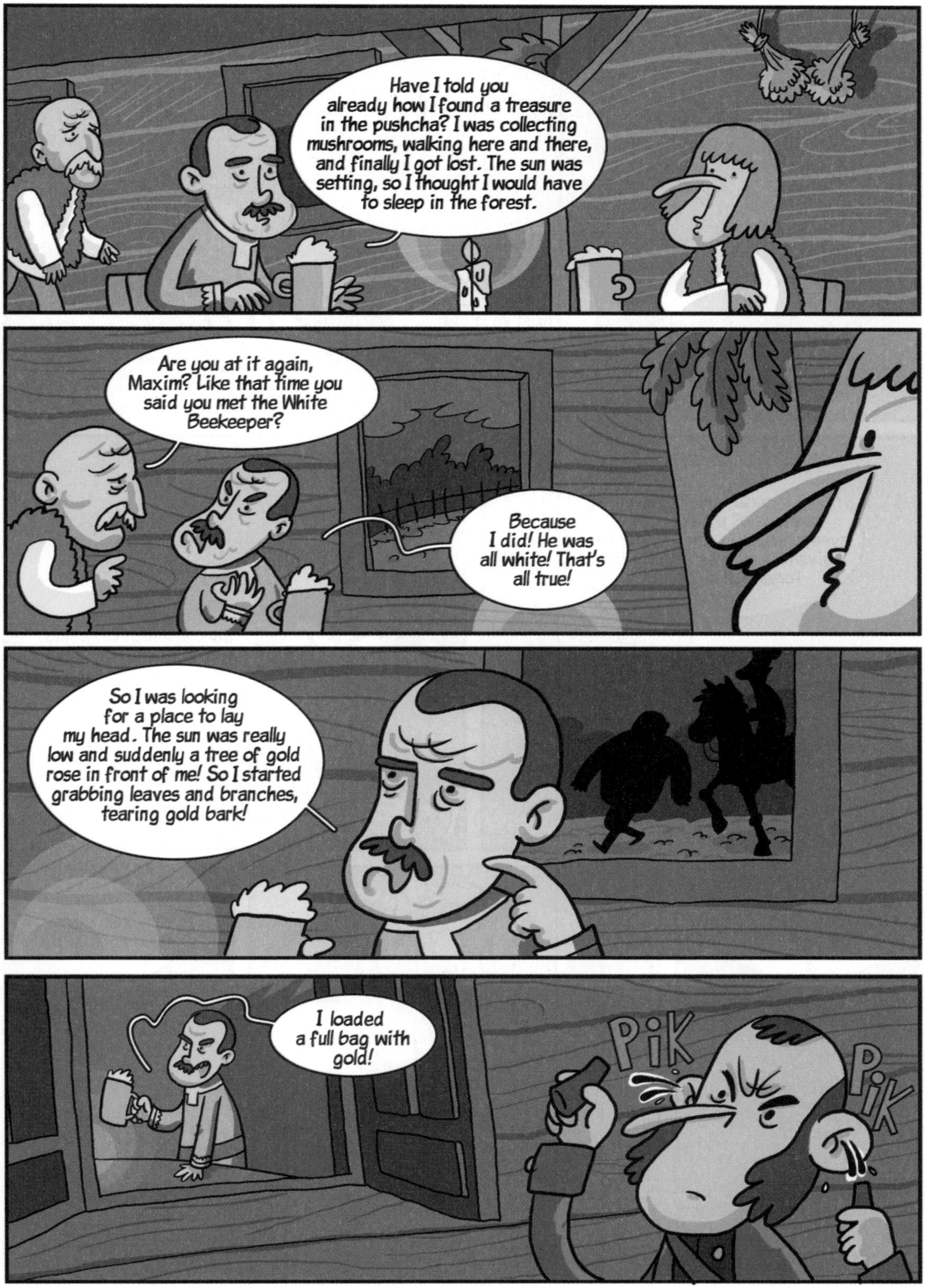
Have I told you already how I found a treasure in the pushcha? I was collecting mushrooms, walking here and there, and finally I got lost. The sun was setting, so I thought I would have to sleep in the forest.
Are you at it again, Maxim? Like that time you said you met the White Beekeeper?
Because I did! He was all white! That's all true!
So I was looking for a place to lay my head. The sun was really low and suddenly a tree of gold rose in front of me! So I started grabbing leaves and branches, tearing gold bark!
I loaded a full bag with gold!
PiK
PiK

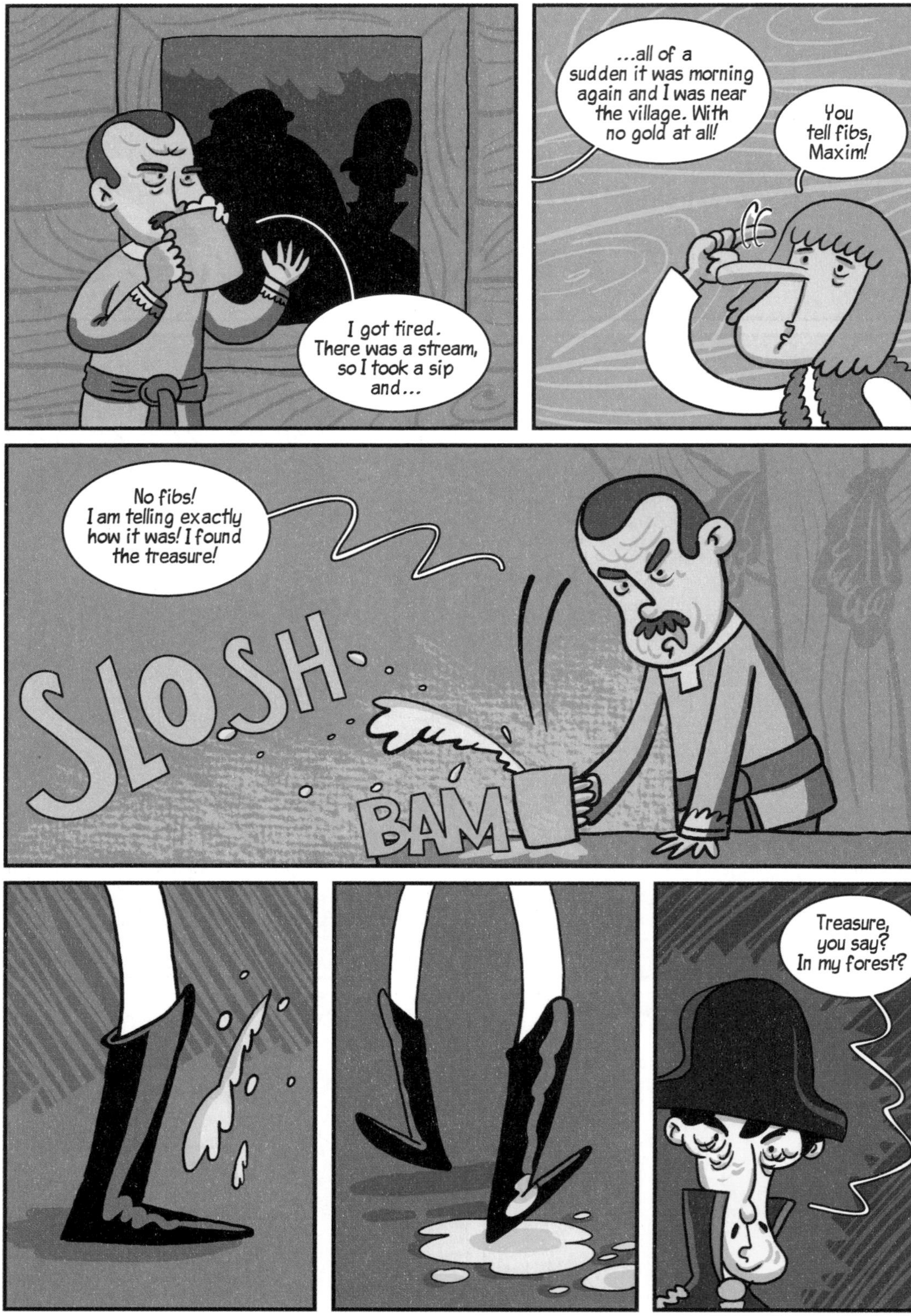
I got tired. There was a stream, so I took a sip and...
...all of a sudden it was morning again and I was near the village. With no gold at all!
You tell fibs, Maxim!
No fibs! I am telling exactly how it was! I found the treasure!
SLOSH
BAM
Treasure, you say? In my forest?

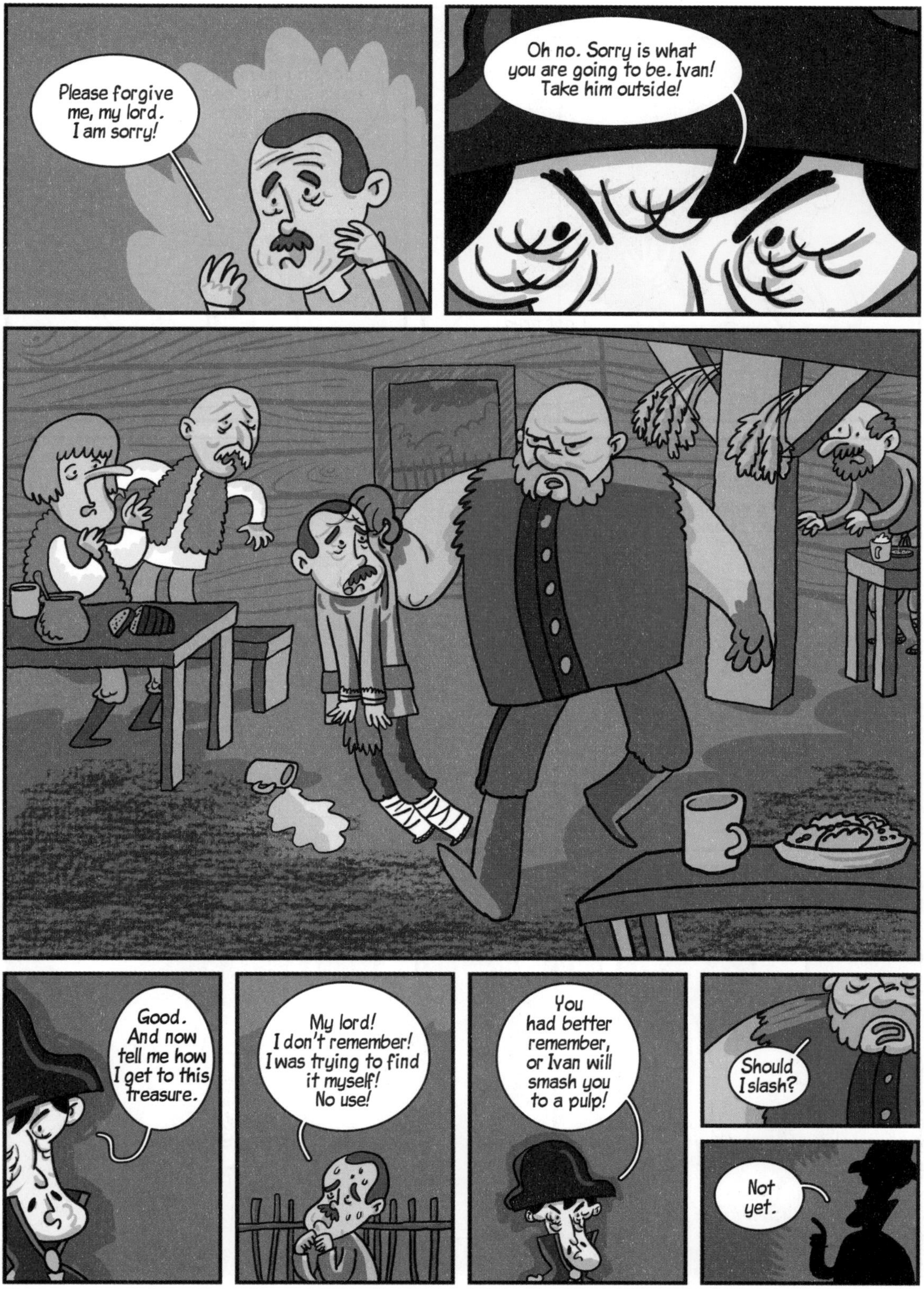
Please forgive me, my lord. I am sorry!
Oh no. Sorry is what you are going to be. Ivan! Take him outside!
Good. And now tell me how I get to this treasure.
My lord! I don't remember! I was trying to find it myself! No use!
You had better remember, or Ivan will smash you to a pulp!
Should I slash?
Not yet.

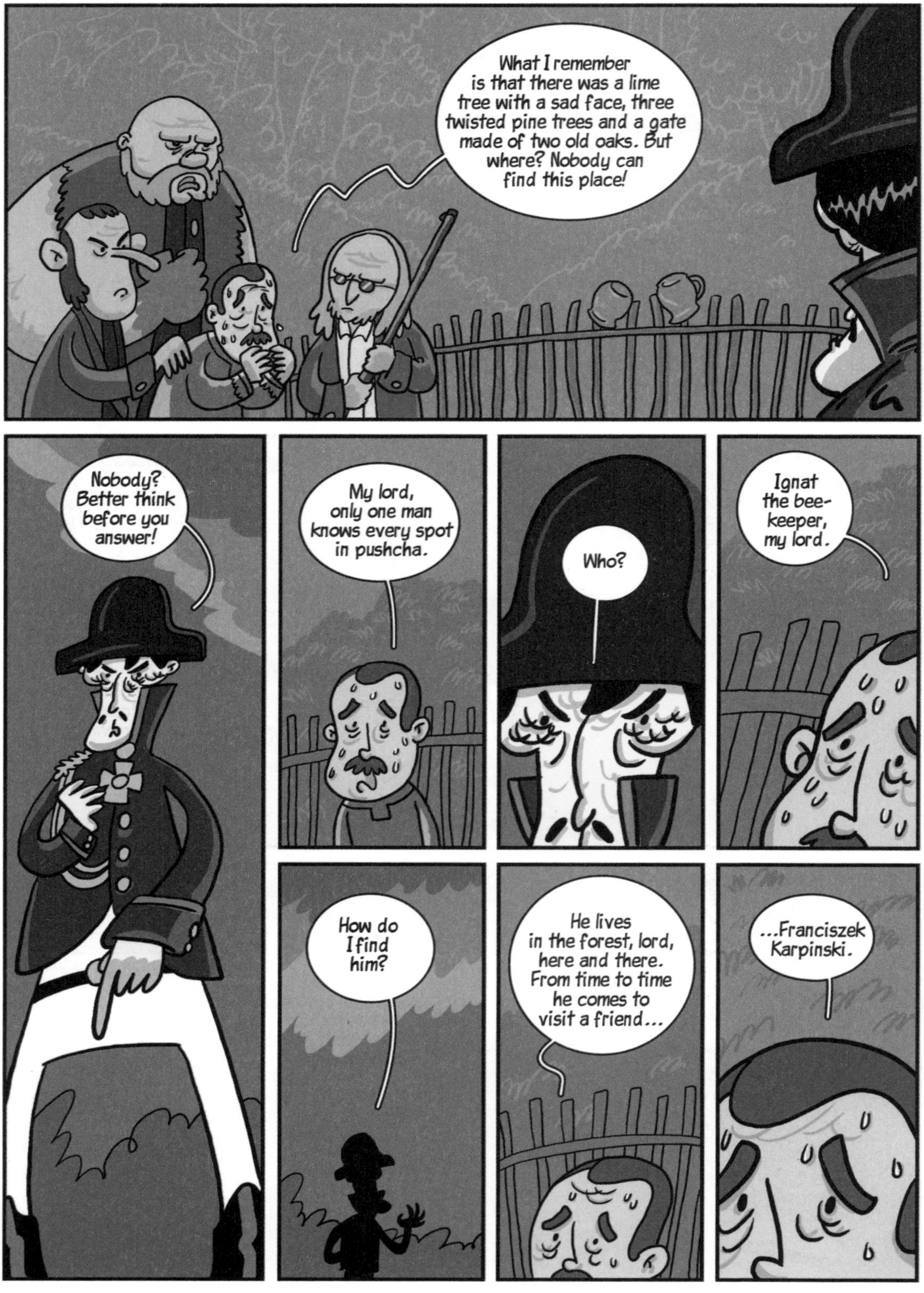
What I remember is that there was a lime tree with a sad face, three twisted pine trees and a gate made of two old oaks. But where? Nobody can find this place!
Nobody? Better think before you answer!
My lord, only one man knows every spot in pushcha.
Who?
Ignat the bee-keeper, my lord.
How do I find him?
He lives in the forest, lord, here and there. From time to time he comes to visit a friend...
...Franciszek Karpinski.

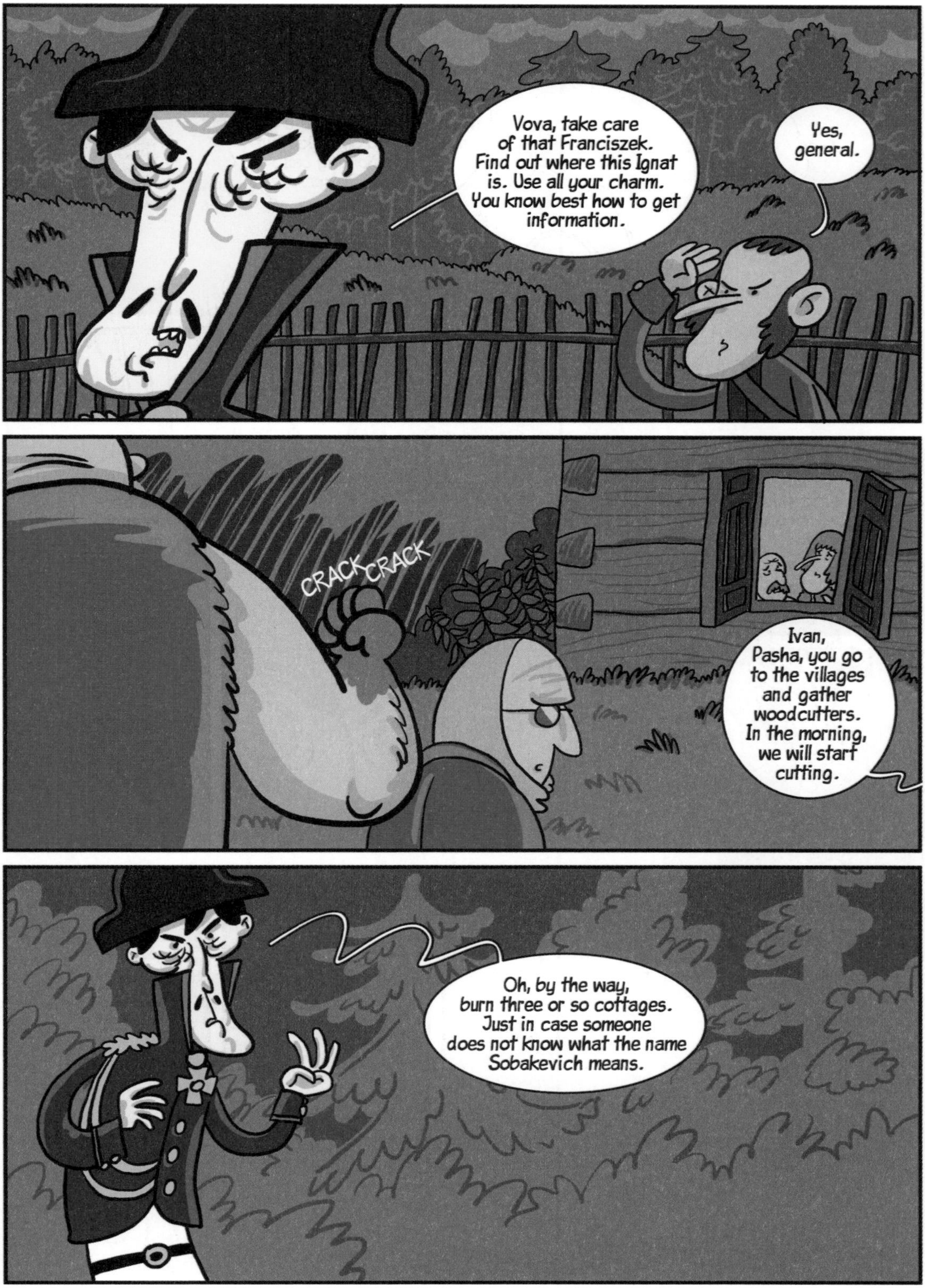
Vova, take care of that Franciszek. Find out where this Ignat is. Use all your charm. You know best how to get information.
Yes, general.
CRACK CRACK
Ivan, Pasha, you go to the villages and gather woodcutters. In the morning, we will start cutting.
Oh, by the way, burn three or so cottages. Just in case someone does not know what the name Sobakevich means.

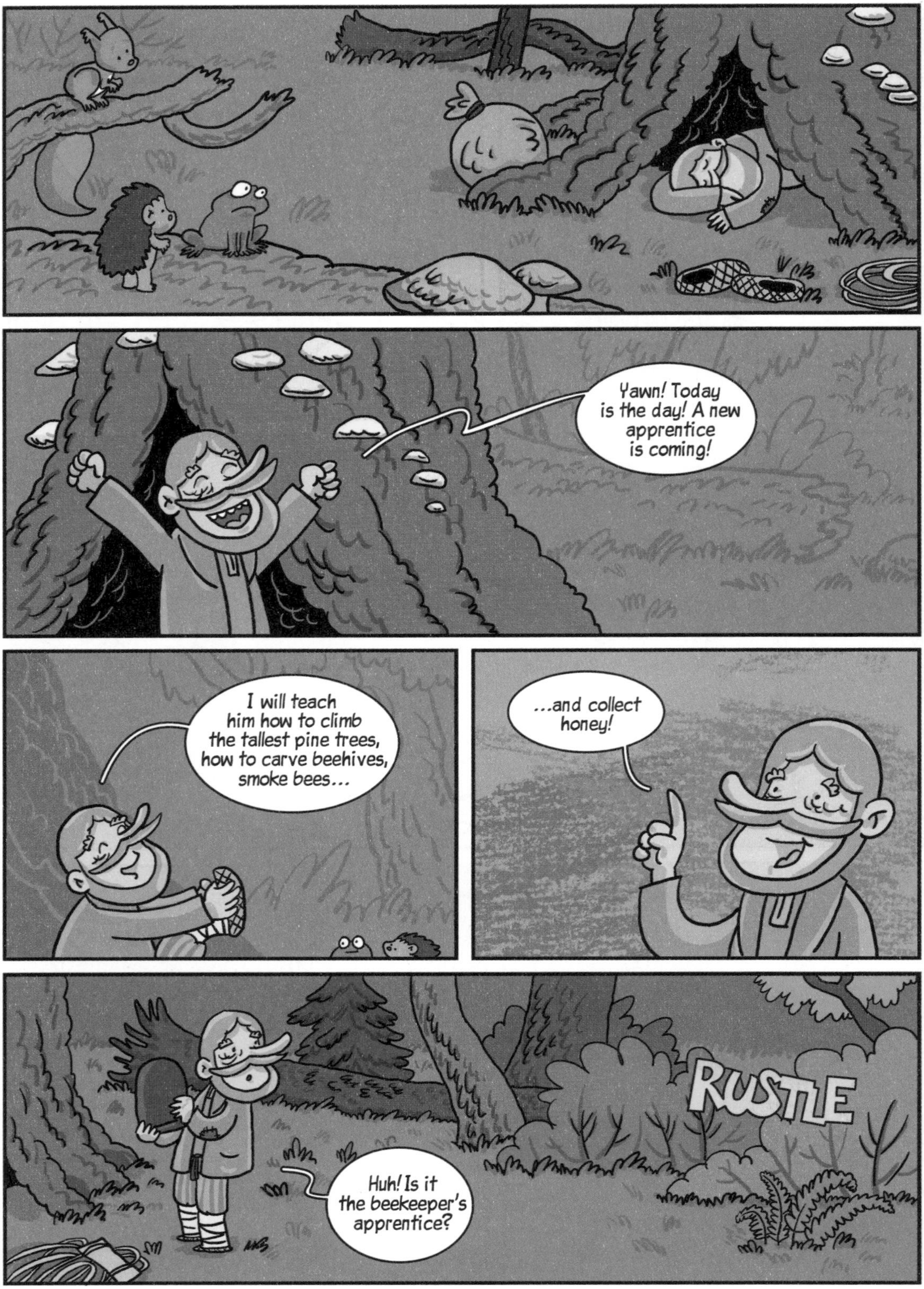
Yawn! Today is the day! A new apprentice is coming!
I will teach him how to climb the tallest pine trees, how to carve beehives, smoke bees...
...and collect honey!
RUSTLE
Huh! Is it the beekeeper's apprentice?

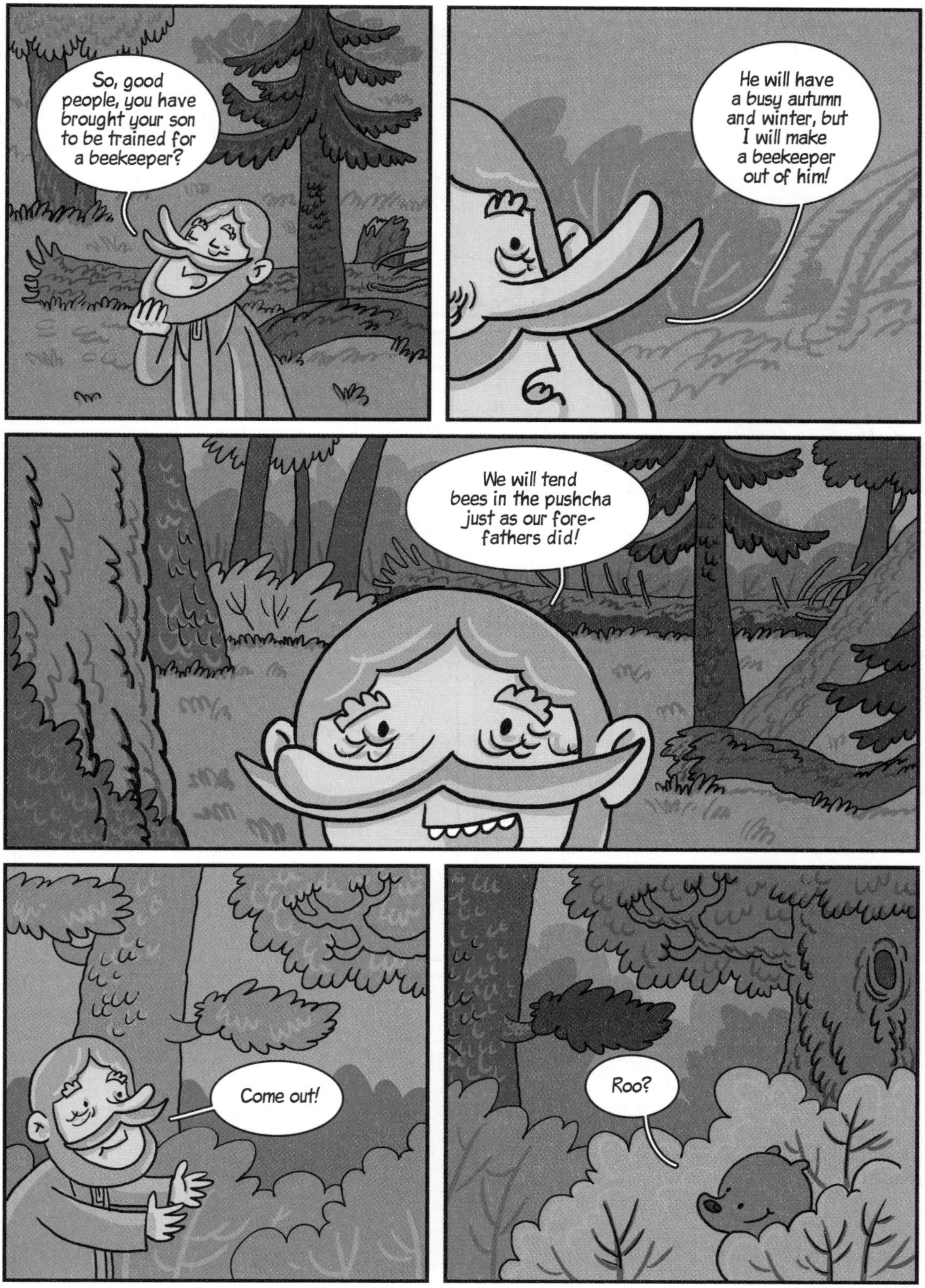
So, good people, you have brought your son to be trained for a beekeeper?
He will have a busy autumn and winter, but I will make a beekeeper out of him!
We will tend bees in the pushcha just as our fore-fathers did!
Come out!
Roo?

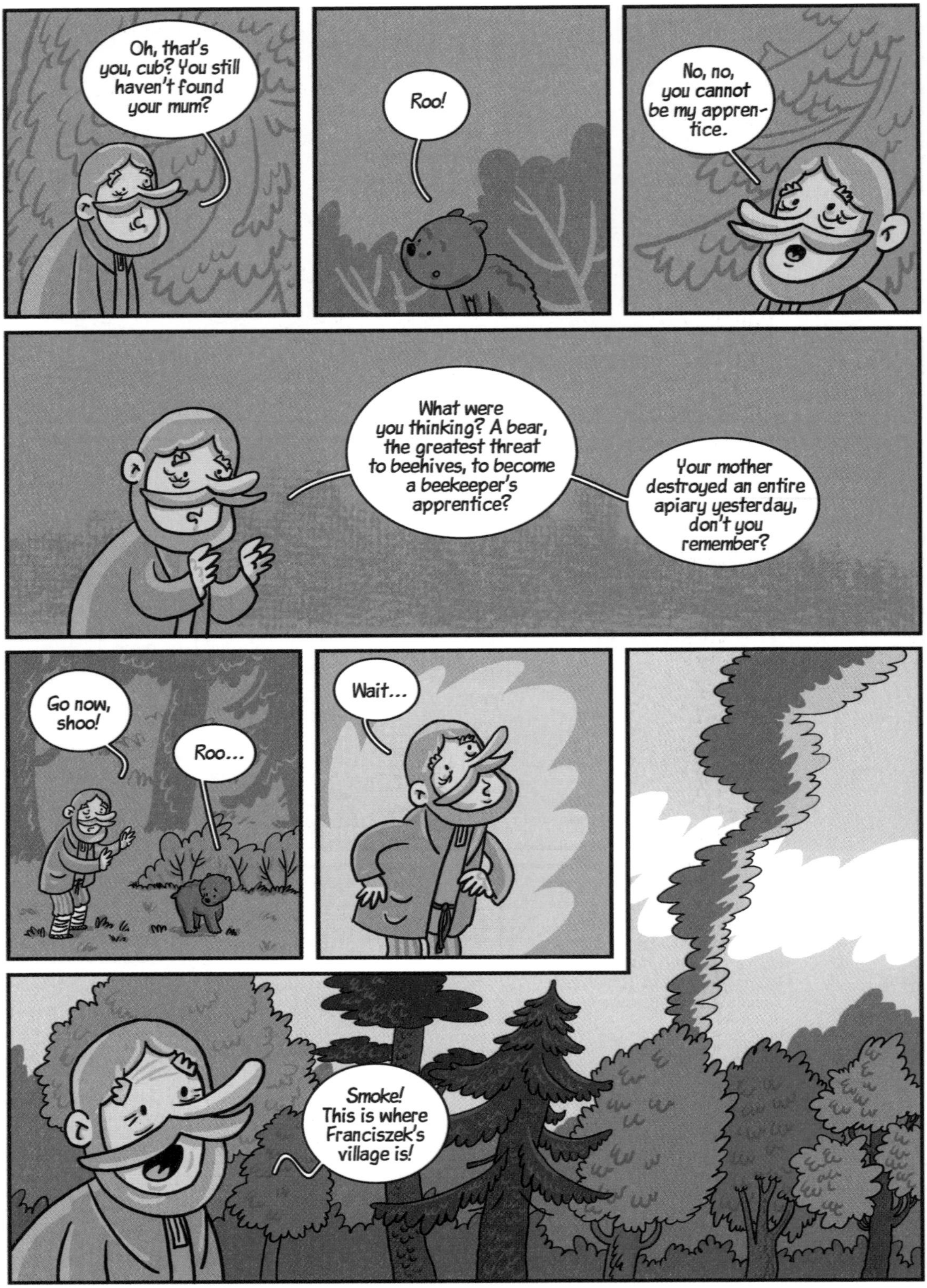

Oh, that's you, cub? You still haven't found your mum?
Roo!
No, no, you cannot be my apprentice.
What were you thinking? A bear, the greatest threat to beehives, to become a beekeeper's apprentice?
Your mother destroyed an entire apiary yesterday, don't you remember?
Go now, shoo!
Roo...
Wait...
Smoke! This is where Franciszek's village is!

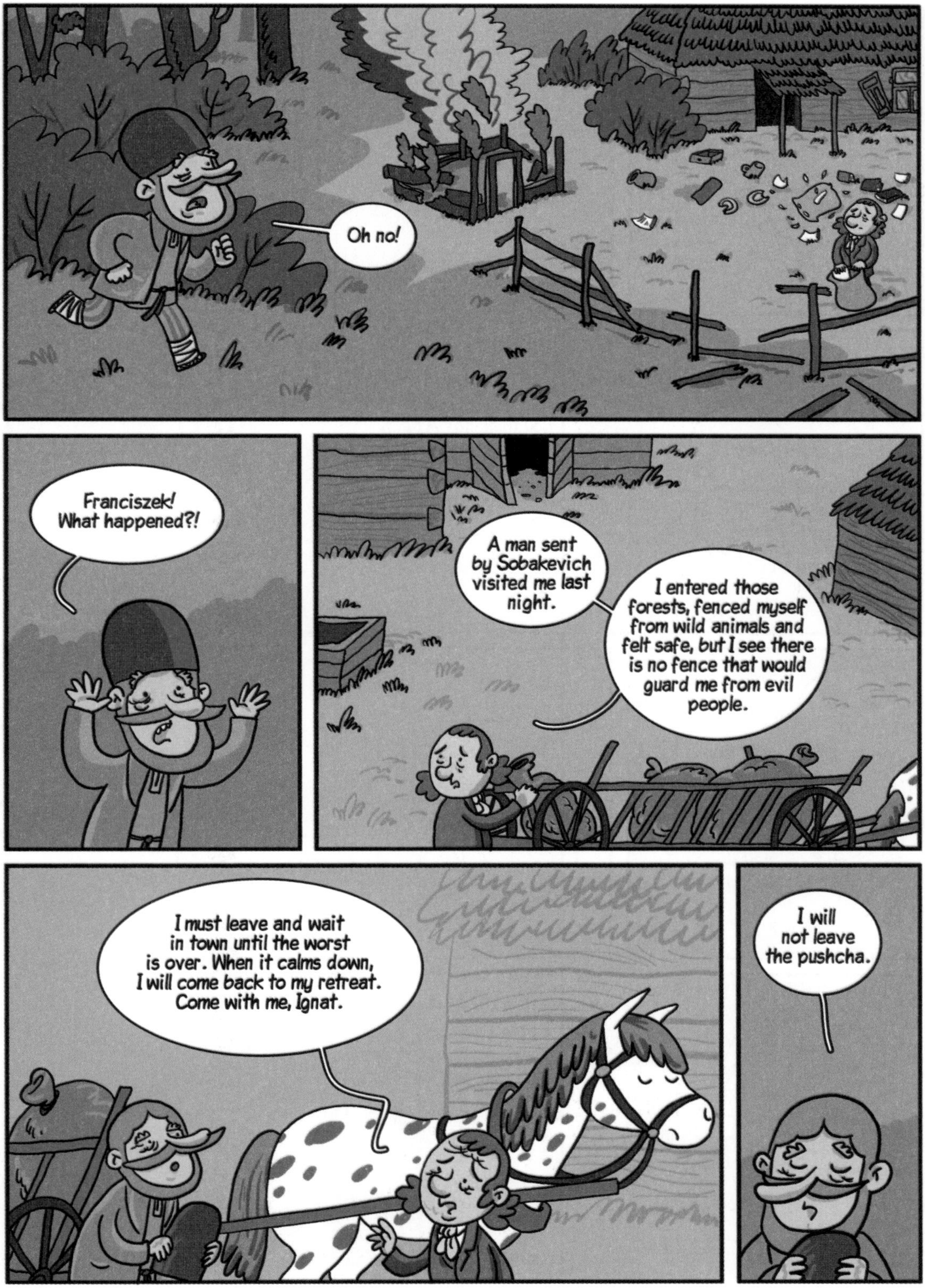
Oh no!
Franciszek! What happened?!
A man sent by Sobakevich visited me last night.
I entered those forests, fenced myself from wild animals and felt safe, but I see there is no fence that would guard me from evil people.
I must leave and wait in town until the worst is over. When it calms down, I will come back to my retreat. Come with me, Ignat.
I will not leave the pushcha.

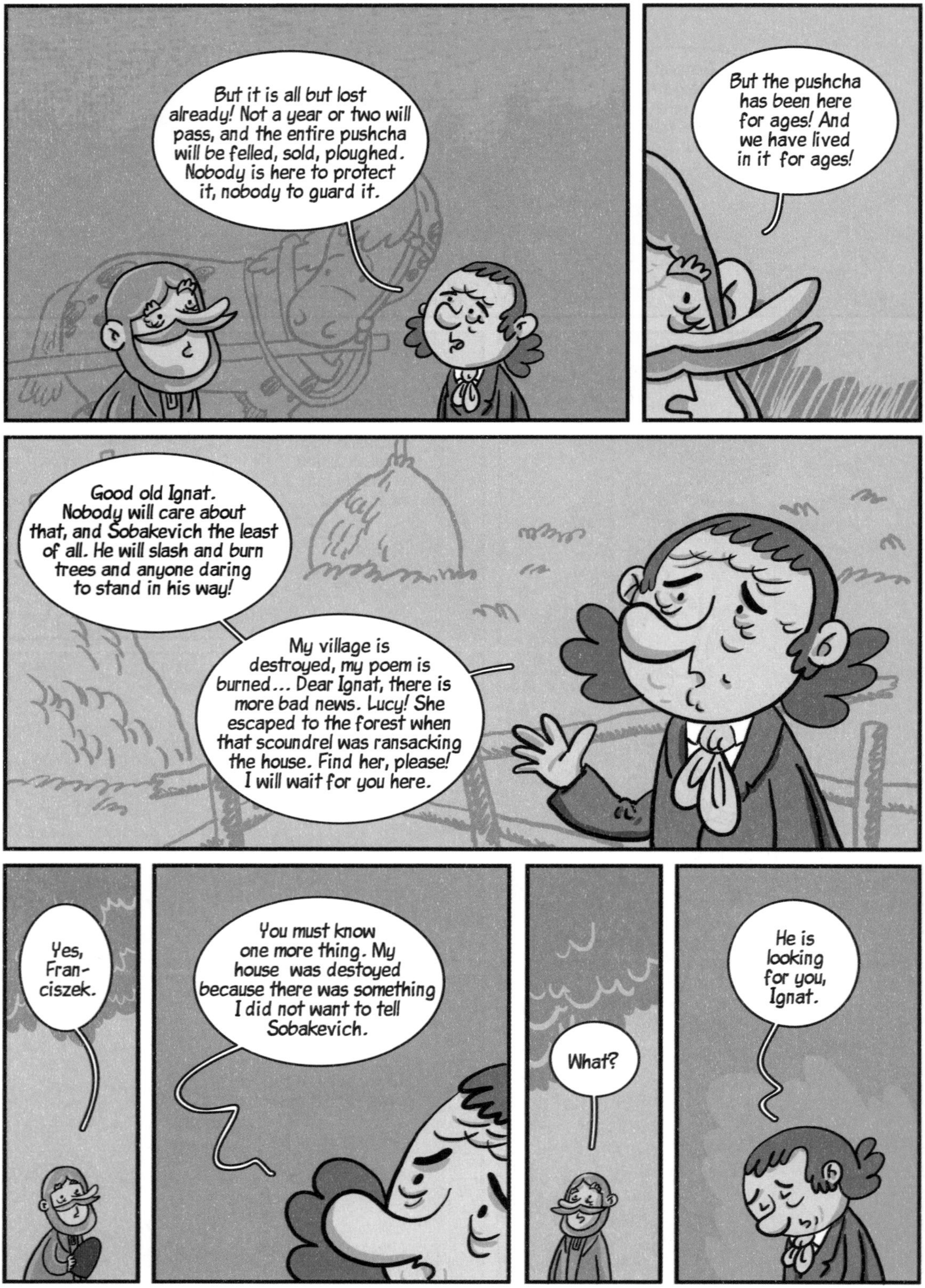
But it is all but lost already! Not a year or two will pass, and the entire pushcha will be felled, sold, ploughed. Nobody is here to protect it, nobody to guard it.
But the pushcha has been here for ages! And we have lived in it for ages!
Good old Ignat. Nobody will care about that, and Sobakevich the least of all. He will slash and burn trees and anyone daring to stand in his way!
My village is destroyed, my poem is burned... Dear Ignat, there is more bad news. Lucy! She escaped to the forest when that scoundrel was ransacking the house. Find her, please! I will wait for you here.
Yes, Fran-ciszek.
You must know one more thing. My house was destoyed because there was something I did not want to tell Sobakevich.
What?
He is looking for you, Ignat.

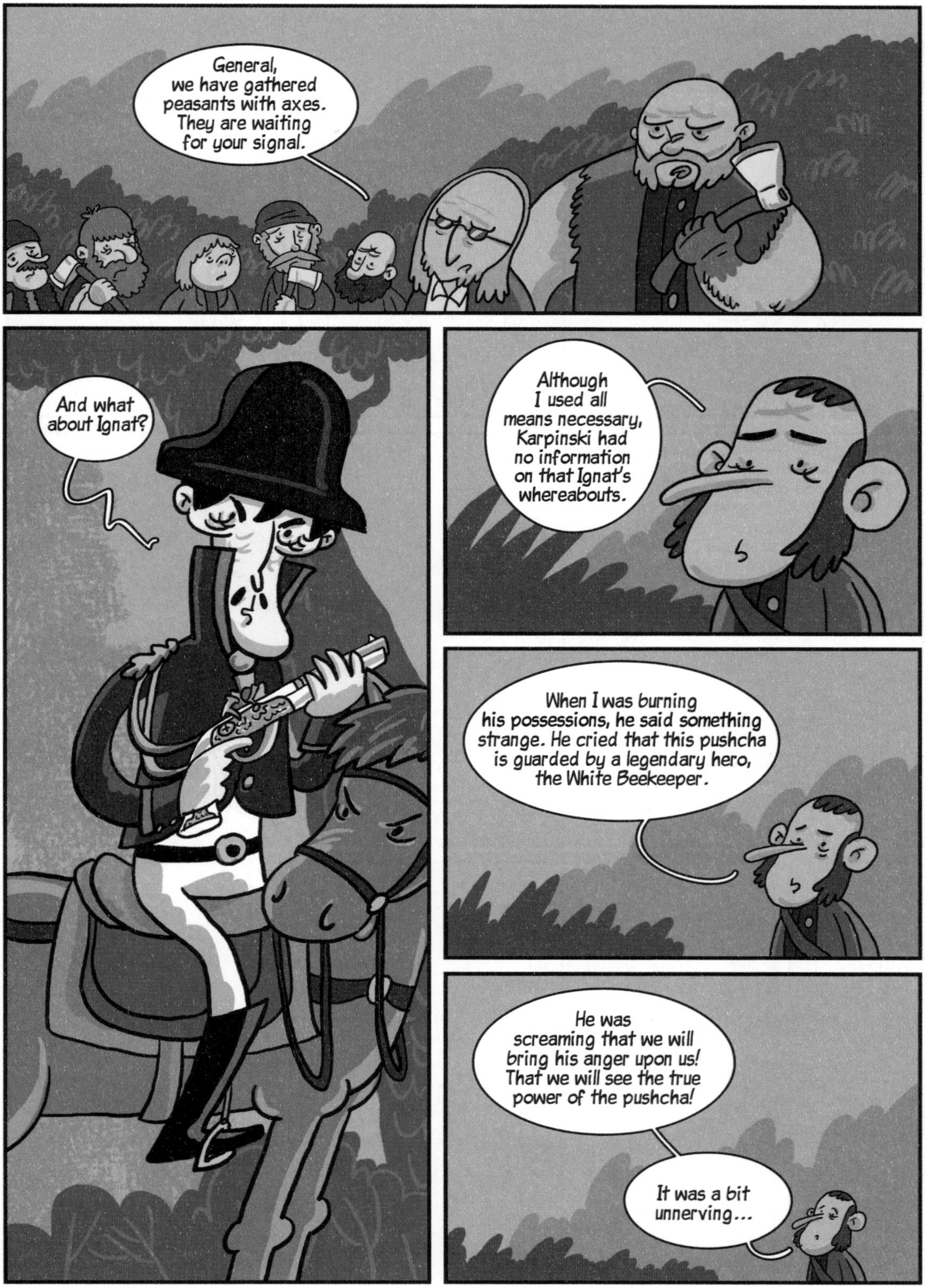
General, we have gathered peasants with axes. They are waiting for your signal.
And what about Ignat?
Although I used all means necessary, Karpinski had no information on that Ignat's whereabouts.
When I was burning his possessions, he said something strange. He cried that this pushcha is guarded by a legendary hero, the White Beekeeper.
He was screaming that we will bring his anger upon us! That we will see the true power of the pushcha!
It was a bit unnerving...

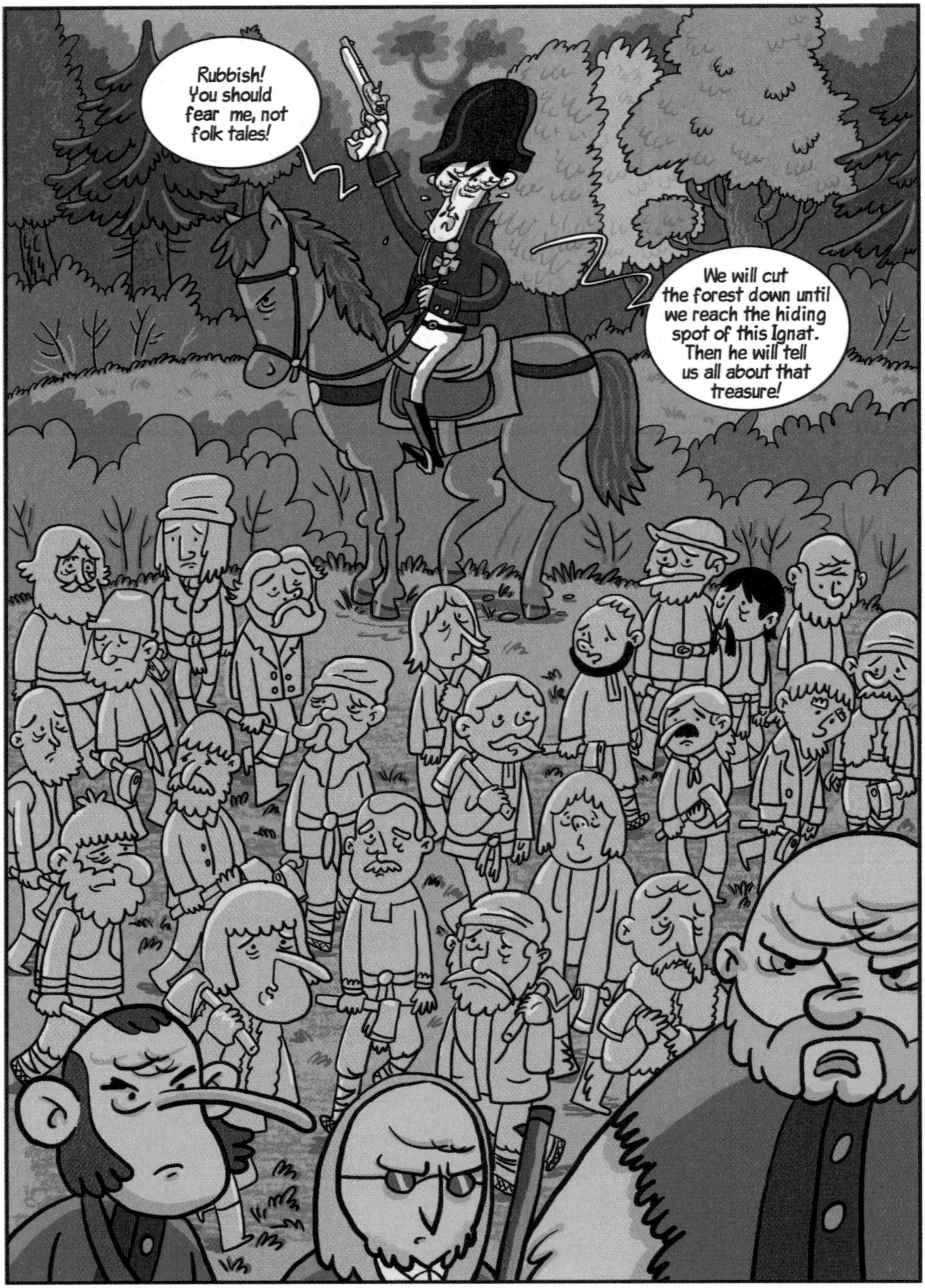
Rubbish! You should fear me, not folk tales!
We will cut the forest down until we reach the hiding spot of this Ignat. Then he will tell us all about that treasure!

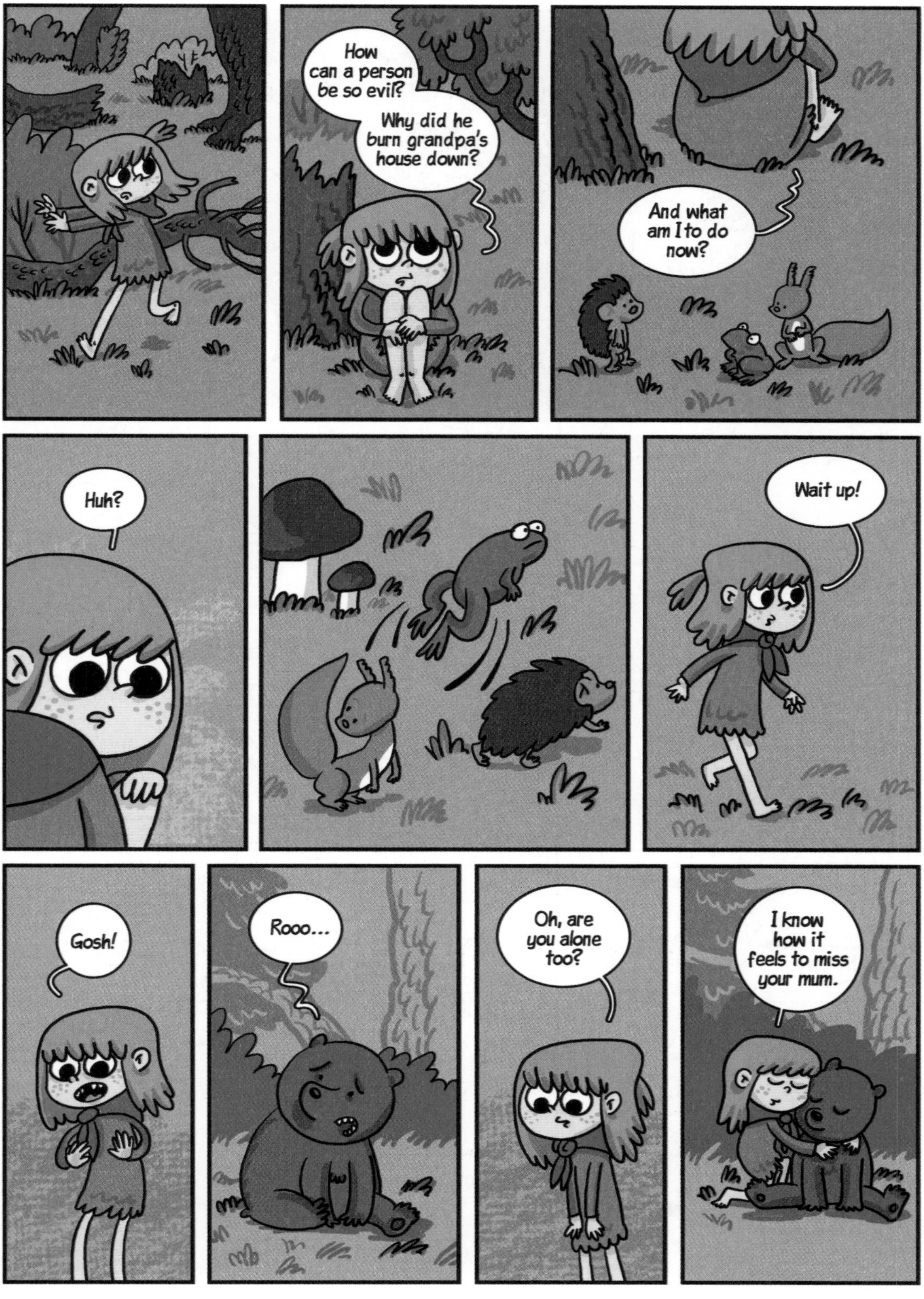
How can a person be so evil?
Why did he burn grandpa's house down?
And what am I to do now?
Huh?
Wait up!
Gosh!
Rooo...
Oh, are you alone too?
I know how it feels to miss your mum.

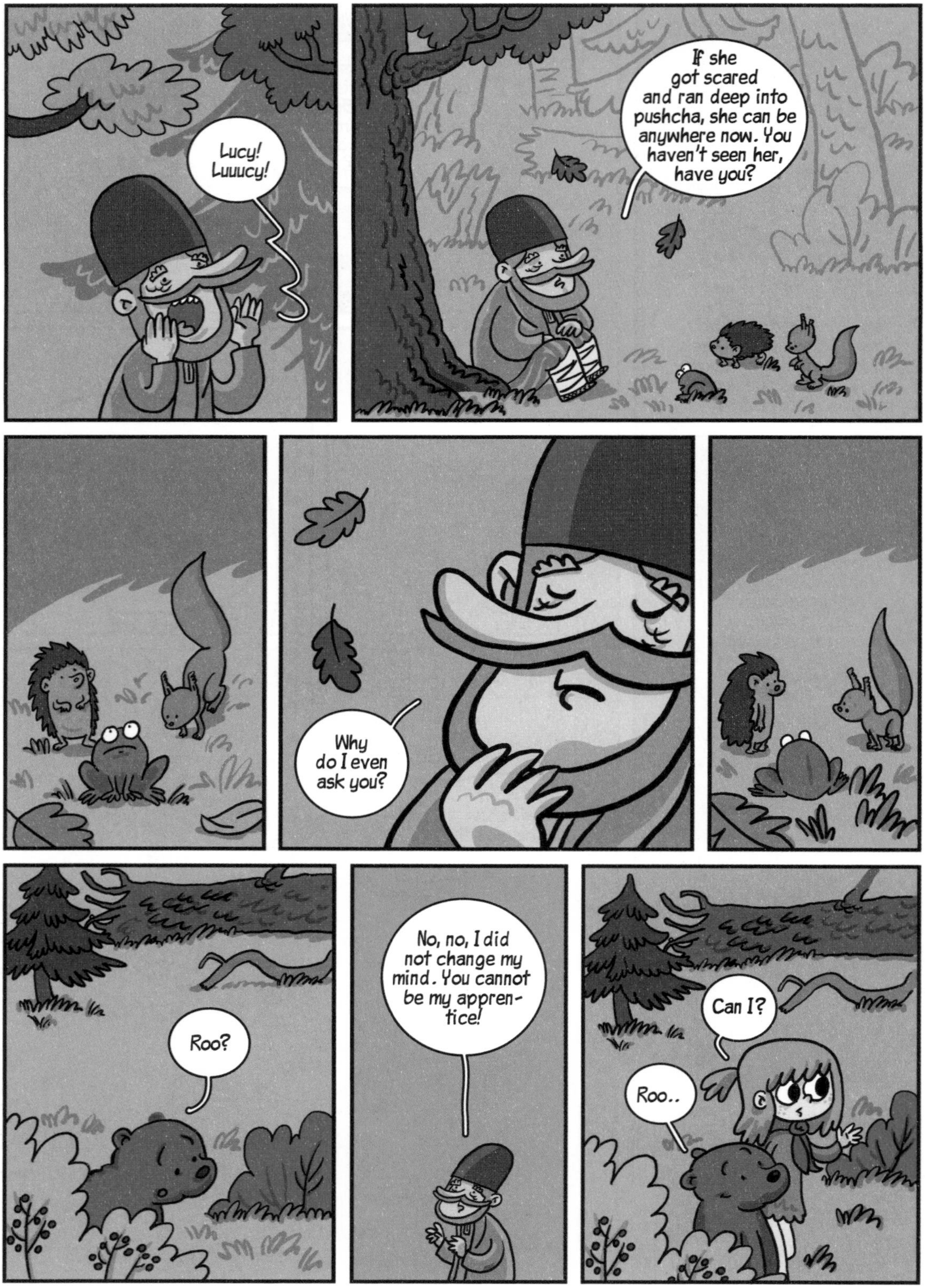
Lucy! Luuucy!
If she got scared and ran deep into pushcha, she can be anywhere now. You haven't seen her, have you?
Why do I even ask you?
Roo?
No, no, I did not change my mind. You cannot be my appren-tice!
Can I?
Roo..

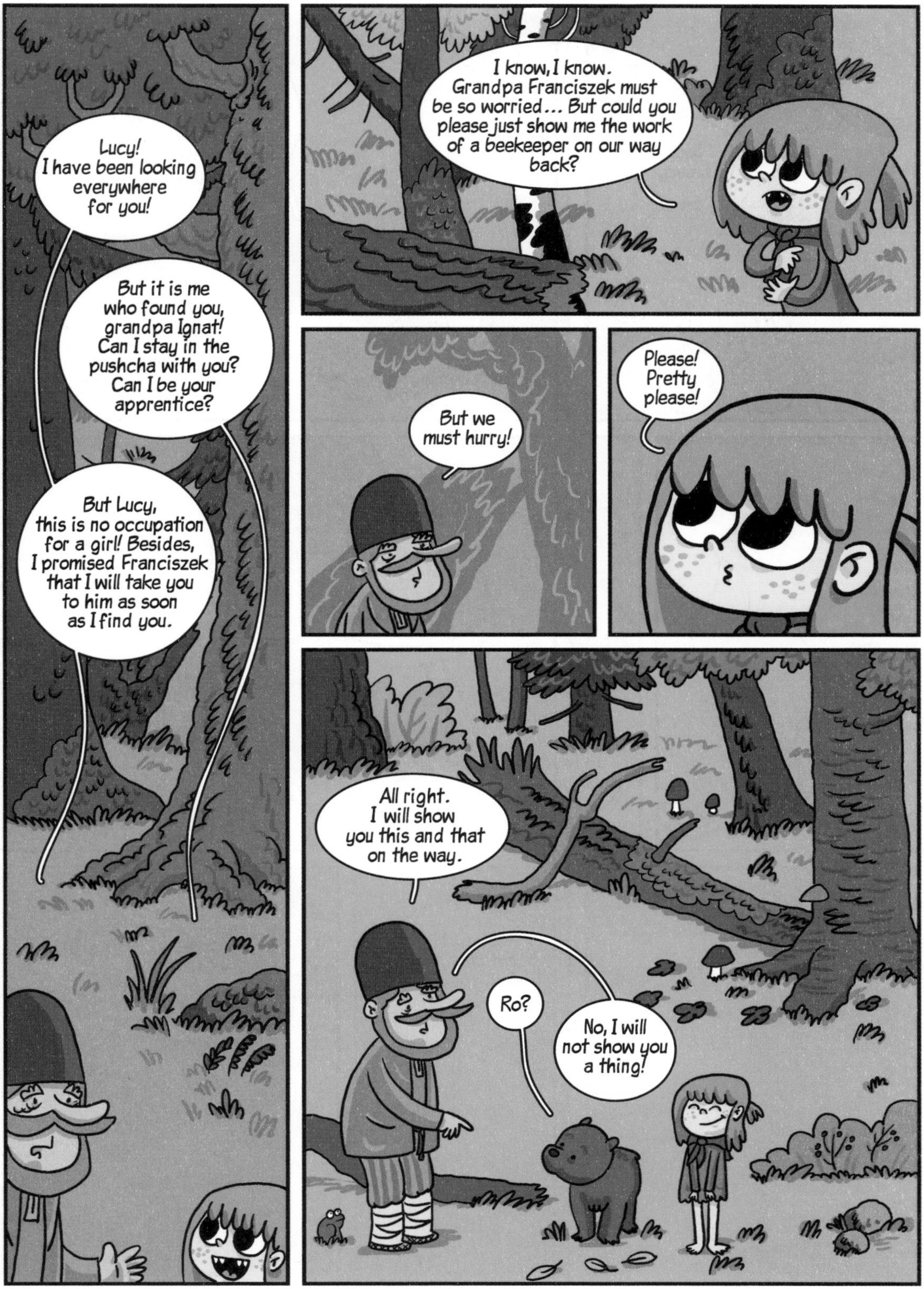
Lucy! I have been looking everywhere for you!
But it is me who found you, grandpa Ignat! Can I stay in the pushcha with you? Can I be your apprentice?
But Lucy, this is no occupation for a girl! Besides, I promised Franciszek that I will take you to him as soon as I find you.
I know, I know. Grandpa Franciszek must be so worried... But could you please just show me the work of a beekeeper on our way back?
But we must hurry!
Please! Pretty please!
All right. I will show you this and that on the way.
Ro?
No, I will not show you a thing!

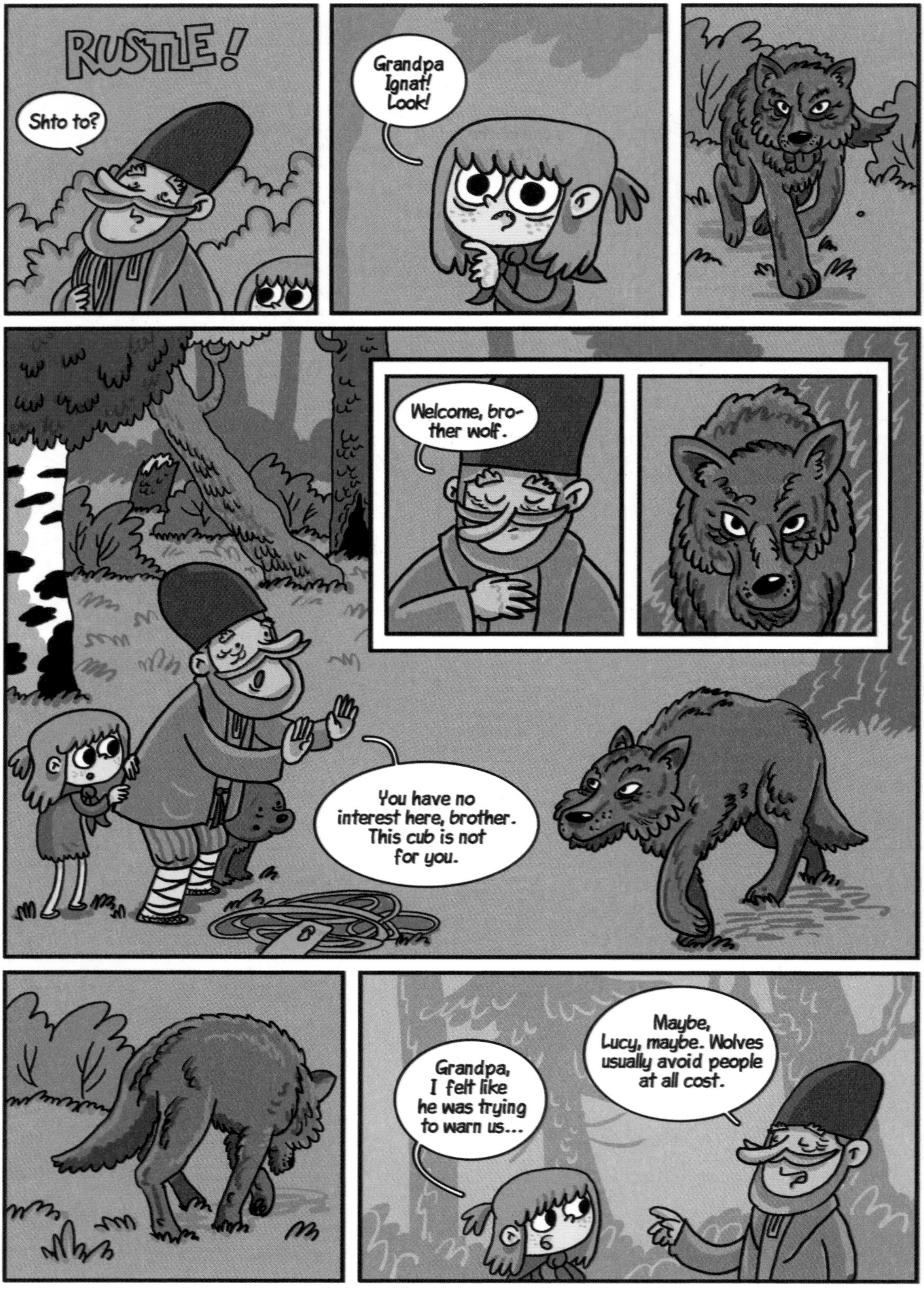
RUSTLE!
Shto to?
Grandpa Ignat! Look!
Welcome, brother wolf.
You have no interest here, brother. This cub is not for you.
Grandpa, I felt like he was trying to warn us...
Maybe, Lucy, maybe. Wolves usually avoid people at all cost.

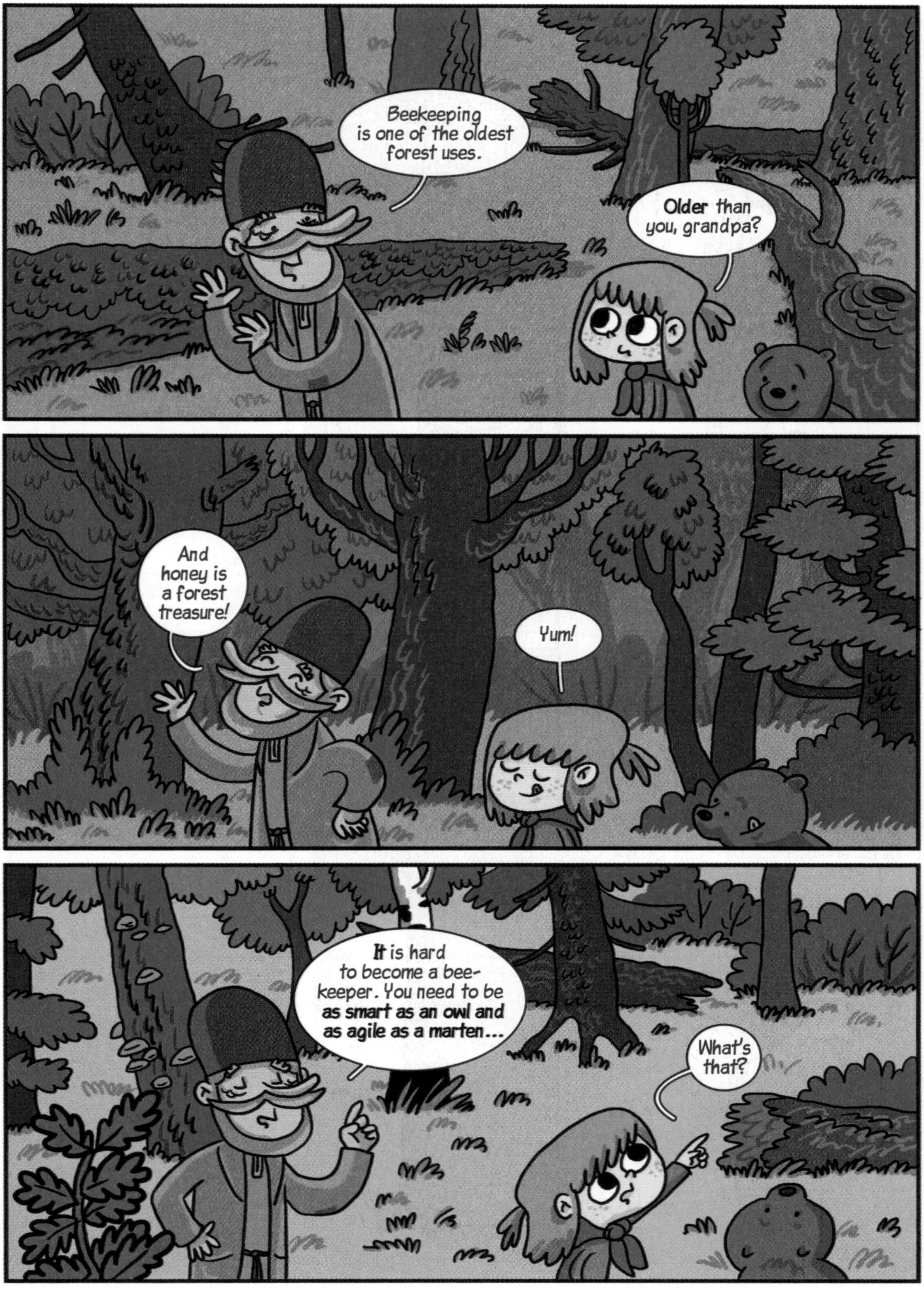
Beekeeping is one of the oldest forest uses.
Older than you, grandpa?
And honey is a forest treasure!
Yum!
It is hard to become a bee-keeper. You need to be **as smart as an owl and as agile as a marten...**
What's that?

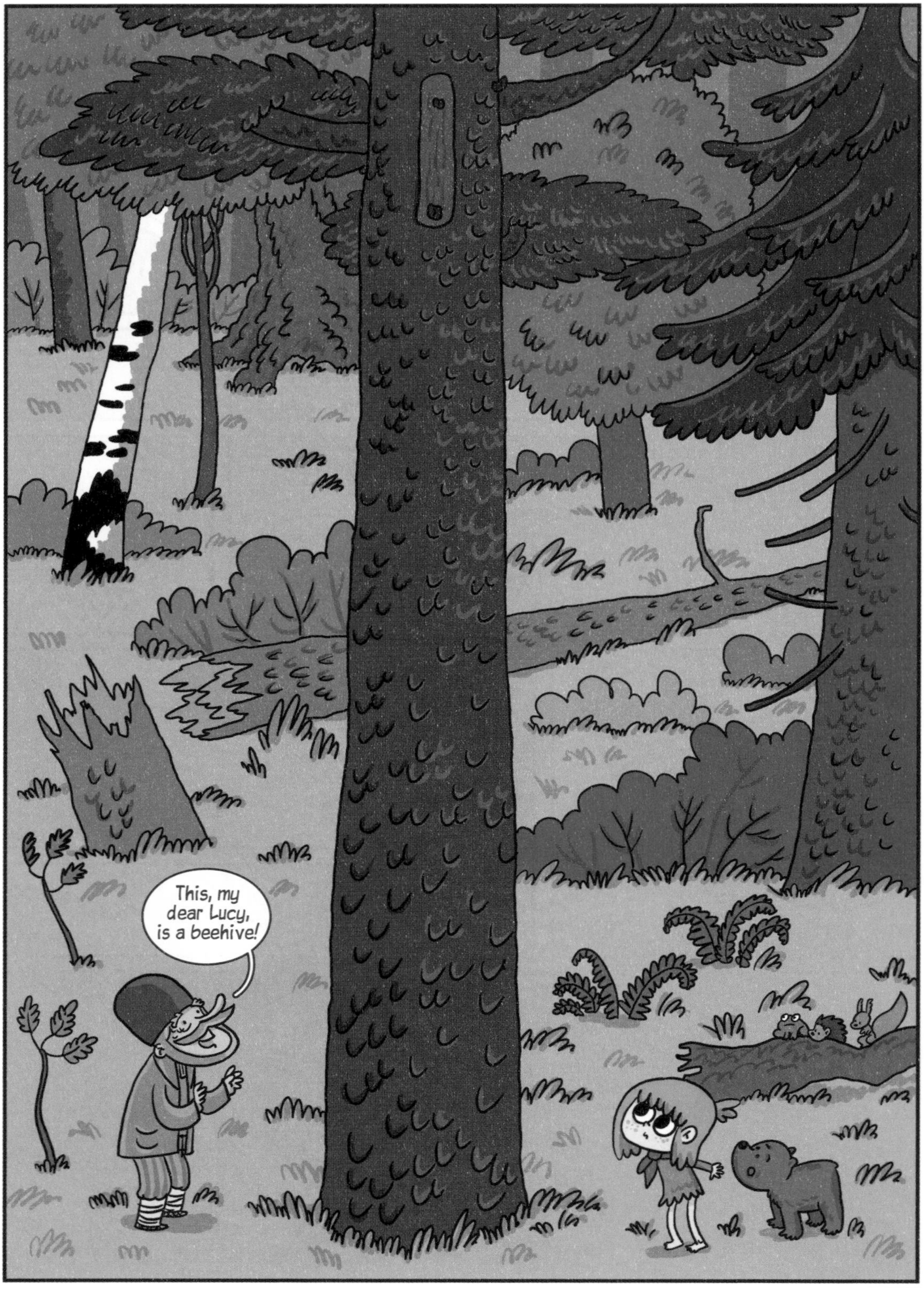
This, my dear Lucy, is a beehive!

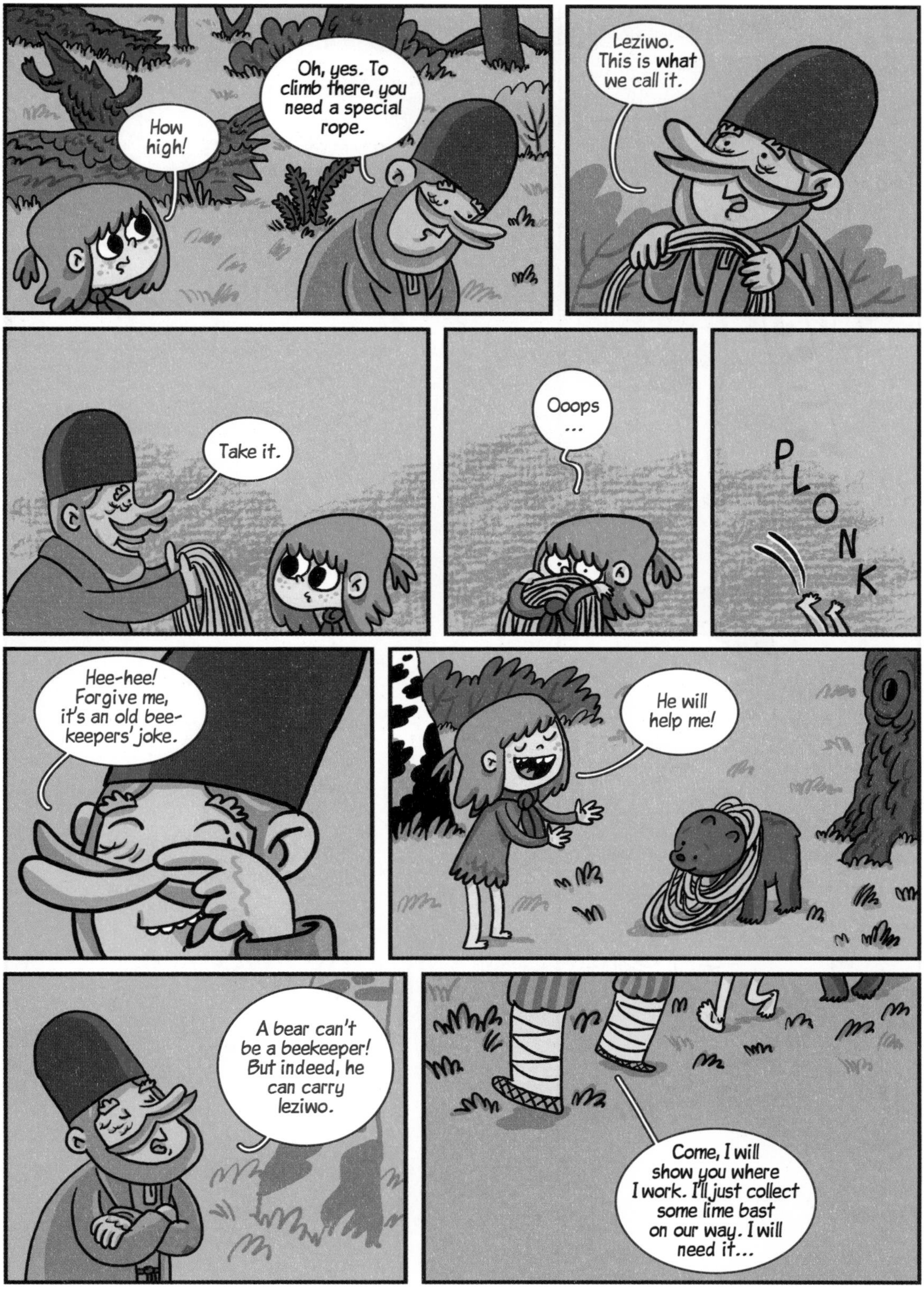
How high!
Oh, yes. To climb there, you need a special rope.
Leziwo. This is what we call it.
Take it.
Ooops ...
PLONK
Hee-hee! Forgive me, it's an old bee-keepers' joke.
He will help me!
A bear can't be a beekeeper! But indeed, he can carry leziwo.
Come, I will show you where I work. I'll just collect some lime bast on our way. I will need it...

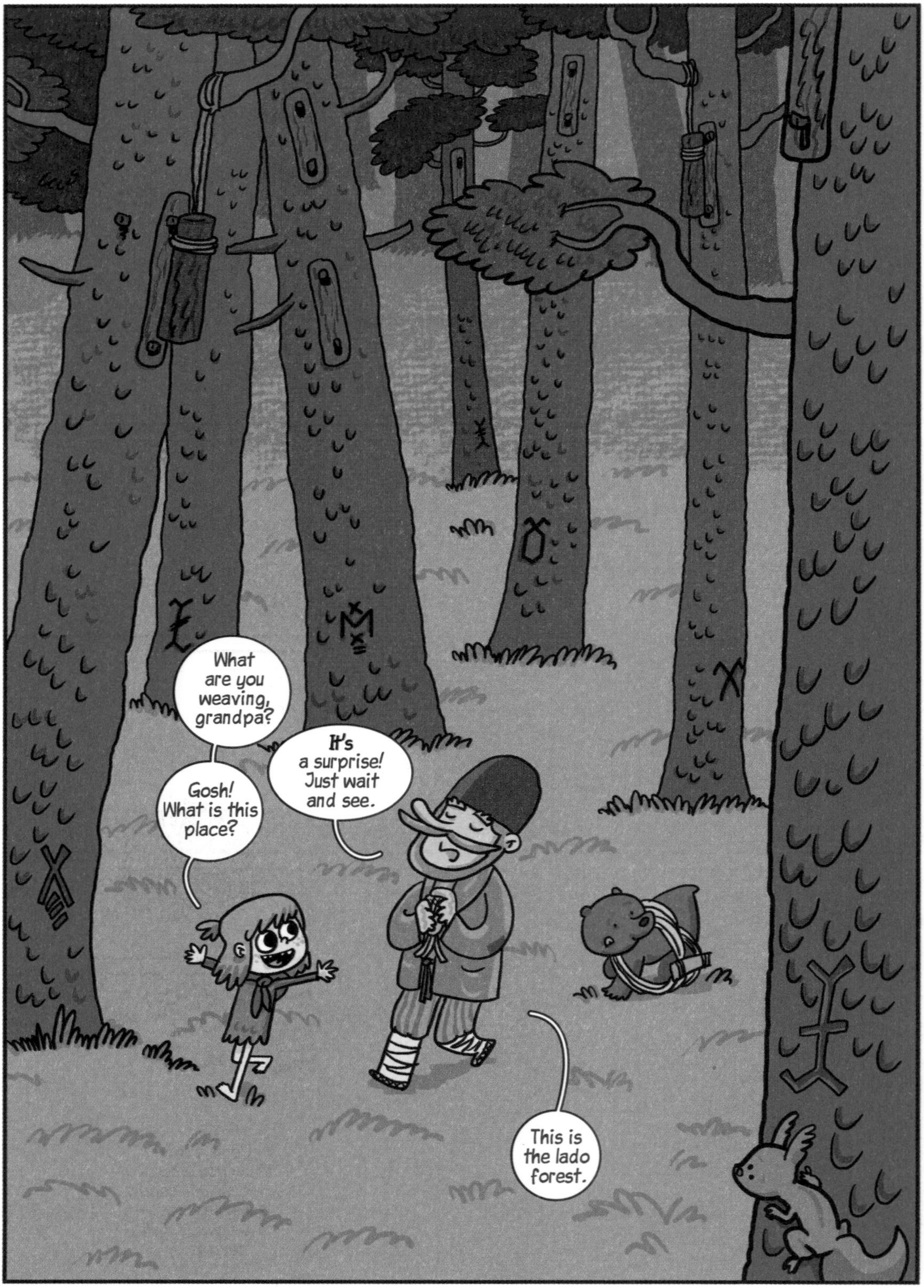
What are you weaving, grandpa?
Gosh! What is this place?
It's a surprise! Just wait and see.
This is the lado forest.

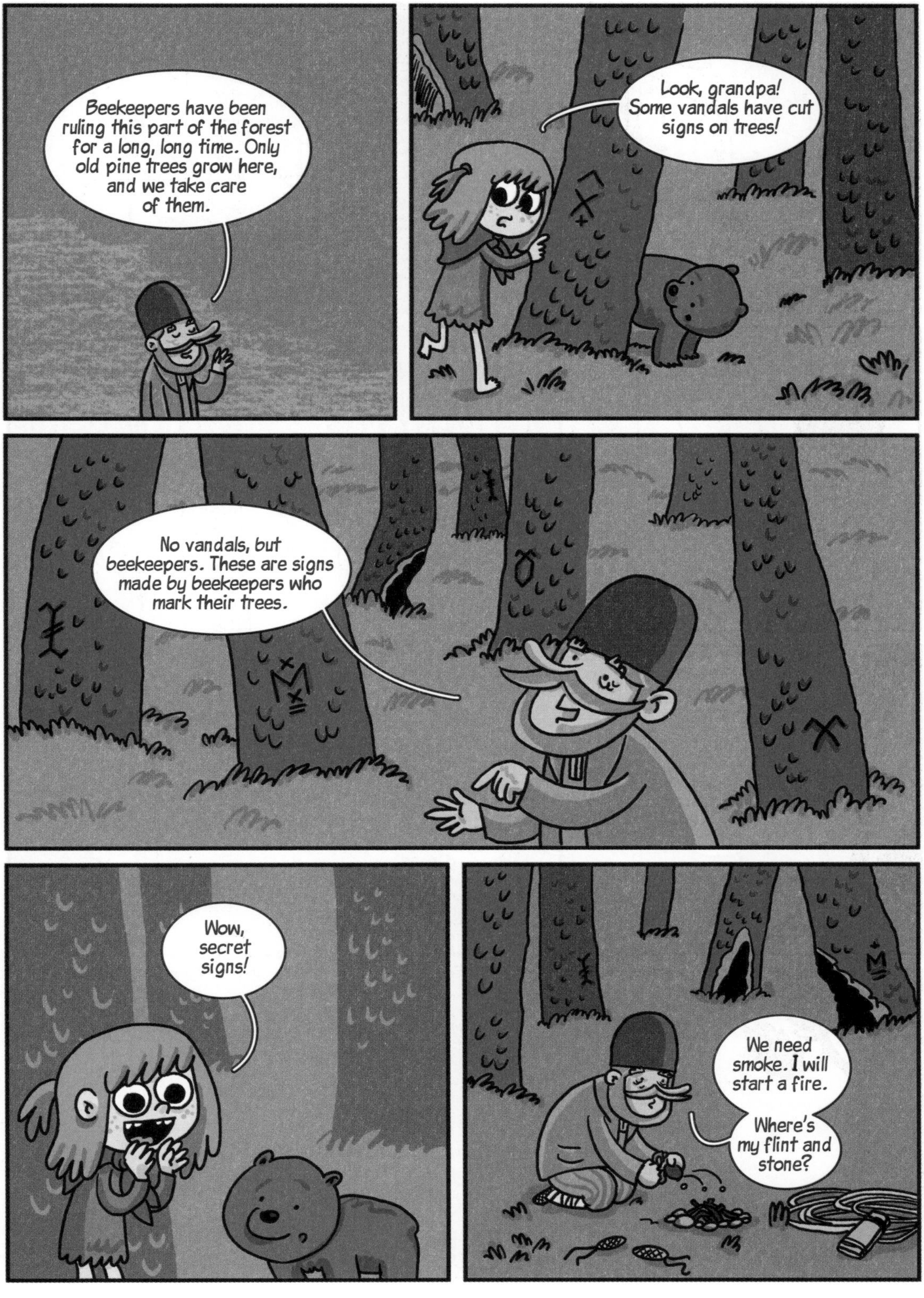
Beekeepers have been ruling this part of the forest for a long, long time. Only old pine trees grow here, and we take care of them.
Look, grandpa! Some vandals have cut signs on trees!
No vandals, but beekeepers. These are signs made by beekeepers who mark their trees.
Wow, secret signs!
We need smoke. I will start a fire.
Where's my flint and stone?

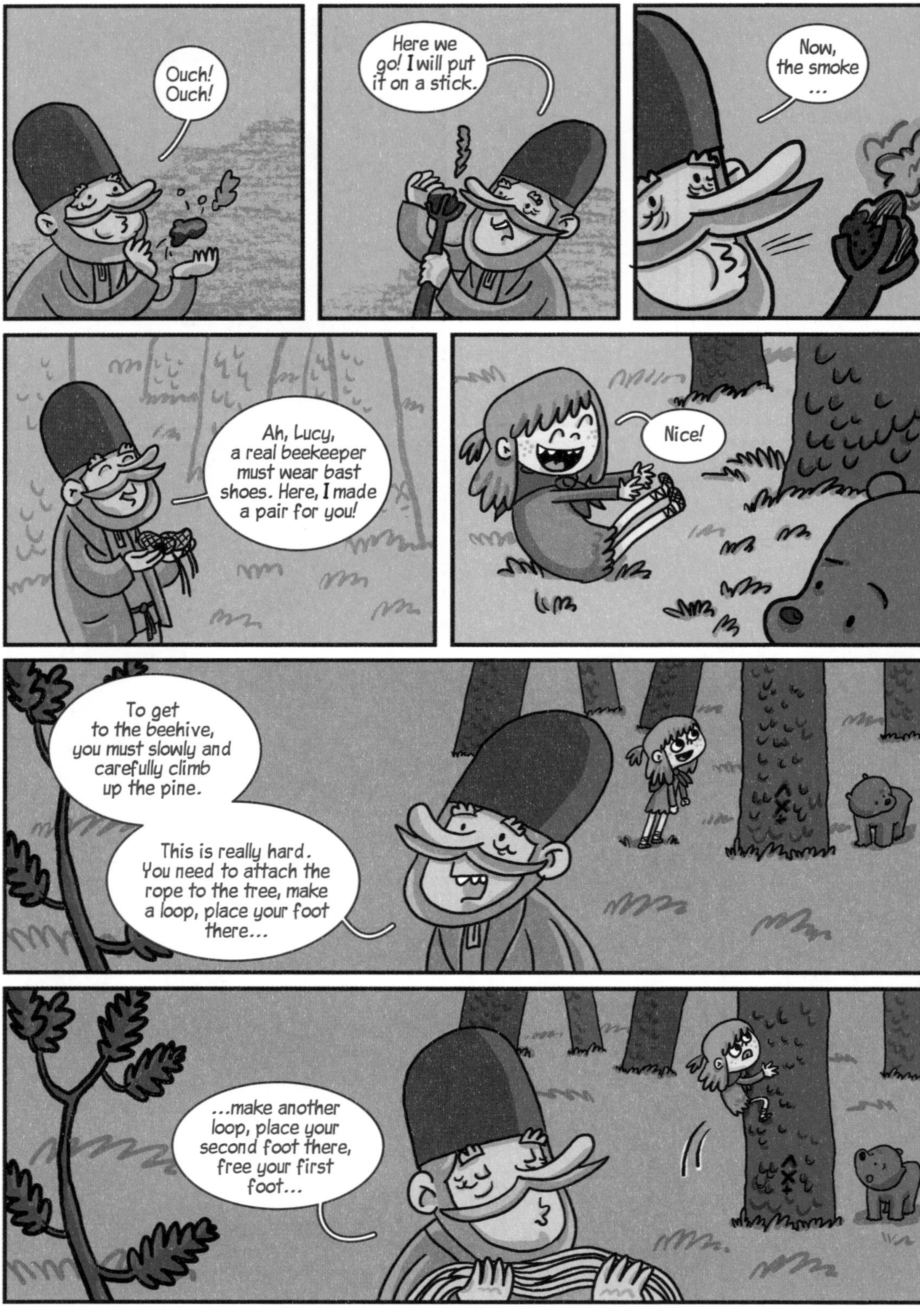
Ouch! Ouch!
Here we go! I will put it on a stick.
Now, the smoke ...
Ah, Lucy, a real beekeeper must wear bast shoes. Here, I made a pair for you!
Nice!
To get to the beehive, you must slowly and carefully climb up the pine.
This is really hard. You need to attach the rope to the tree, make a loop, place your foot there...
...make another loop, place your second foot there, free your first foot...

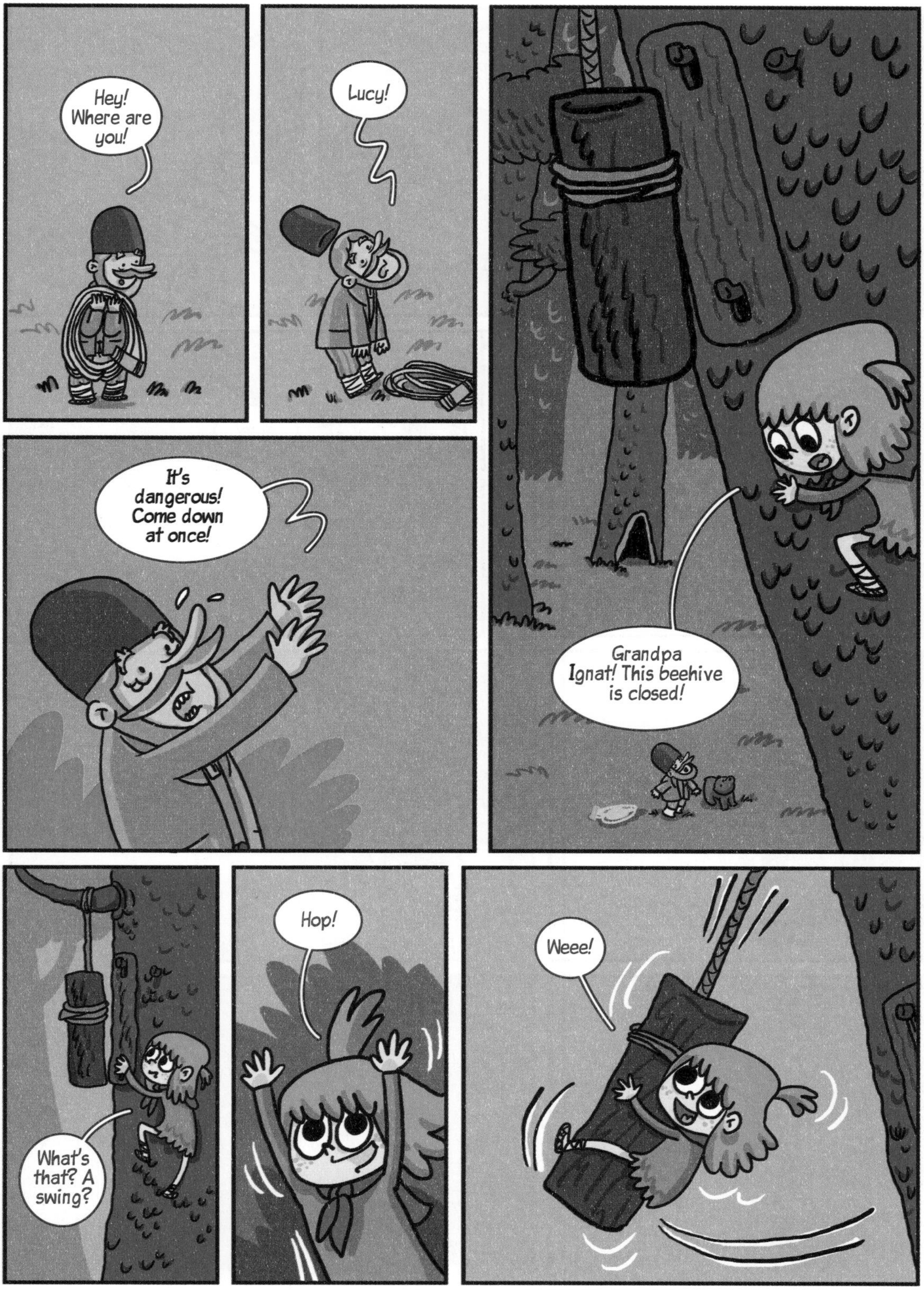
Hey! Where are you!
Lucy!
It's dangerous! Come down at once!
Grandpa Ignat! This beehive is closed!
What's that? A swing?
Hop!
Weee!

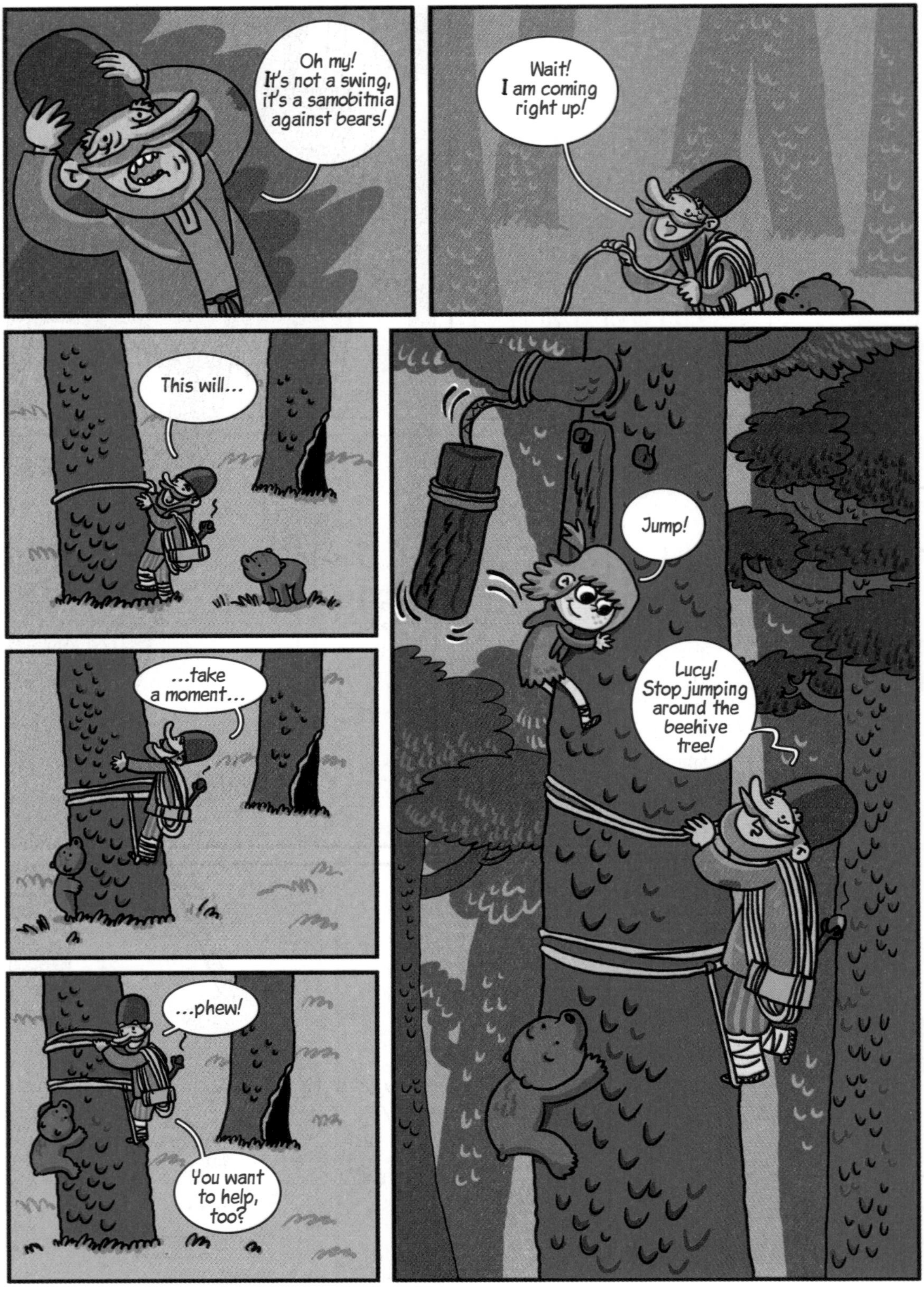
Oh my! It's not a swing, it's a samobitnia against bears!
Wait! I am coming right up!
This will...
...take a moment...
...phew!
You want to help, too?
Jump!
Lucy! Stop jumping around the beehive tree!

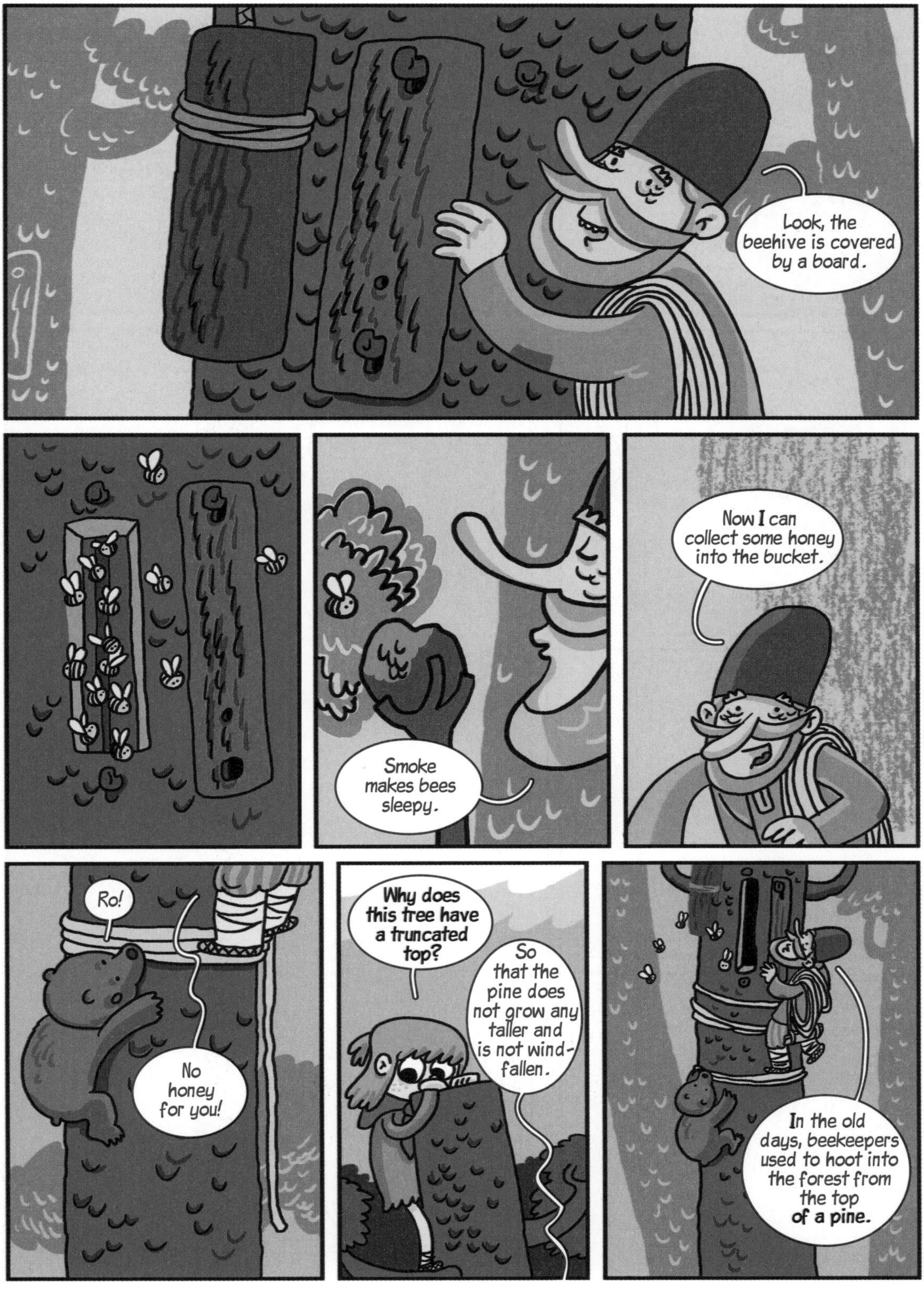
Look, the beehive is covered by a board.
Smoke makes bees sleepy.
Now I can collect some honey into the bucket.
Ro!
No honey for you!
Why does this tree have a truncated top?
So that the pine does not grow any taller and is not wind-fallen.
In the old days, beekeepers used to hoot into the forest from the top of a pine.

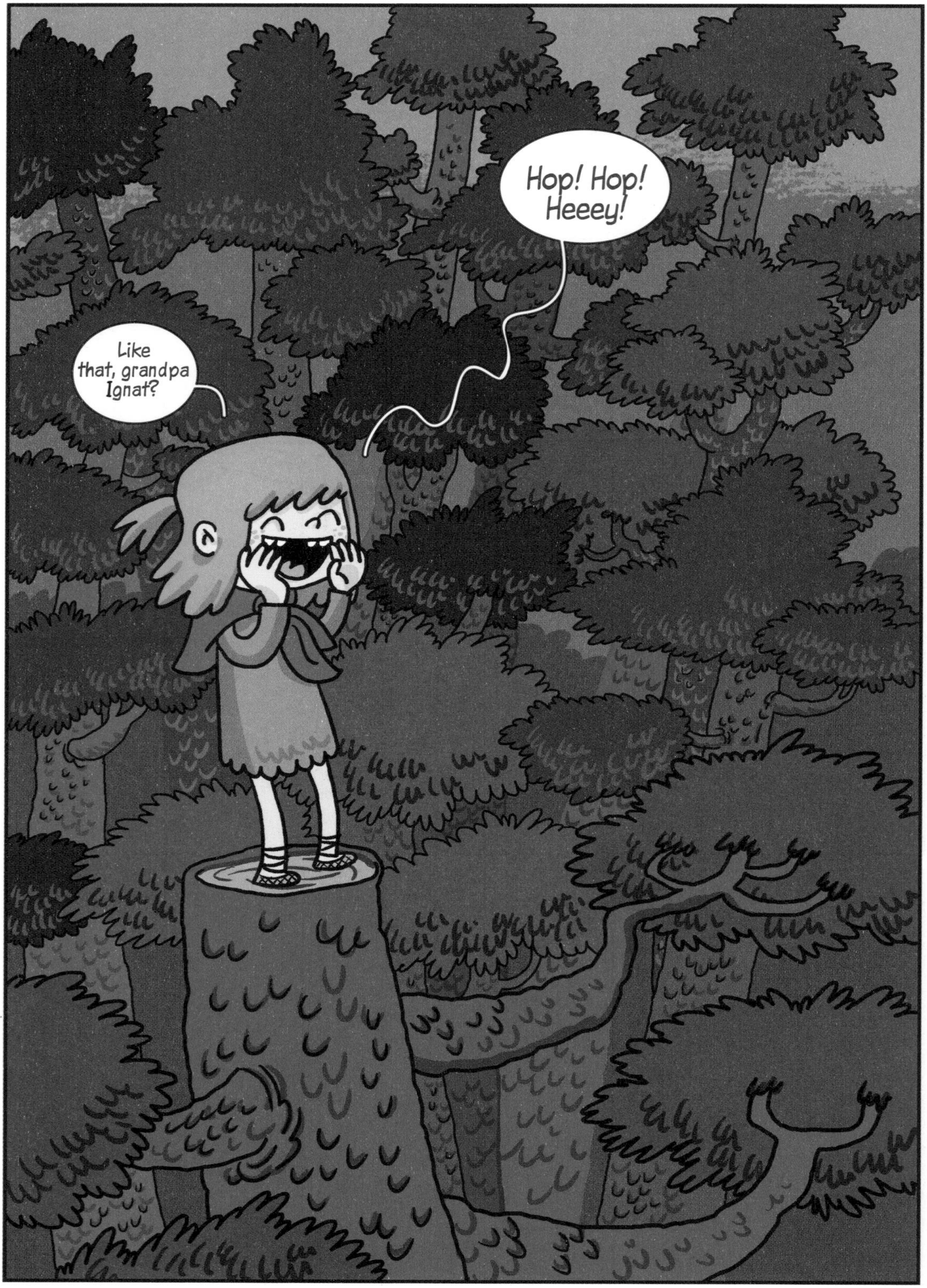
Like that, grandpa Ignat?
Hop! Hop! Heeey!

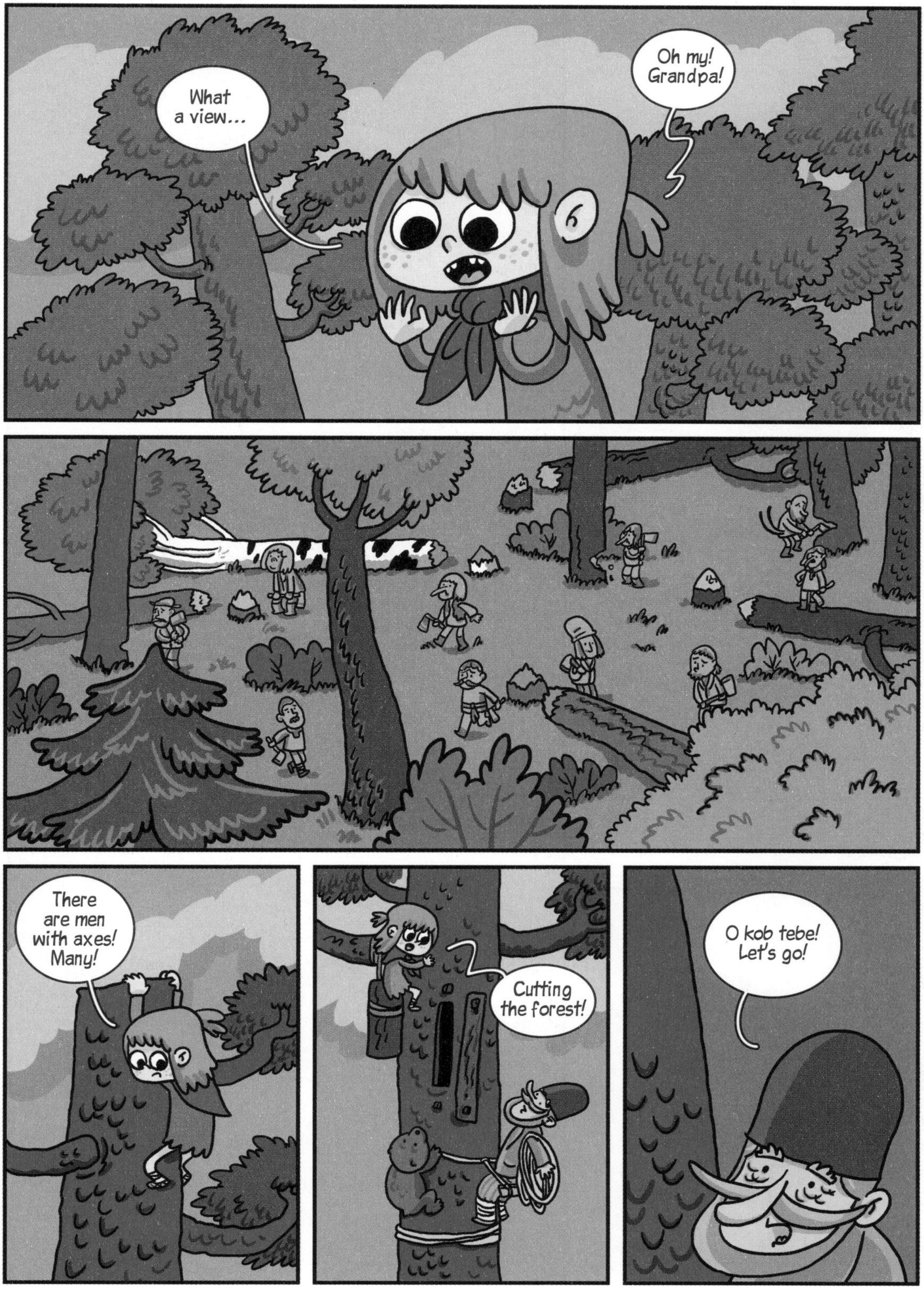
What a view...
Oh my! Grandpa!
There are men with axes! Many!
Cutting the forest!
O kob tebe! Let's go!

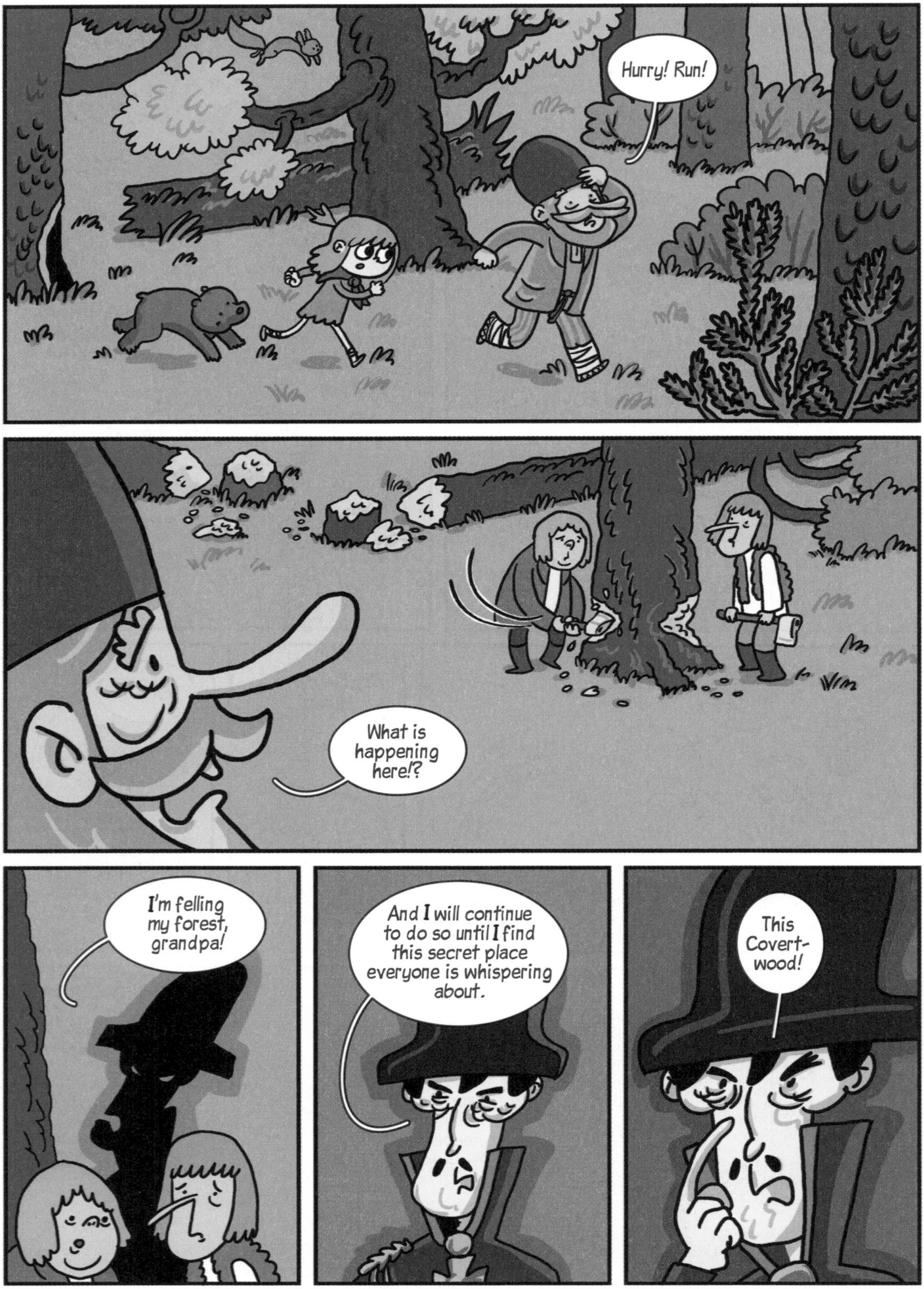
Hurry! Run!
What is happening here!?
I'm felling my forest, grandpa!
And I will continue to do so until I find this secret place everyone is whispering about.
This Covert-wood!

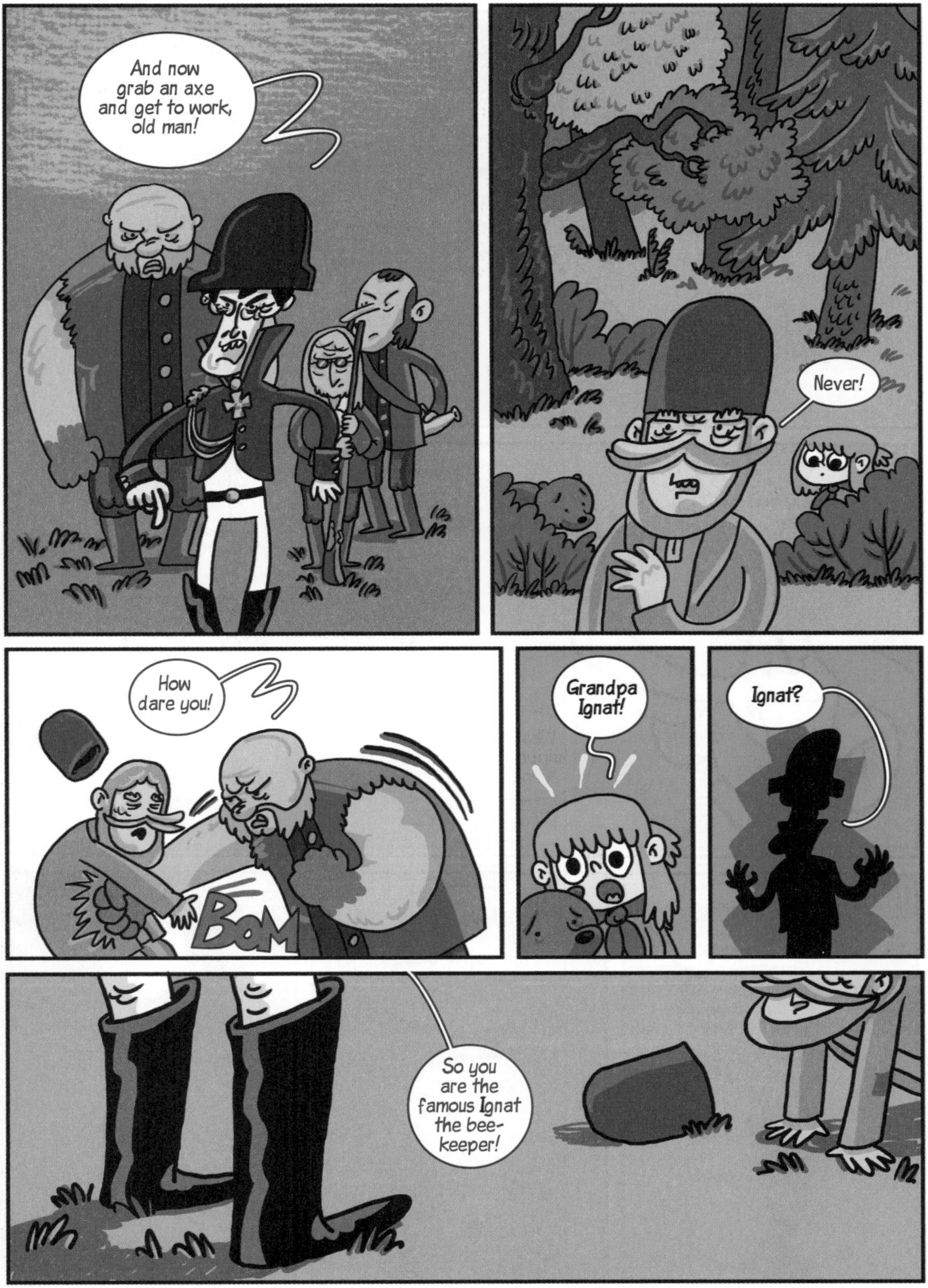
And now grab an axe and get to work, old man!
Never!
How dare you!
BOM
Grandpa Ignat!
Ignat?
So you are the famous Ignat the bee-keeper!

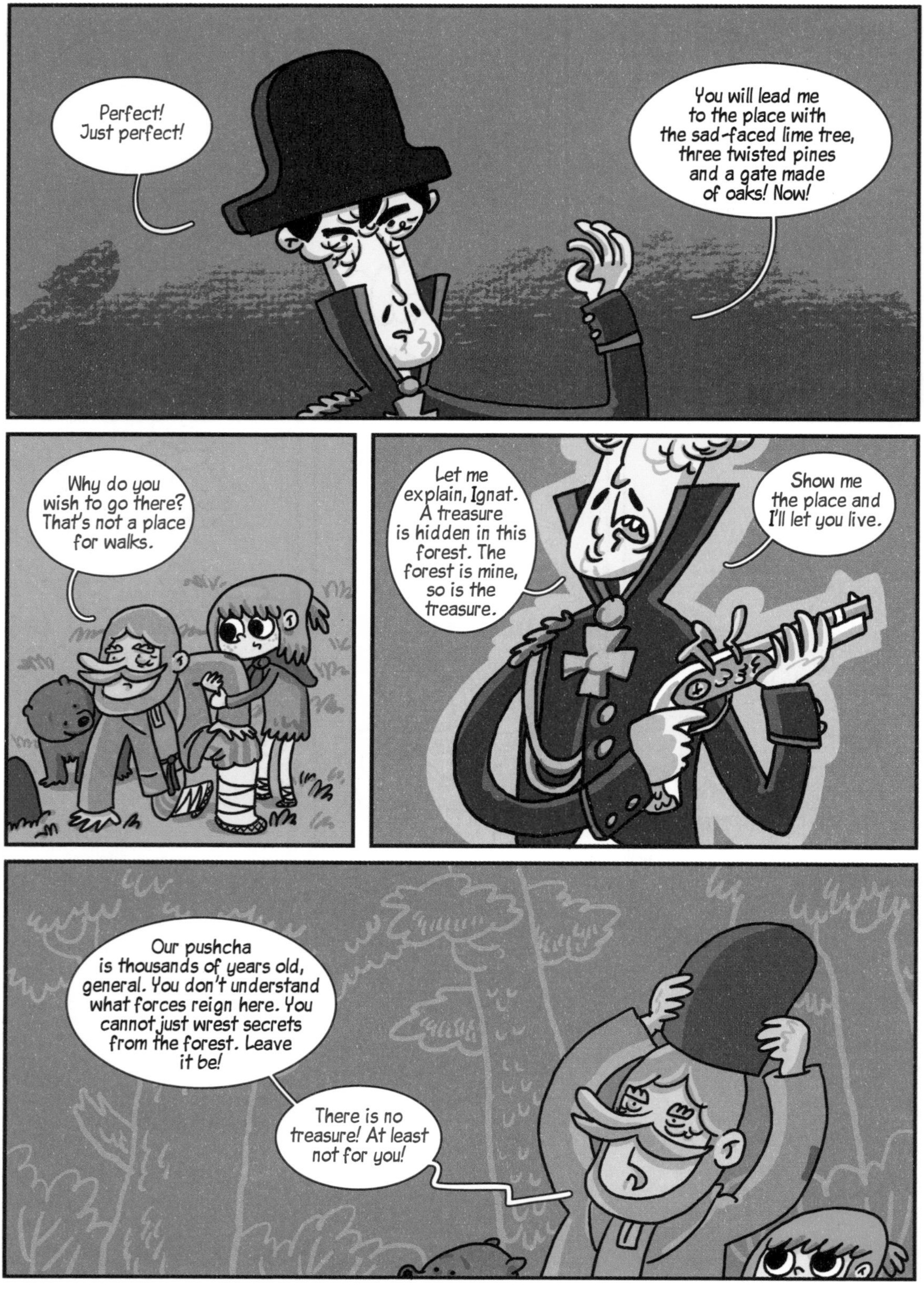

Perfect! Just perfect!
You will lead me to the place with the sad-faced lime tree, three twisted pines and a gate made of oaks! Now!
Why do you wish to go there? That's not a place for walks.
Let me explain, Ignat. A treasure is hidden in this forest. The forest is mine, so is the treasure.
Show me the place and I'll let you live.
Our pushcha is thousands of years old, general. You don't understand what forces reign here. You cannot just wrest secrets from the forest. Leave it be!
There is no treasure! At least not for you!

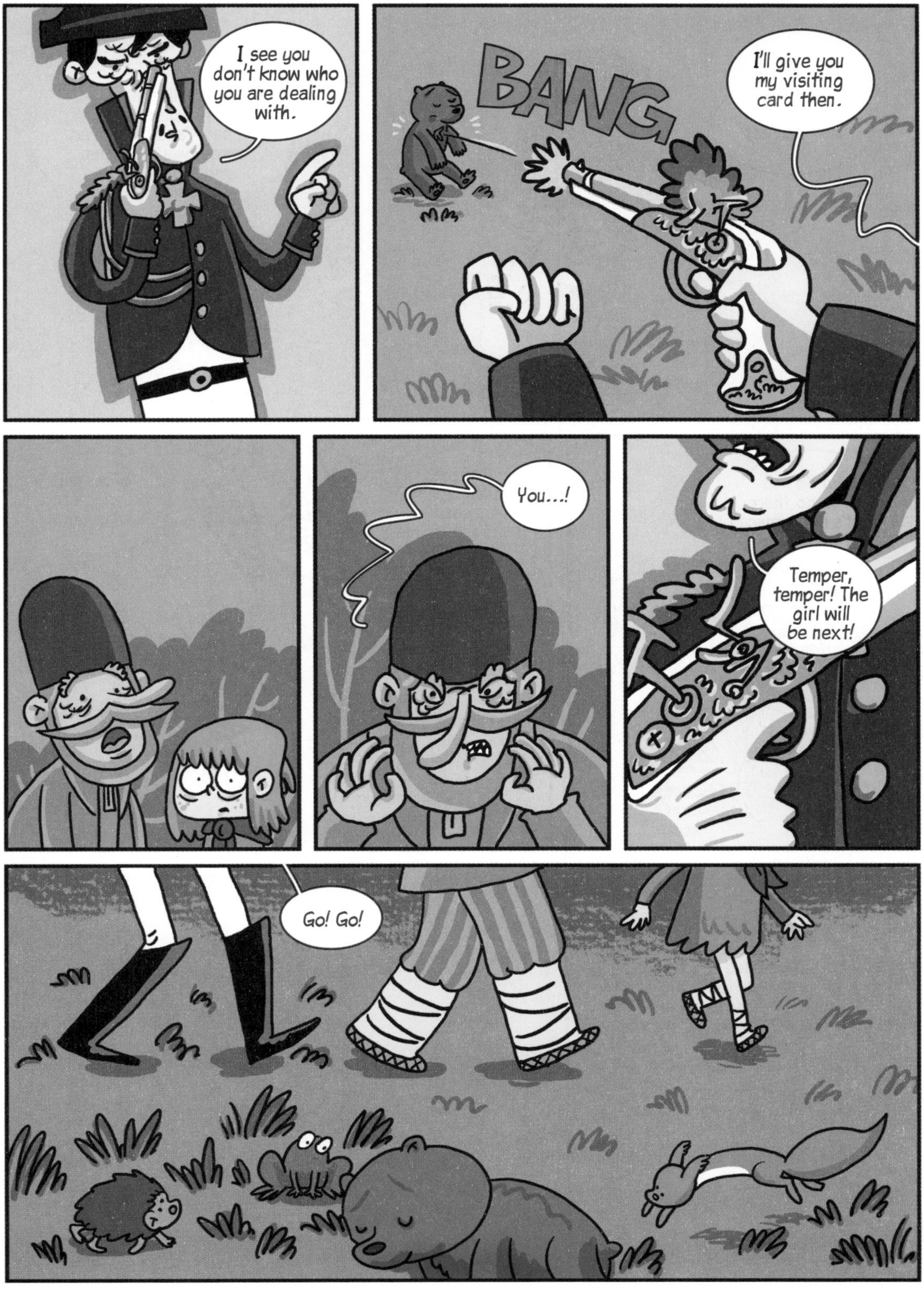
I see you don't know who you are dealing with.
BANG
I'll give you my visiting card then.
You...!
Temper, temper! The girl will be next!
Go! Go!

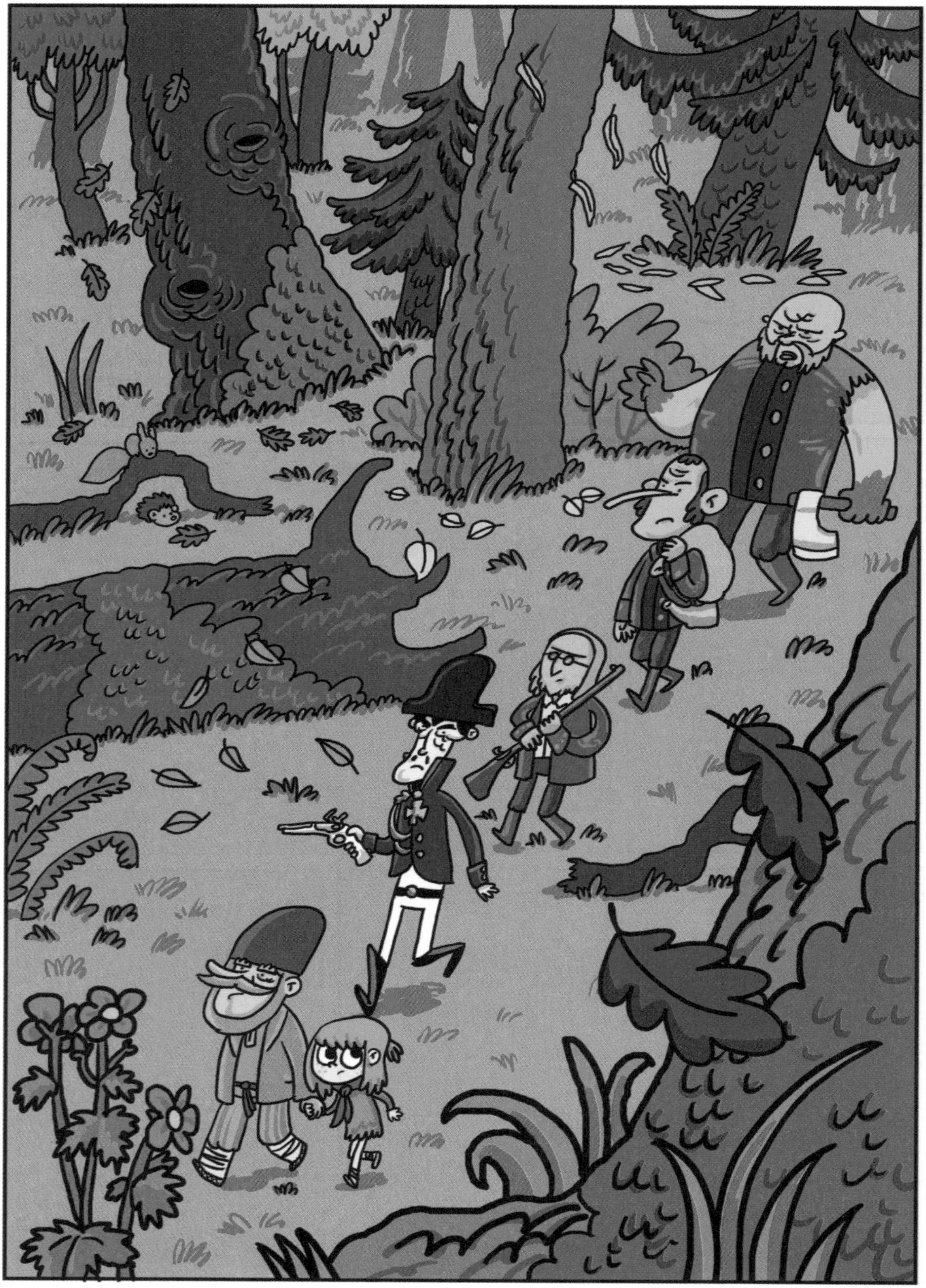

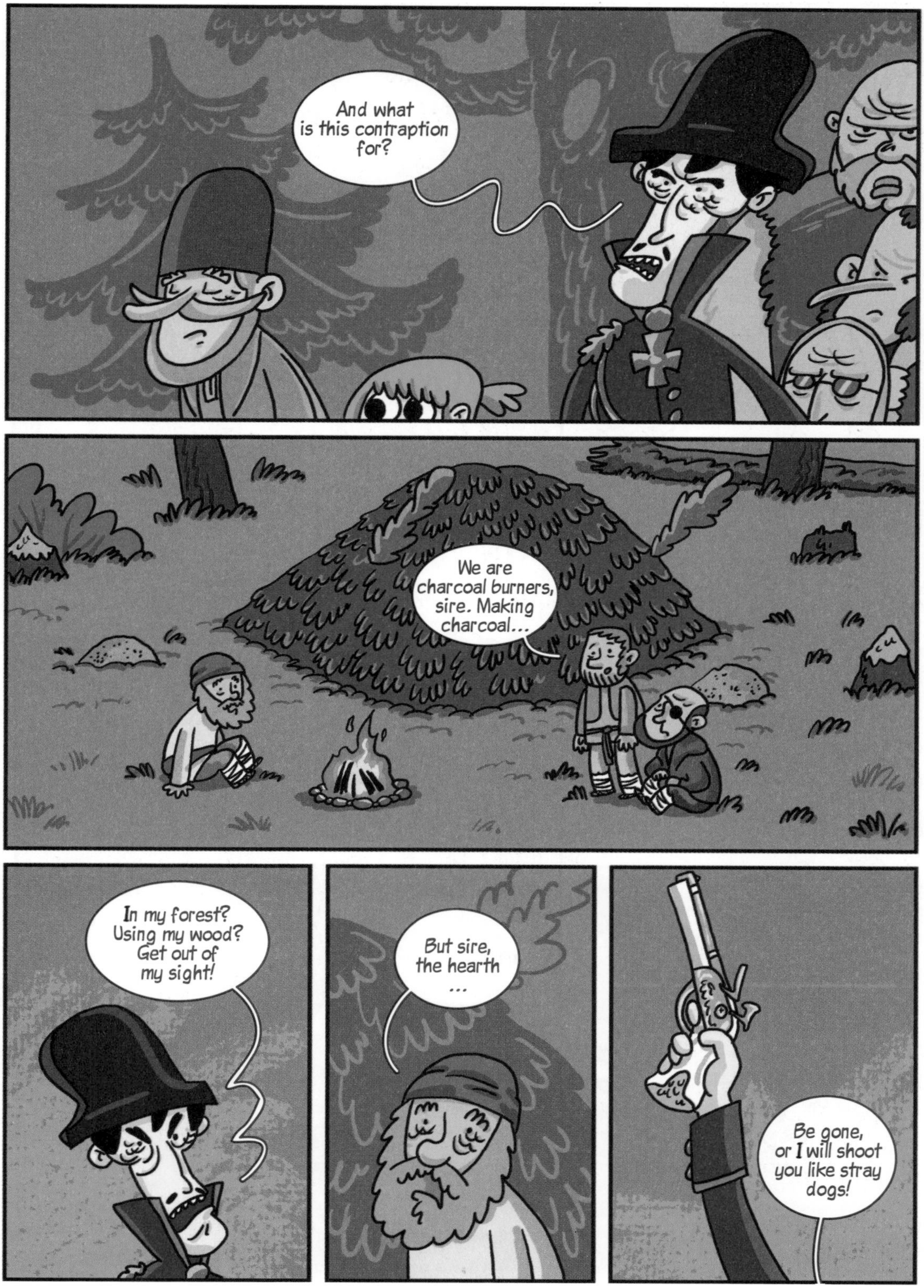
And what is this contraption for?
We are charcoal burners, sire. Making charcoal...
In my forest? Using my wood? Get out of my sight!
But sire, the hearth ...
Be gone, or I will shoot you like stray dogs!

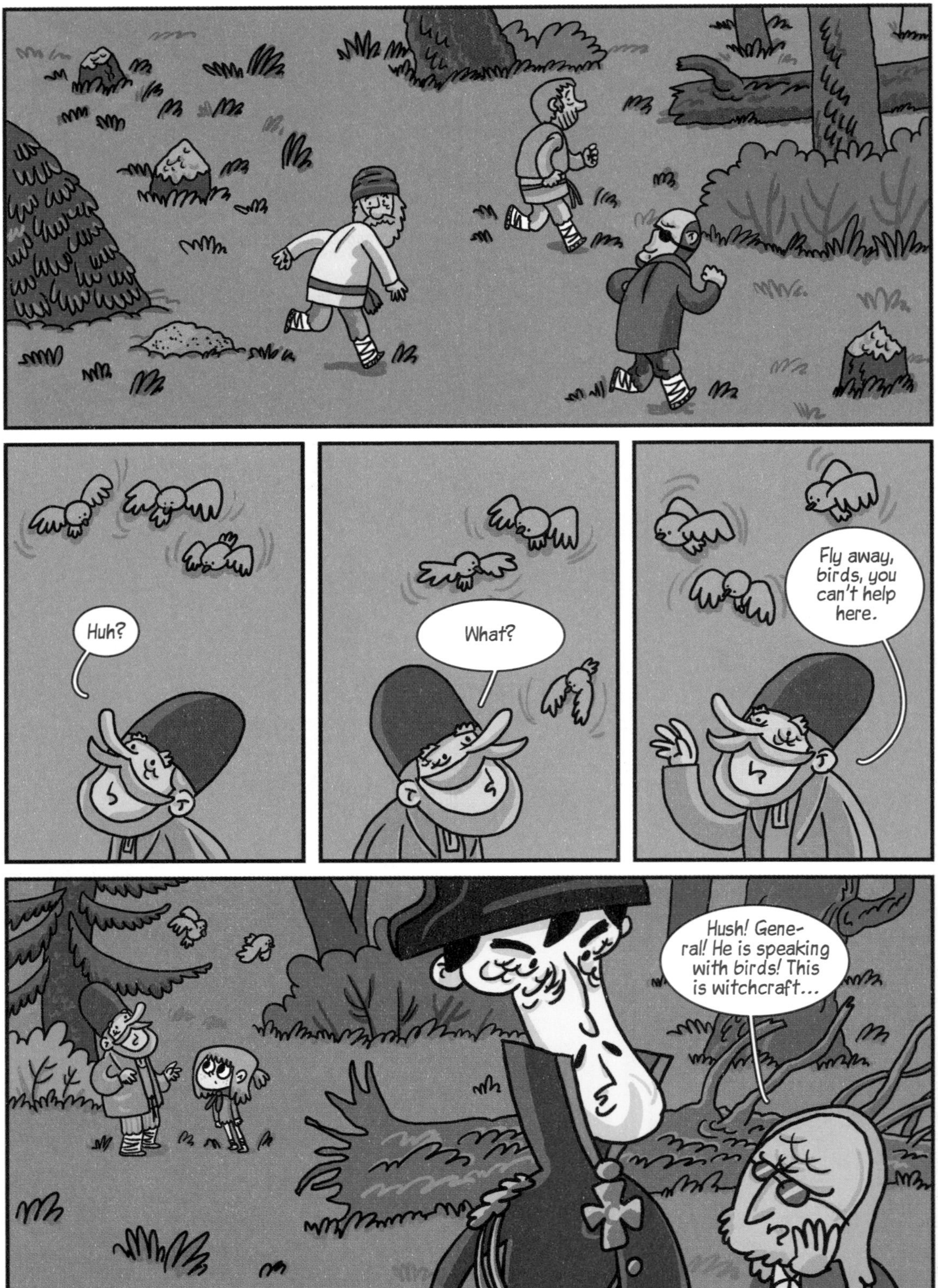
Huh?
What?
Fly away, birds, you can't help here.
Hush! General! He is speaking with birds! This is witchcraft...

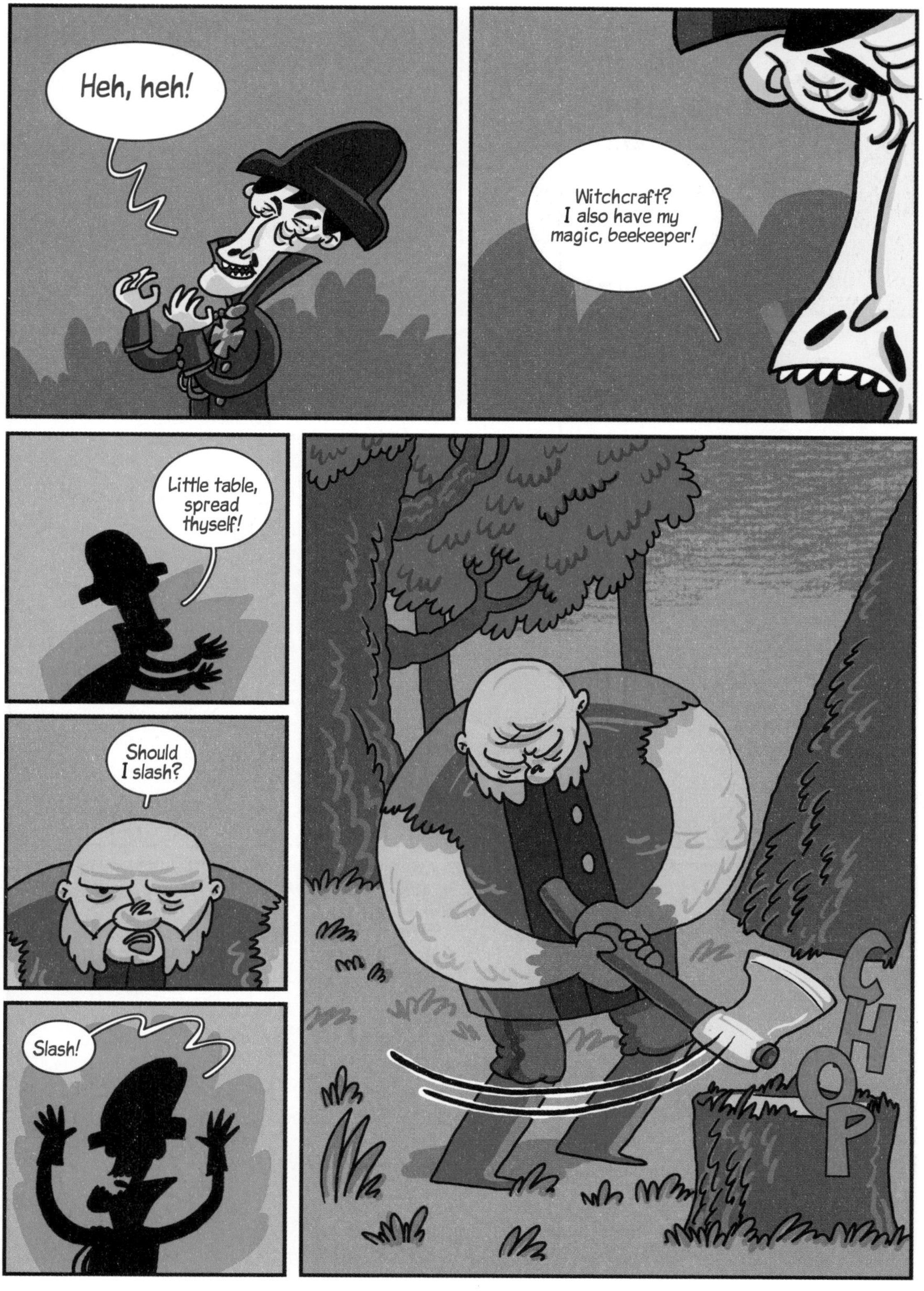
Heh, heh!
Witchcraft? I also have my magic, beekeeper!
Little table, spread thyself!
Should I slash?
Slash!
CHOP

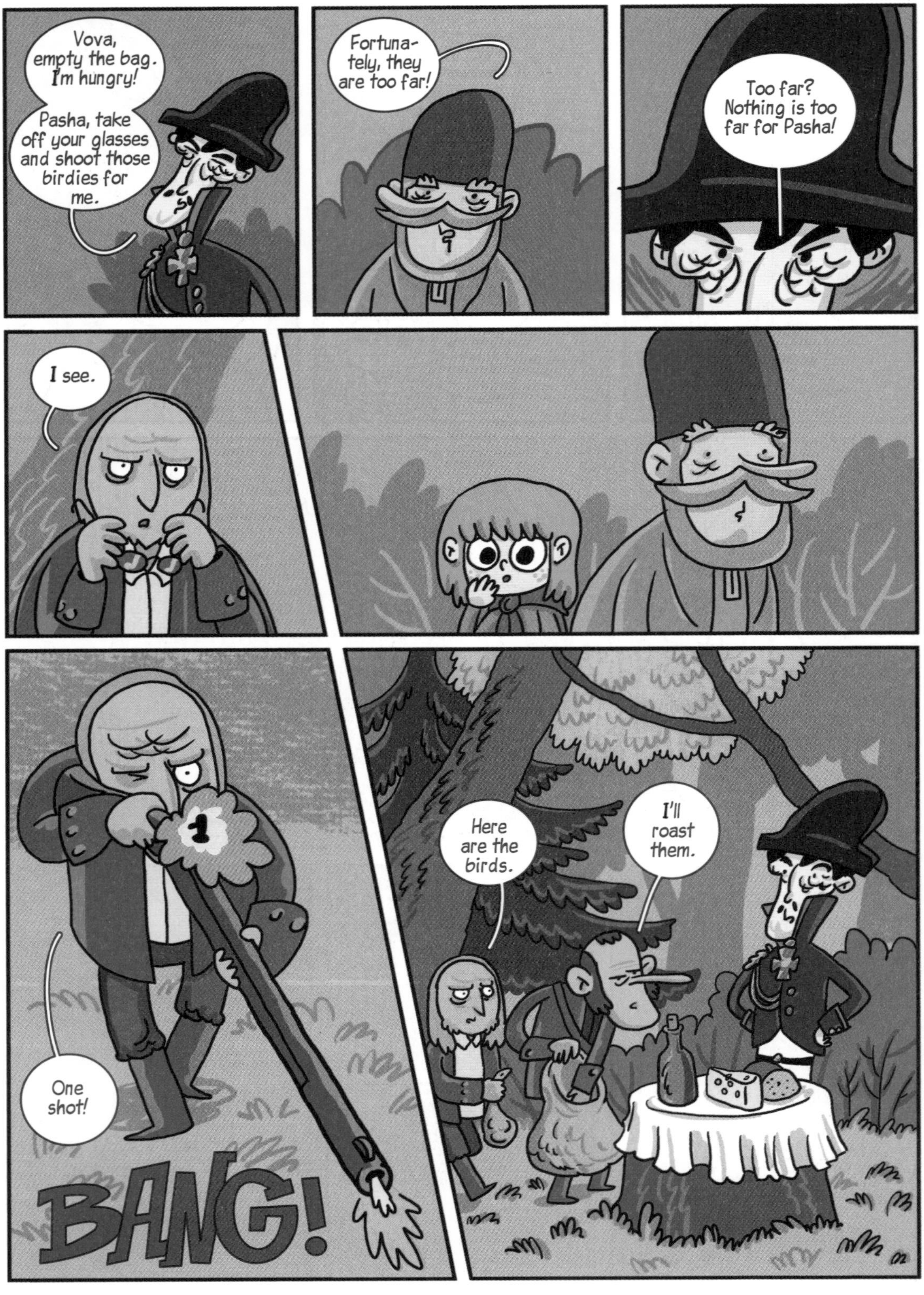
Vova, empty the bag. I'm hungry!
Pasha, take off your glasses and shoot those birdies for me.
Fortunately, they are too far!
Too far? Nothing is too far for Pasha!
I see.
One shot!
BANG!
Here are the birds.
I'll roast them.

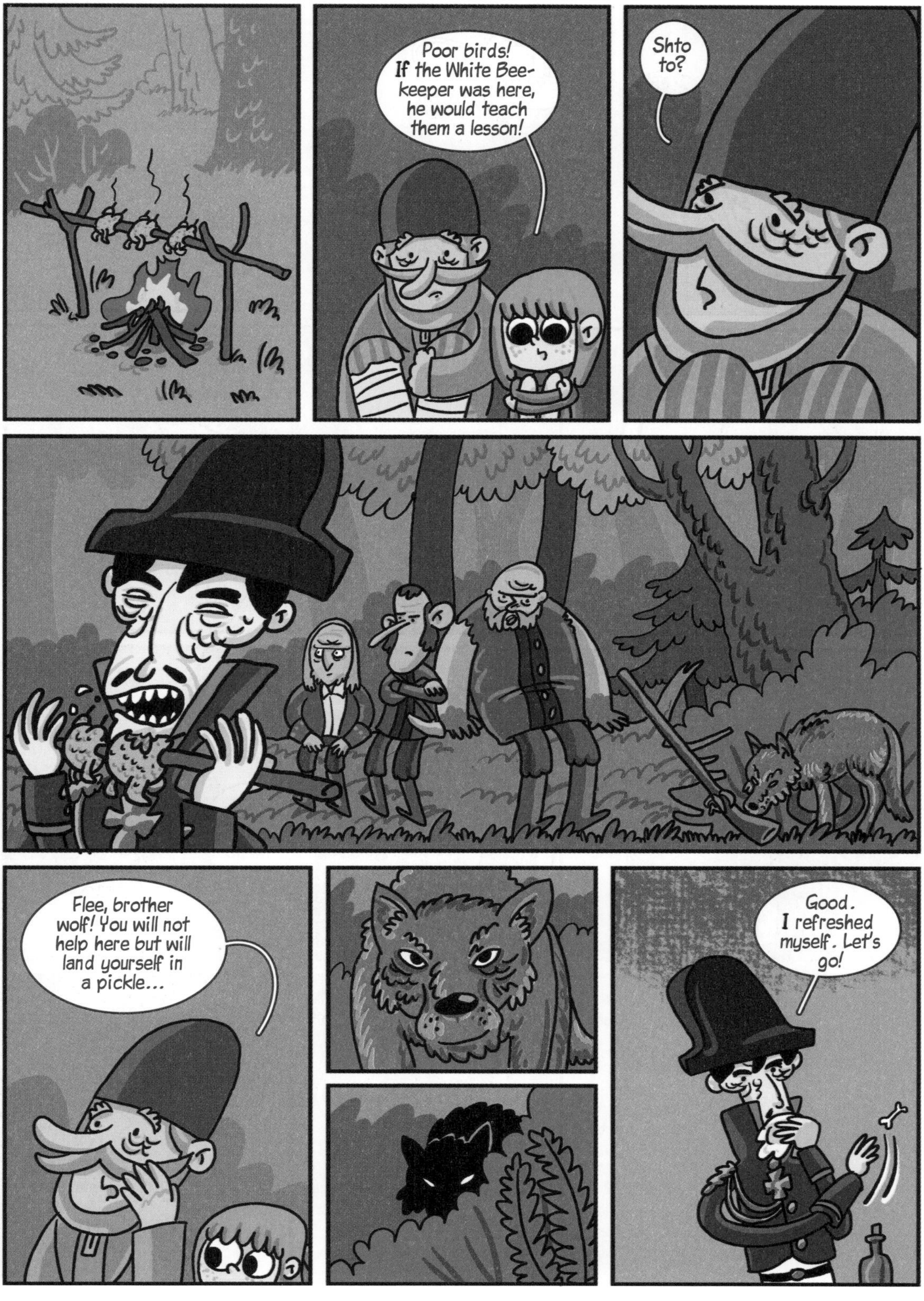
Poor birds! If the White Bee-keeper was here, he would teach them a lesson!
Shto to?
Flee, brother wolf! You will not help here but will land yourself in a pickle...
Good. I refreshed myself. Let's go!

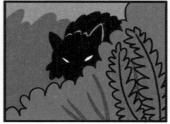

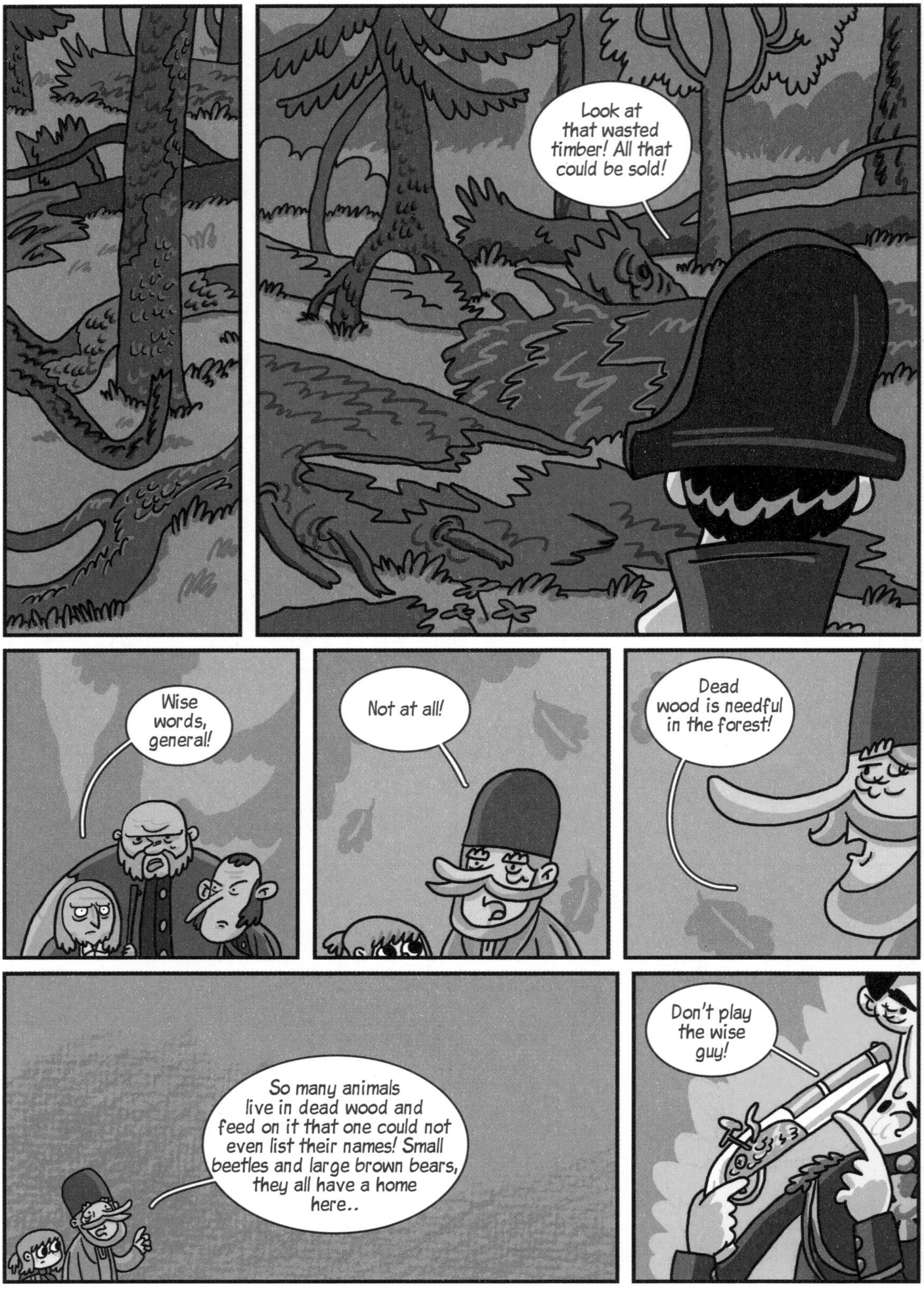
Look at that wasted timber! All that could be sold!
Wise words, general!
Not at all!
Dead wood is needful in the forest!
So many animals live in dead wood and feed on it that one could not even list their names! Small beetles and large brown bears, they all have a home here..
Don't play the wise guy!

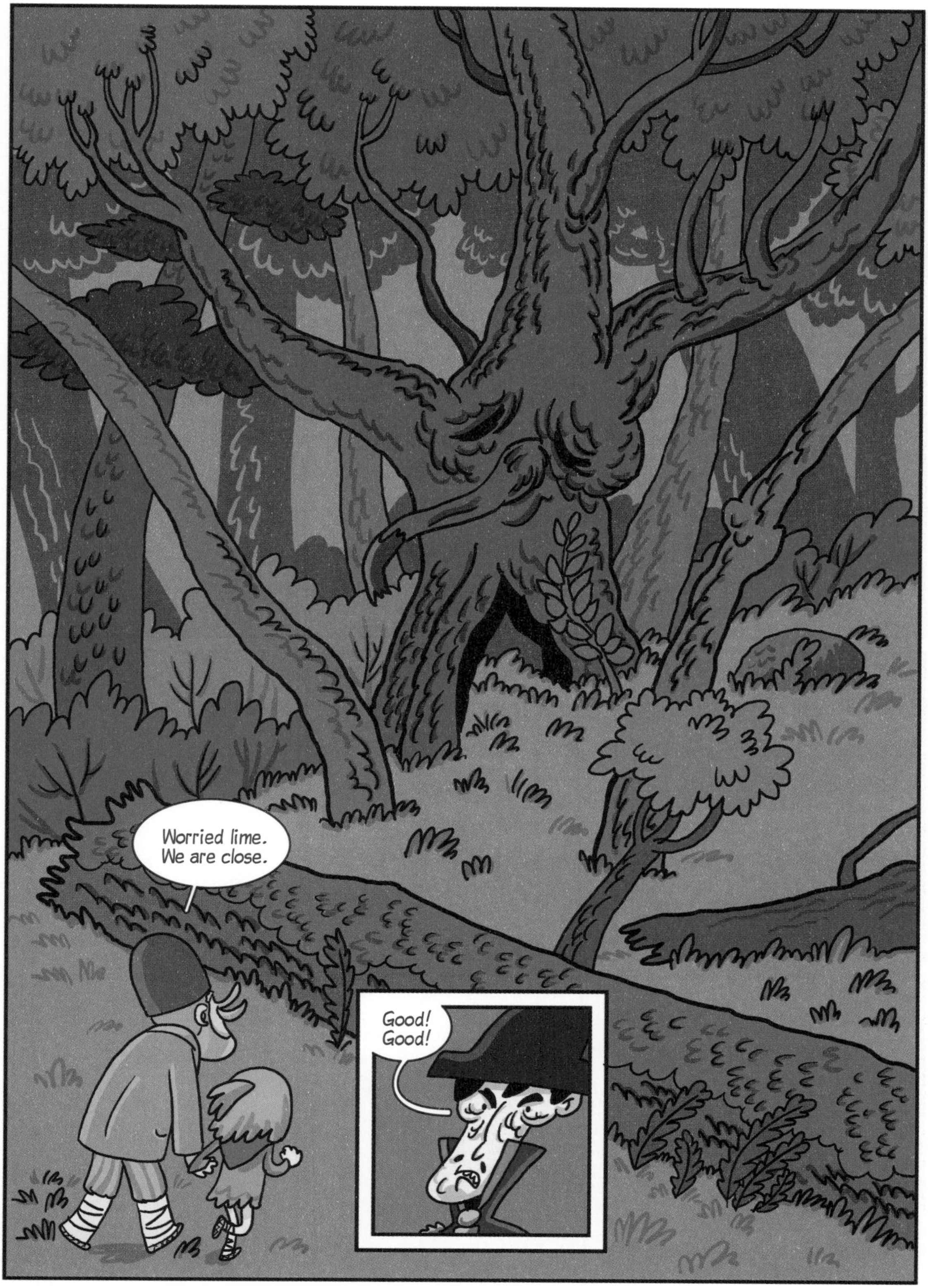
Worried lime.
We are close.
Good!
Good!

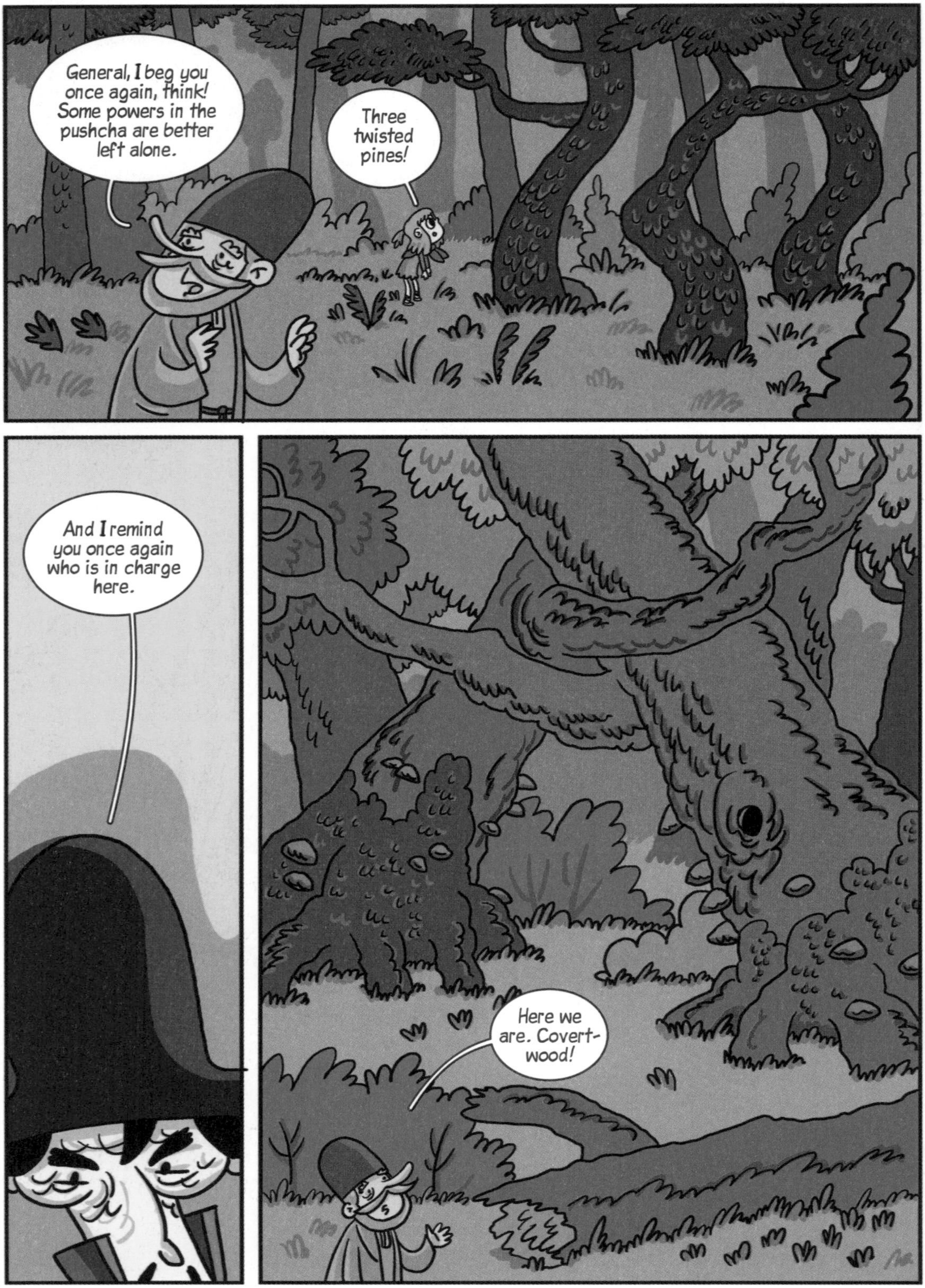
General, I beg you once again, think! Some powers in the pushcha are better left alone.
Three twisted pines!
And I remind you once again who is in charge here.
Here we are. Covert-wood!

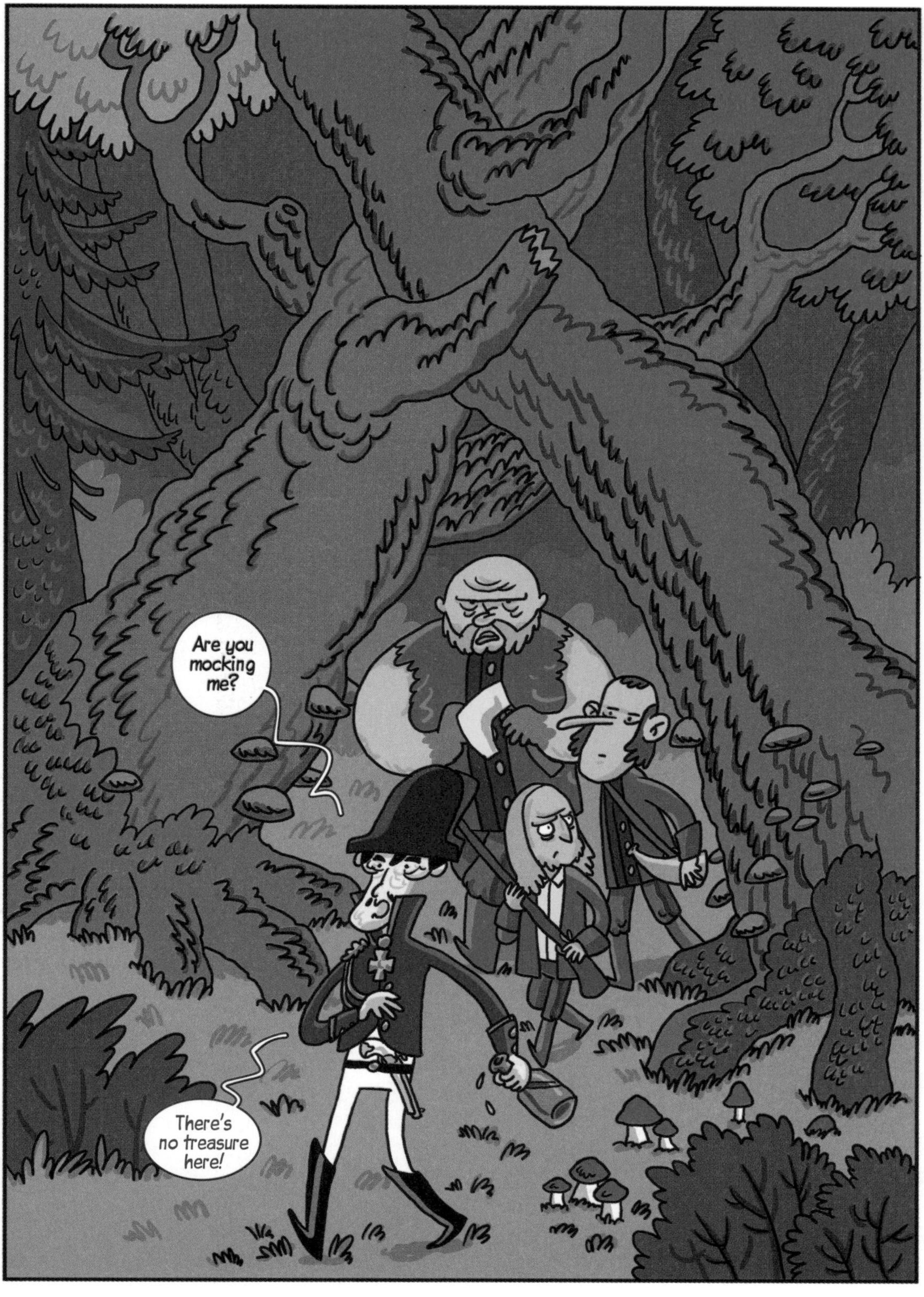
Are you mocking me?
There's no treasure here!

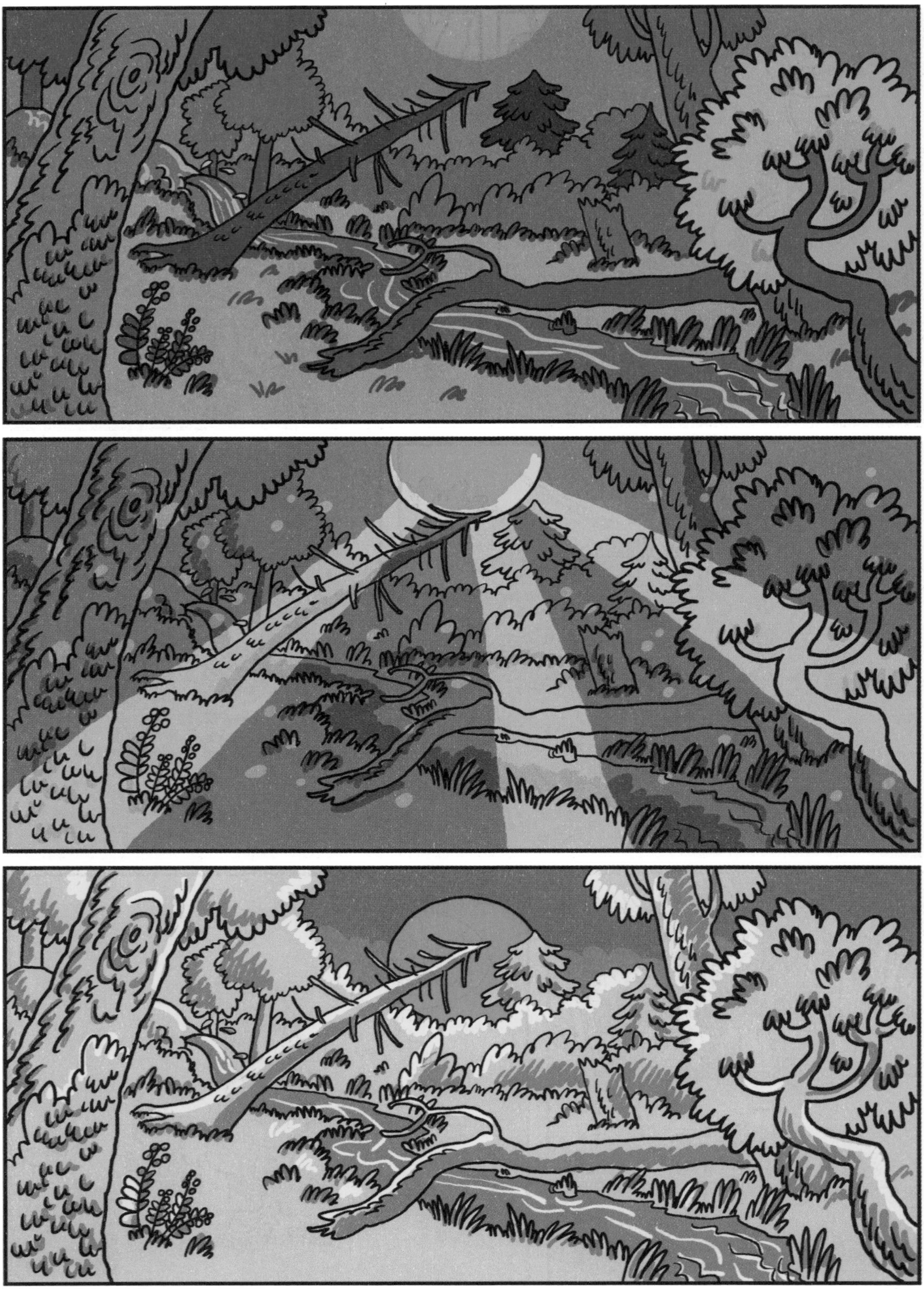

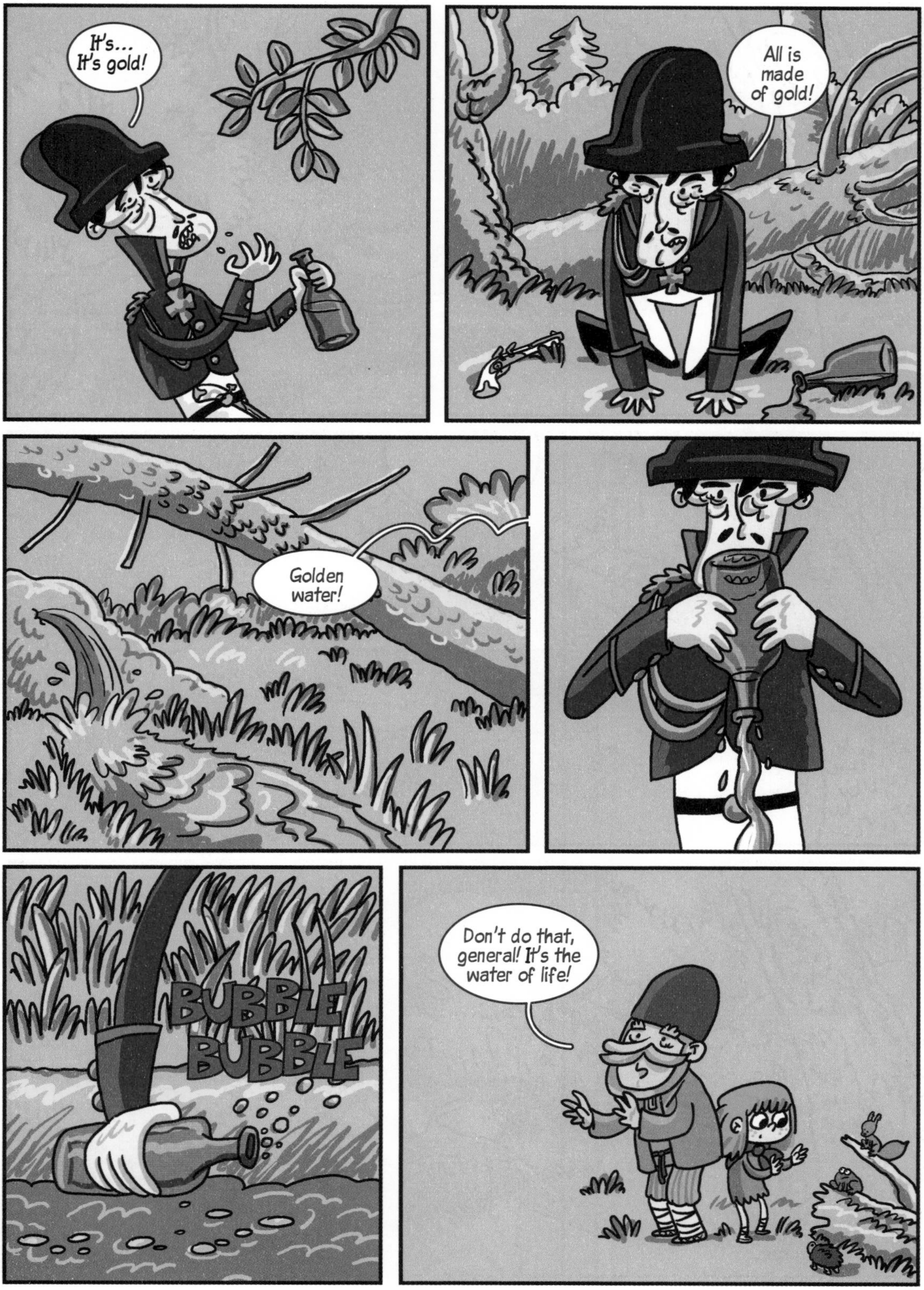
It's... It's gold!
All is made of gold!
Golden water!
BUBBLE BUBBLE
Don't do that, general! It's the water of life!

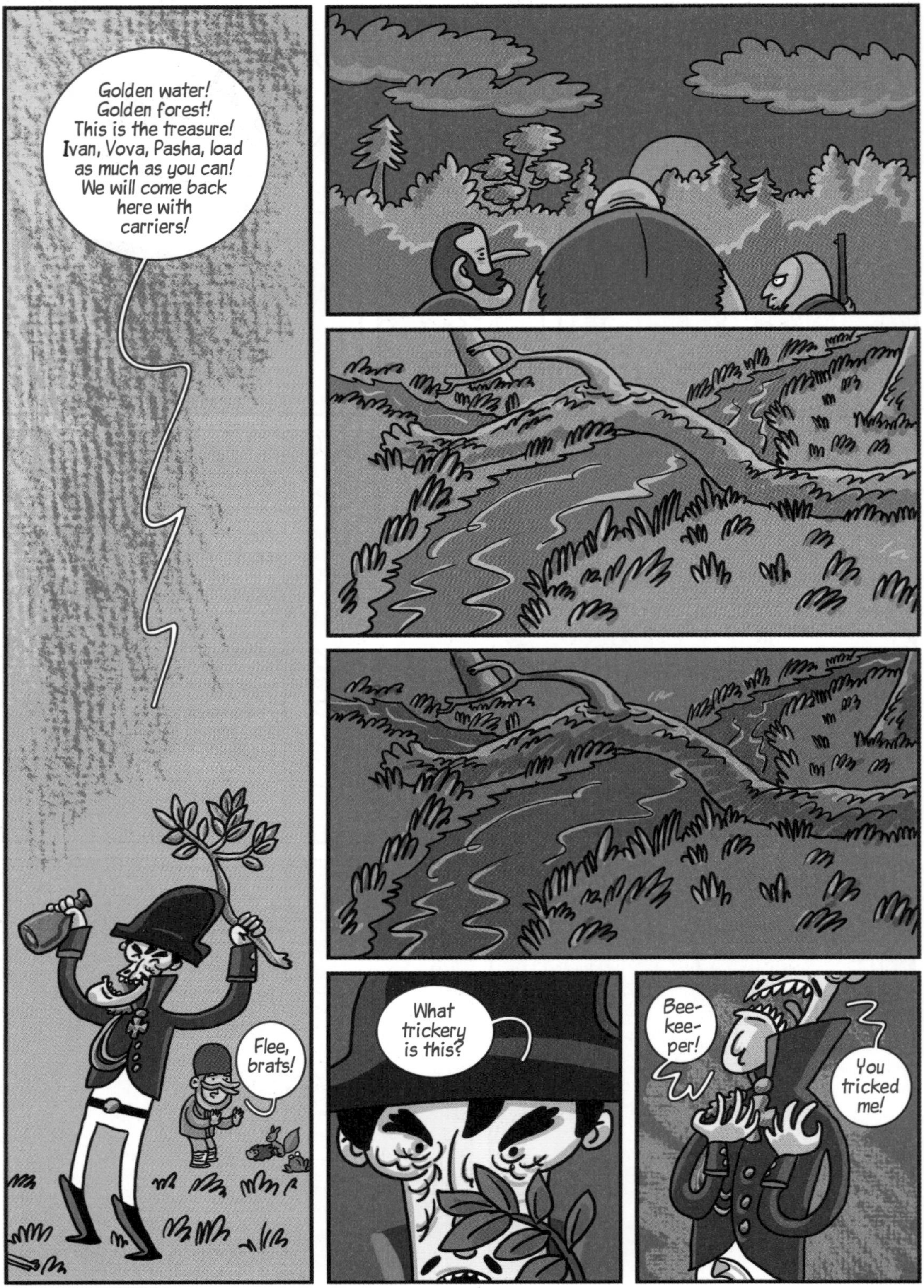
Golden water! Golden forest! This is the treasure! Ivan, Vova, Pasha, load as much as you can! We will come back here with carriers!
Flee, brats!
What trickery is this?
Bee-keeper!
You tricked me!

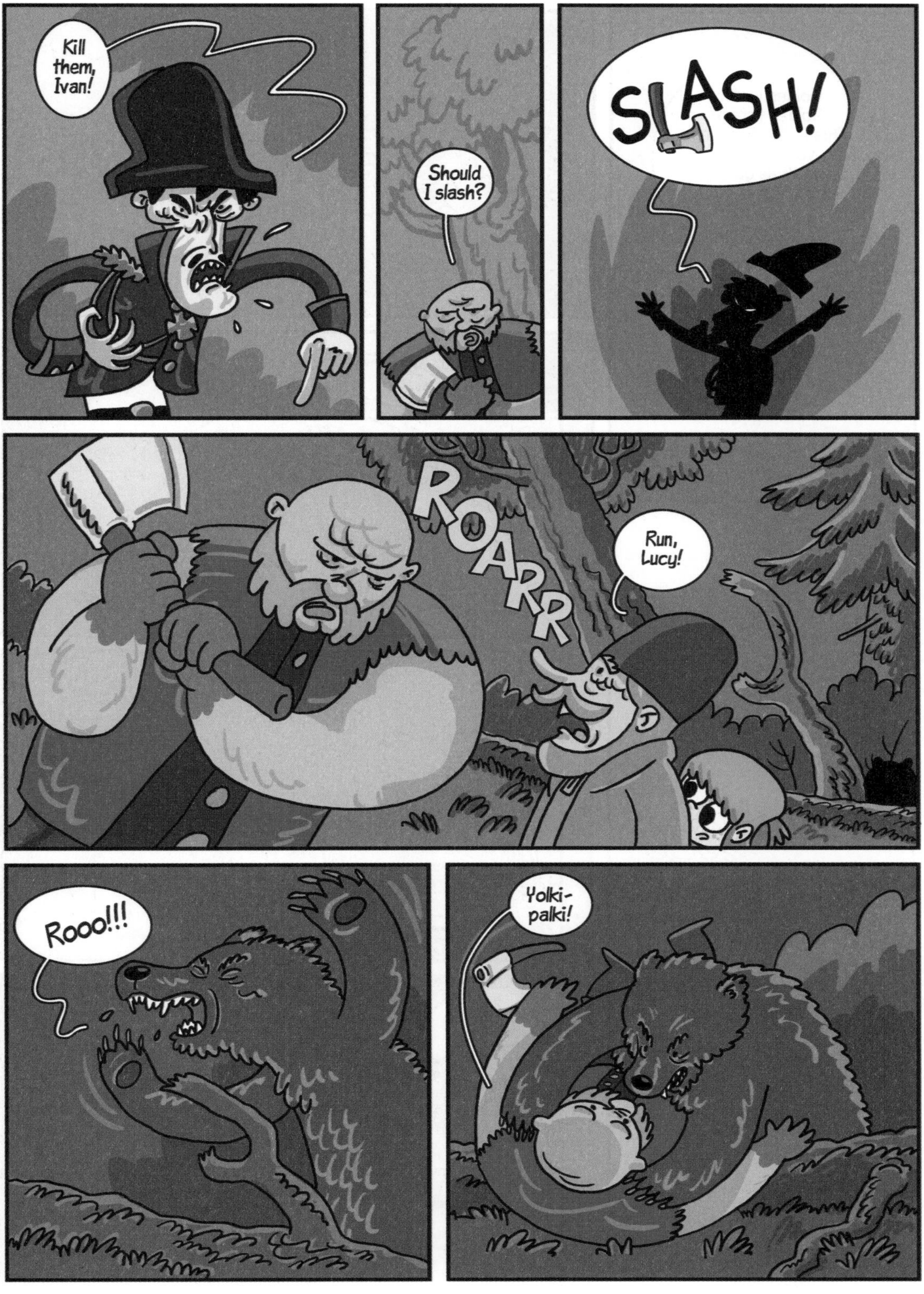
Kill them, Ivan!
Should I slash?
SLASH!
ROARR
Run, Lucy!
Rooo!!!
Yolki-palki!

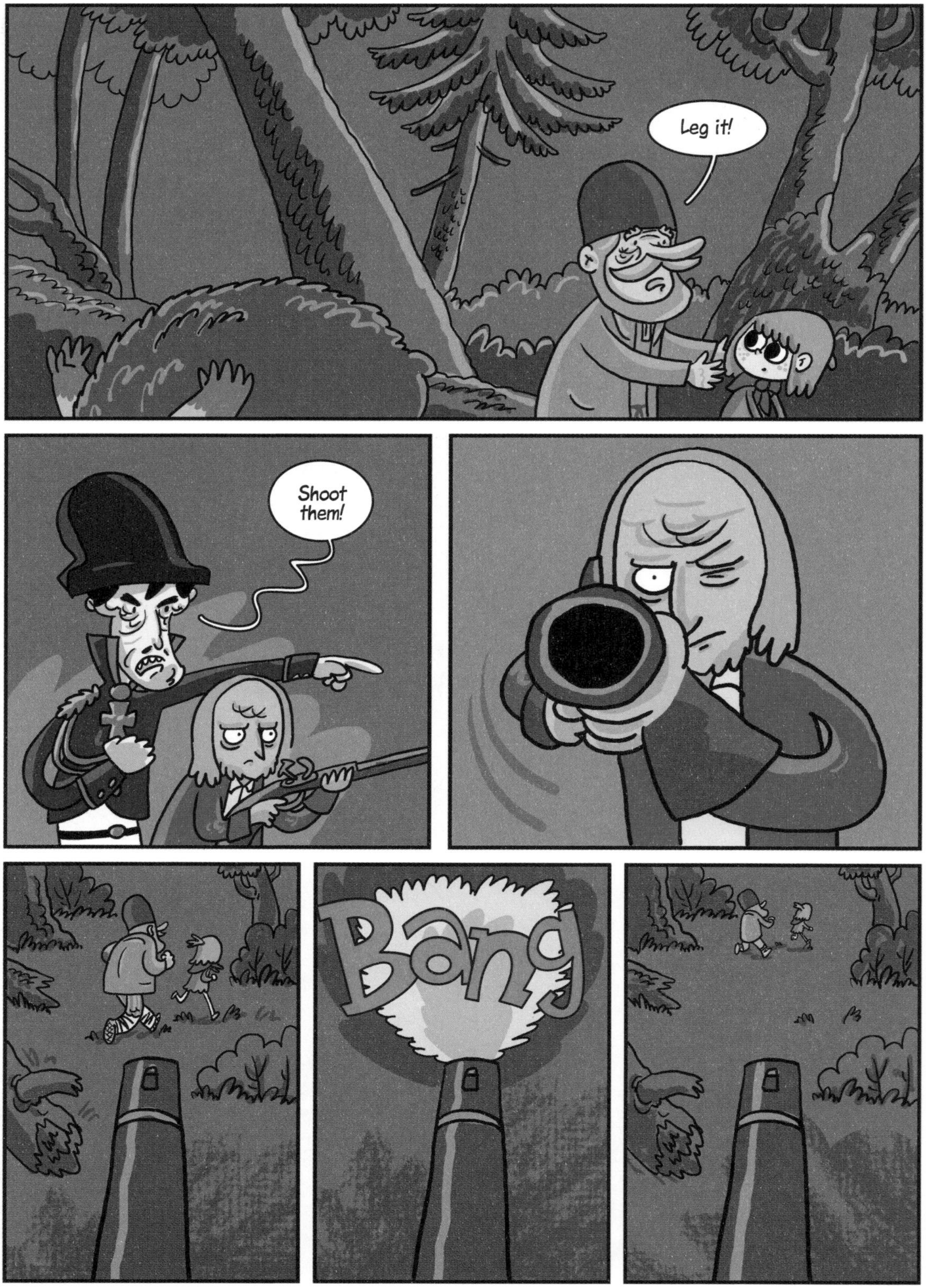
Leg it!
Shoot them!
Bang

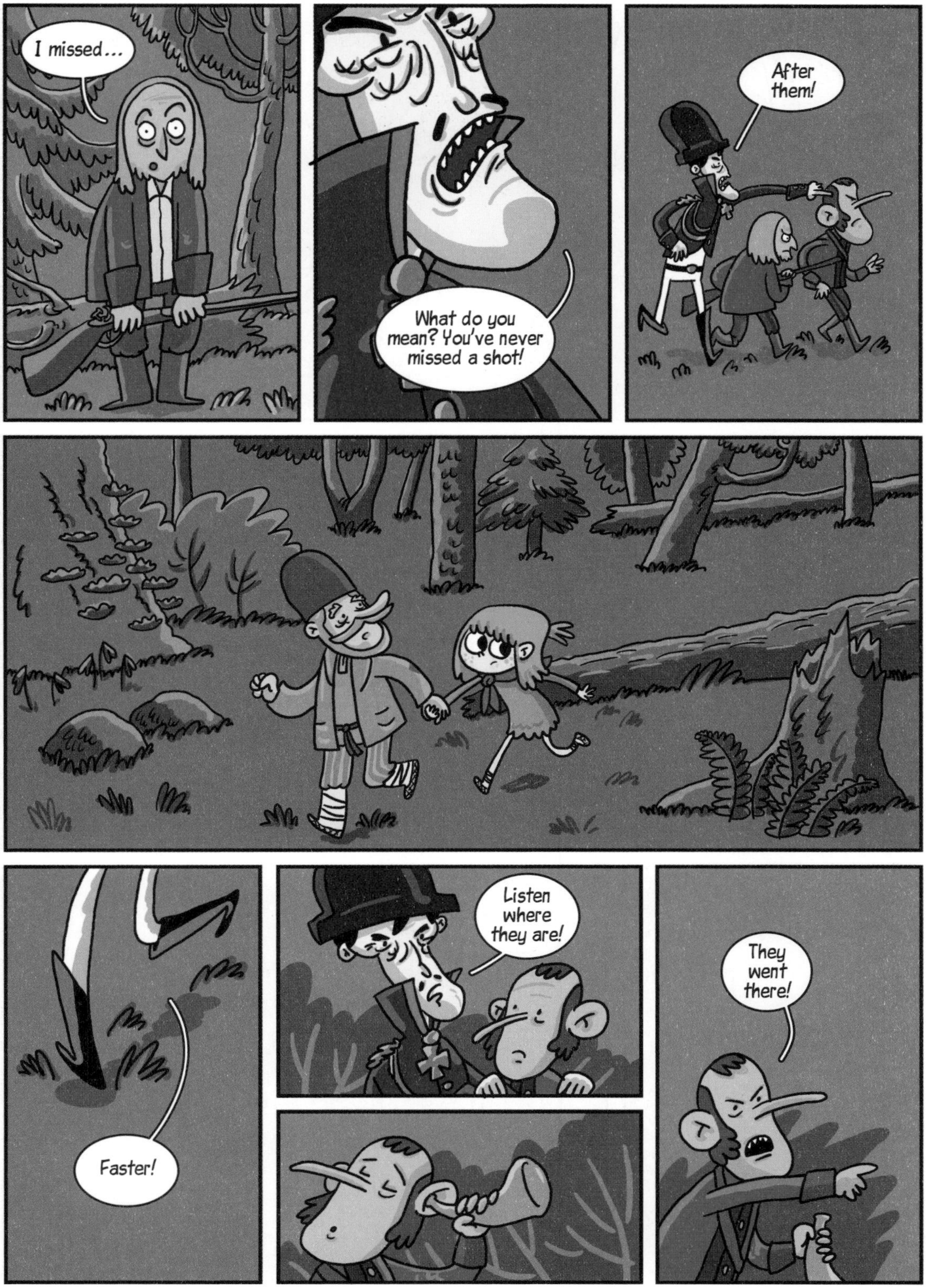
I missed...
What do you mean? You've never missed a shot!
After them!
Faster!
Listen where they are!
They went there!

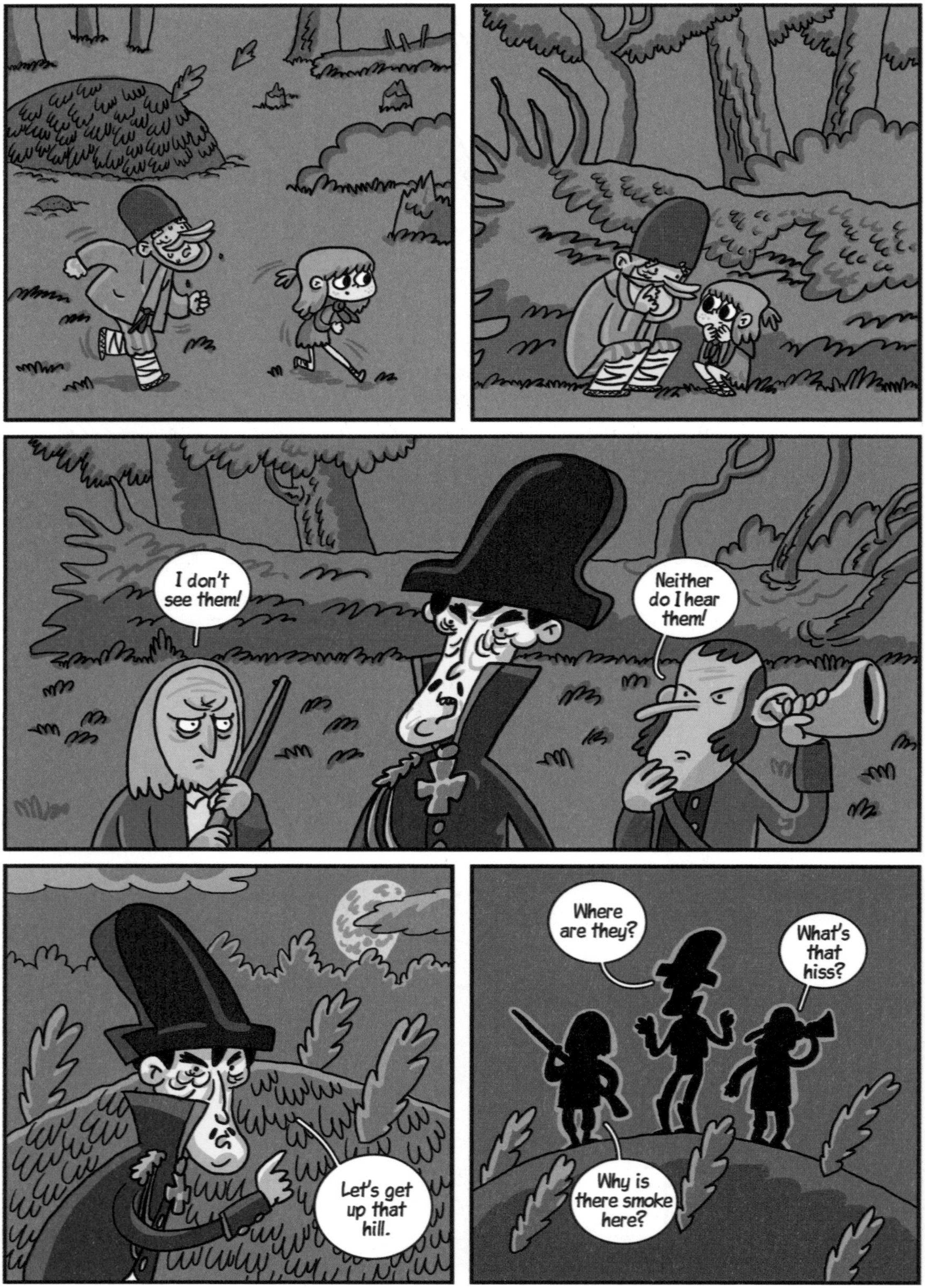
I don't see them!
Neither do I hear them!
Let's get up that hill.
Where are they?
What's that hiss?
Why is there smoke here?

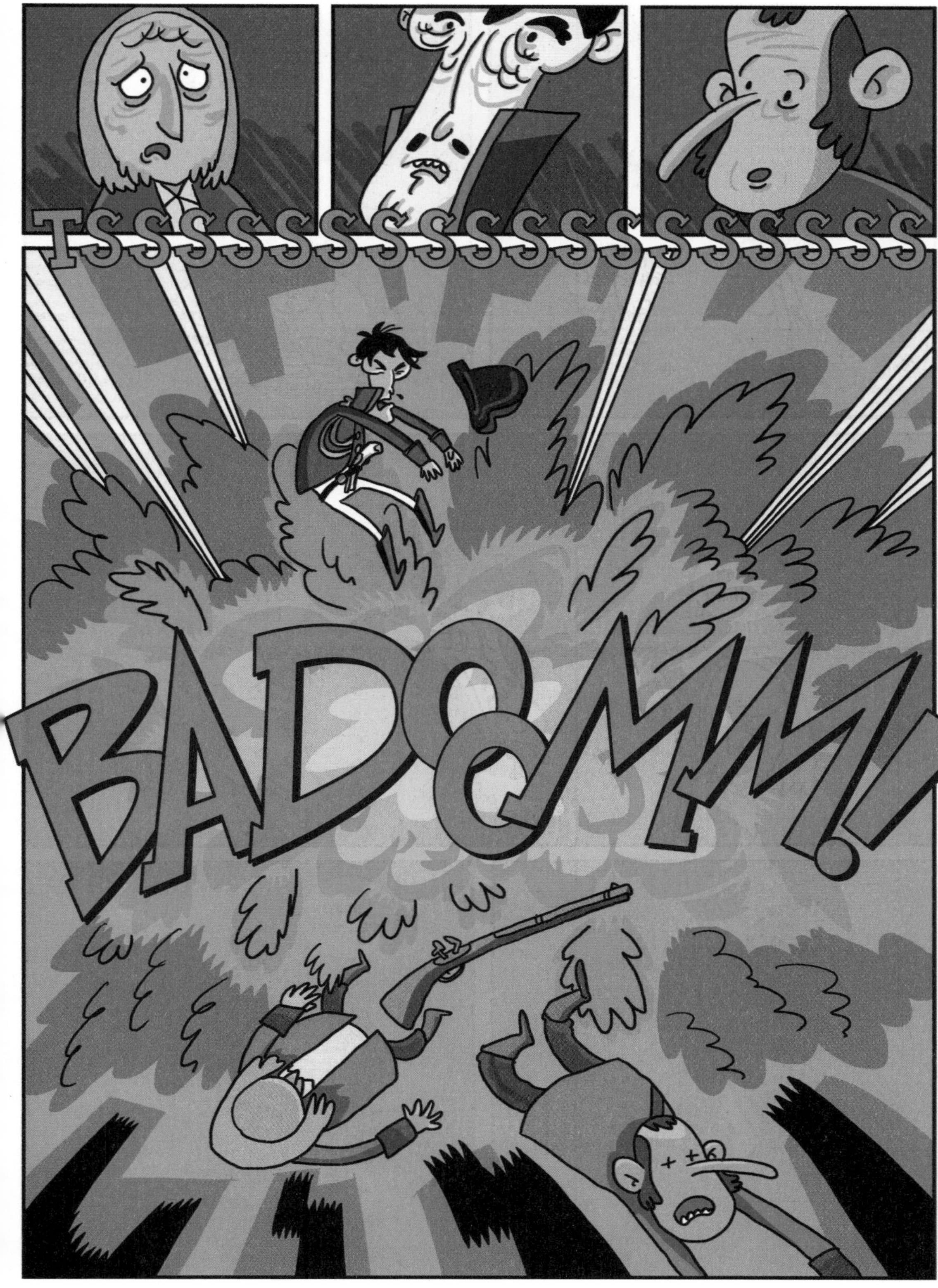
TSSSSSSSSSSSSSSSSS
BADOOMM!

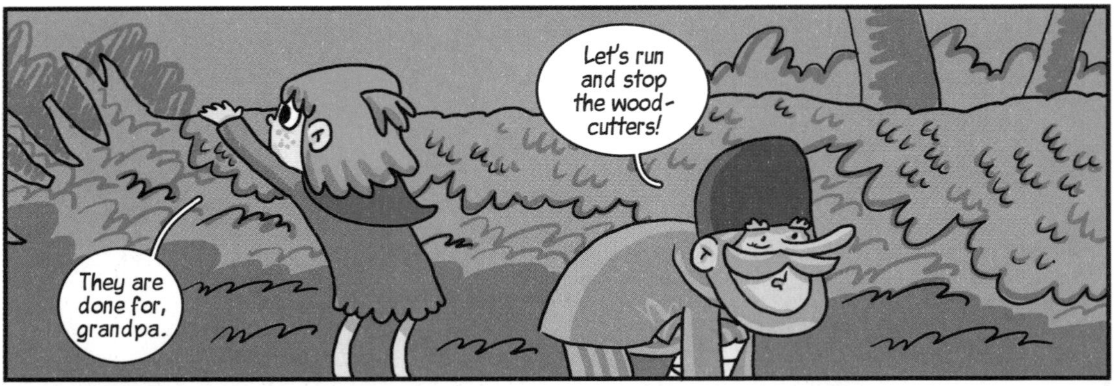
Let's run and stop the wood-cutters!
They are done for, grandpa.

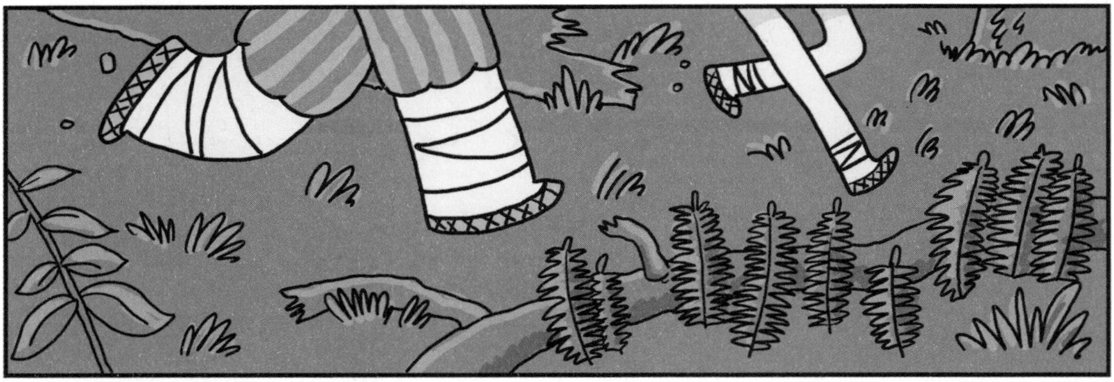

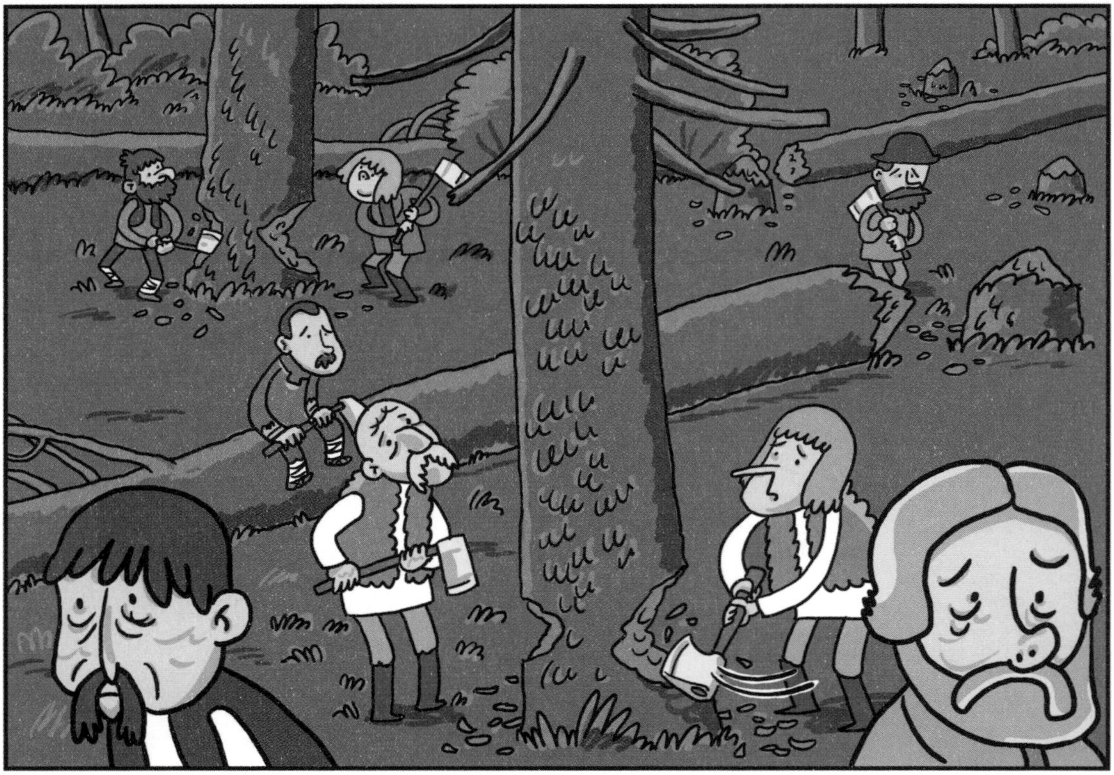

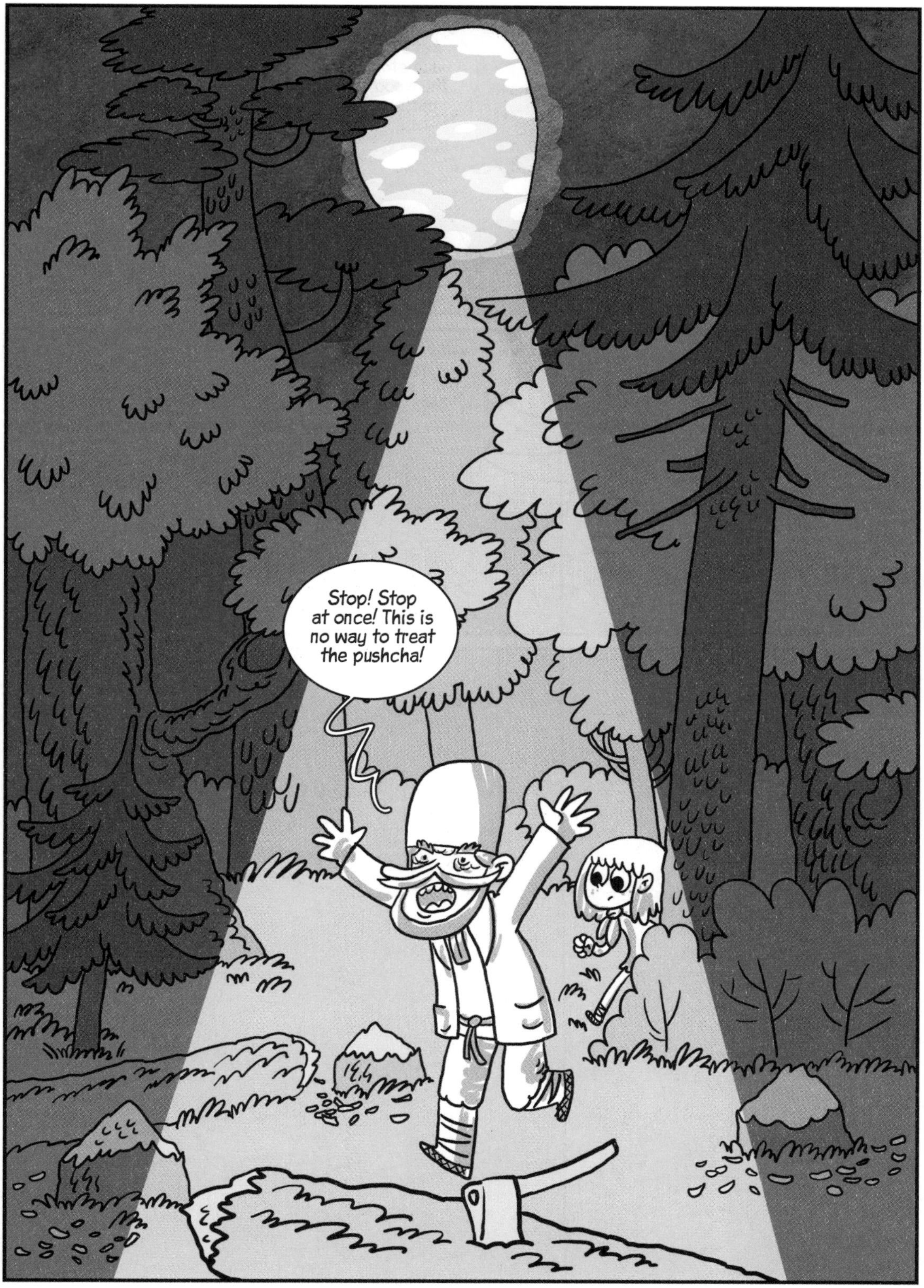
Stop! Stop at once! This is no way to treat the pushcha!

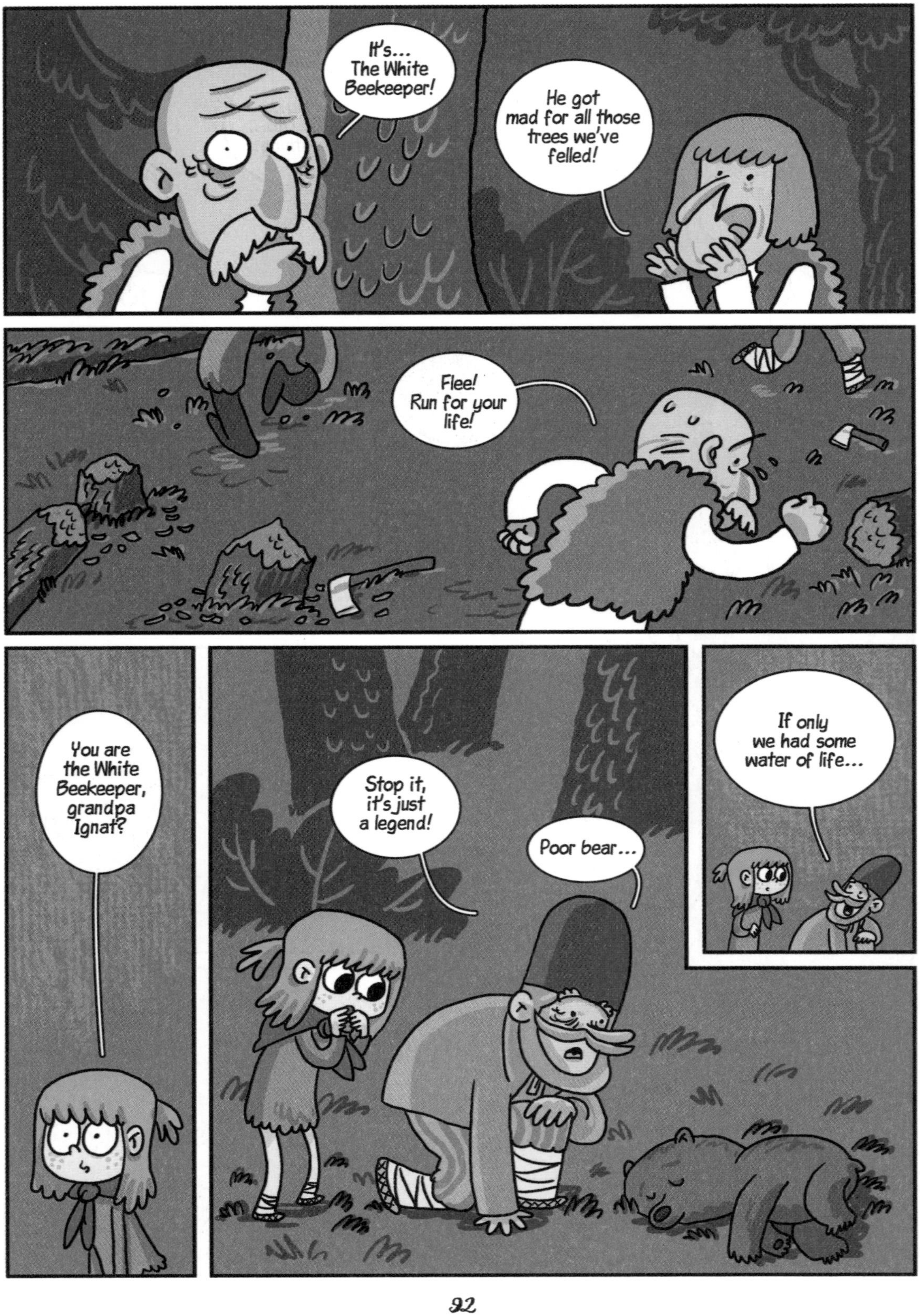
It's... The White Beekeeper!
He got mad for all those trees we've felled!
Flee! Run for your life!
You are the White Beekeeper, grandpa Ignat?
Stop it, it's just a legend!
Poor bear...
If only we had some water of life...

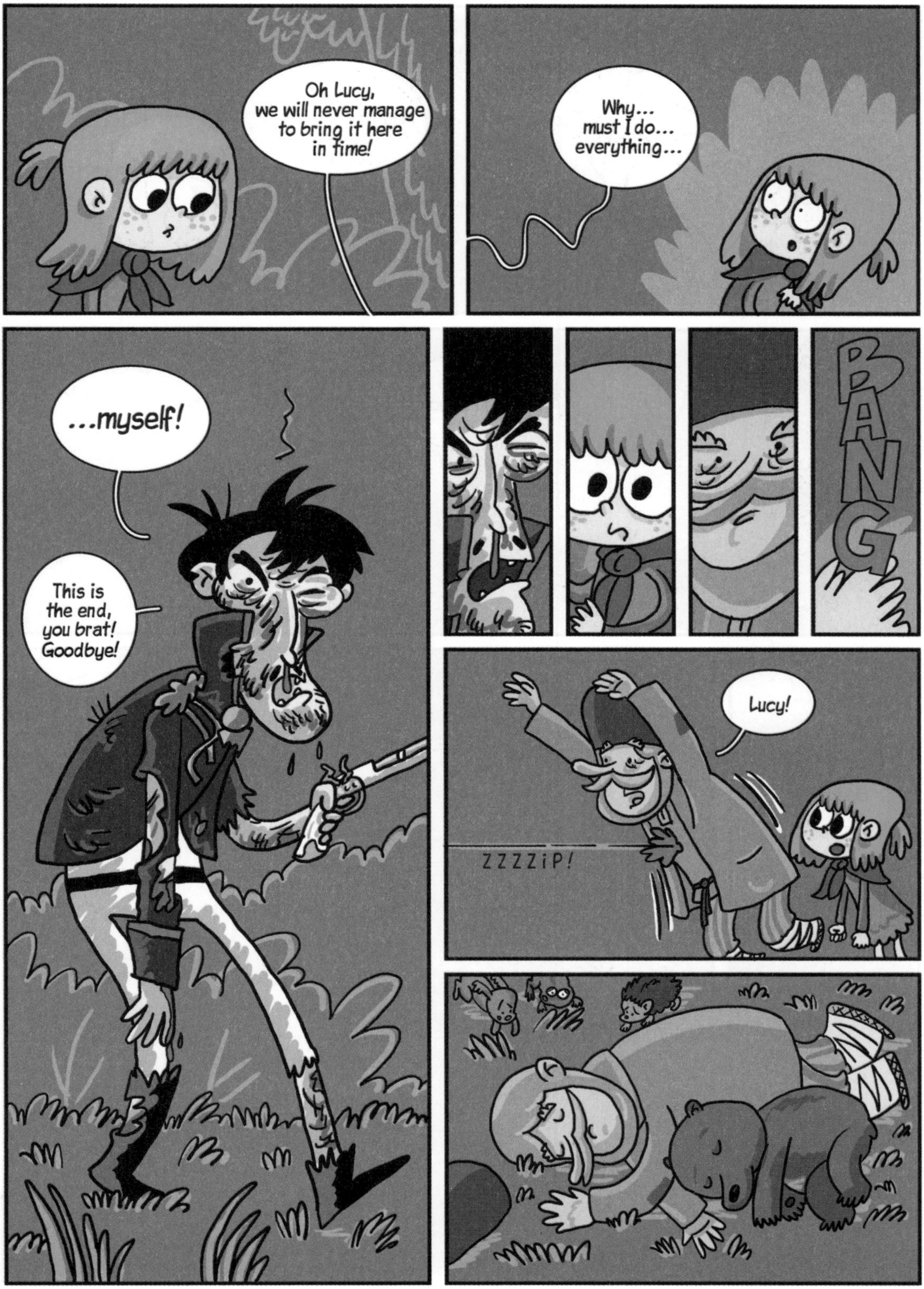
Oh Lucy, we will never manage to bring it here in time!
Why... must I do... everything...
...myself!
This is the end, you brat! Goodbye!
BANG
Lucy!
ZZZZiP!

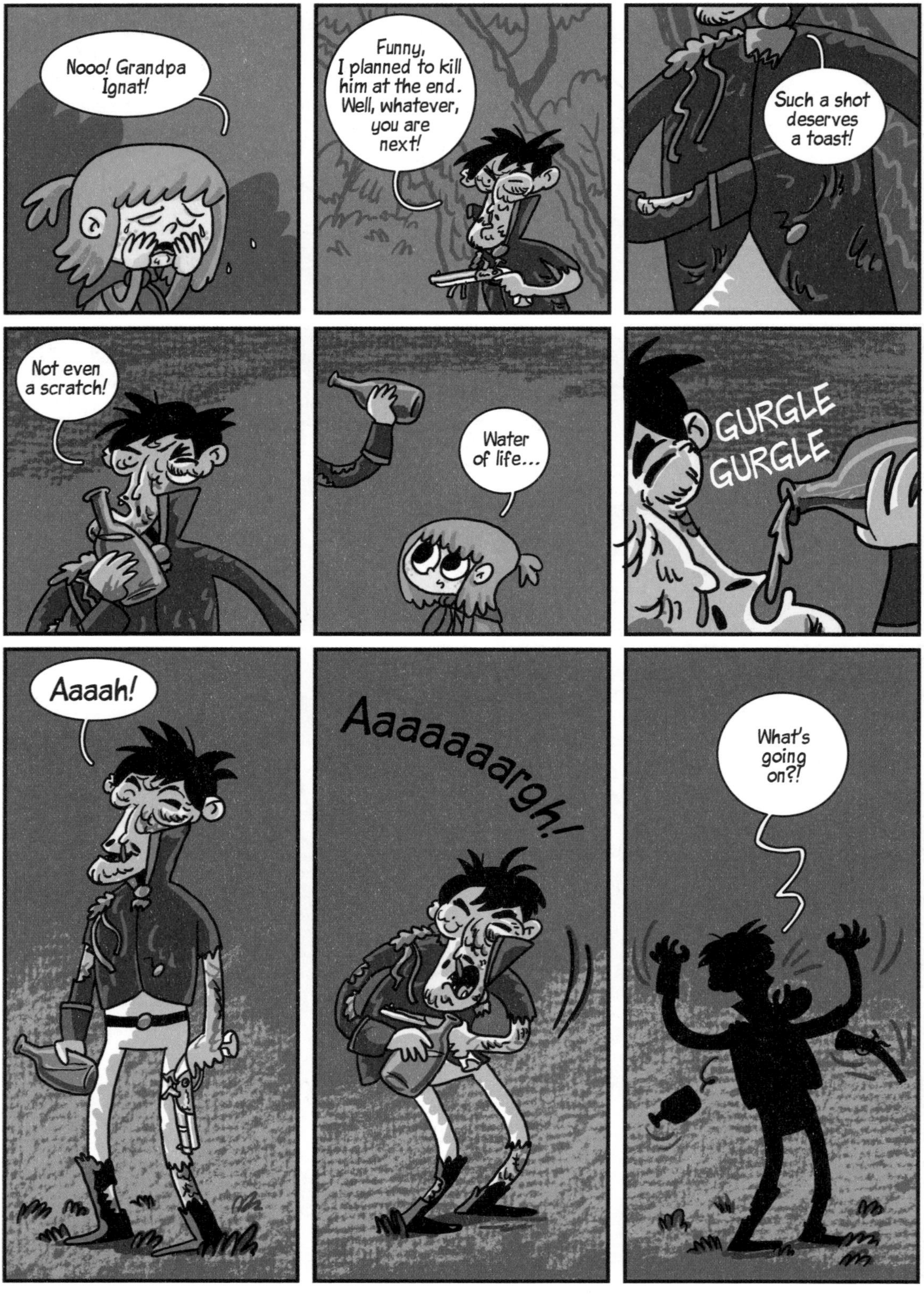
Nooo! Grandpa Ignat!
Funny, I planned to kill him at the end. Well, whatever, you are next!
Such a shot deserves a toast!
Not even a scratch!
Water of life...
GURGLE GURGLE
Aaaah!
Aaaaaaaargh!
What's going on?!

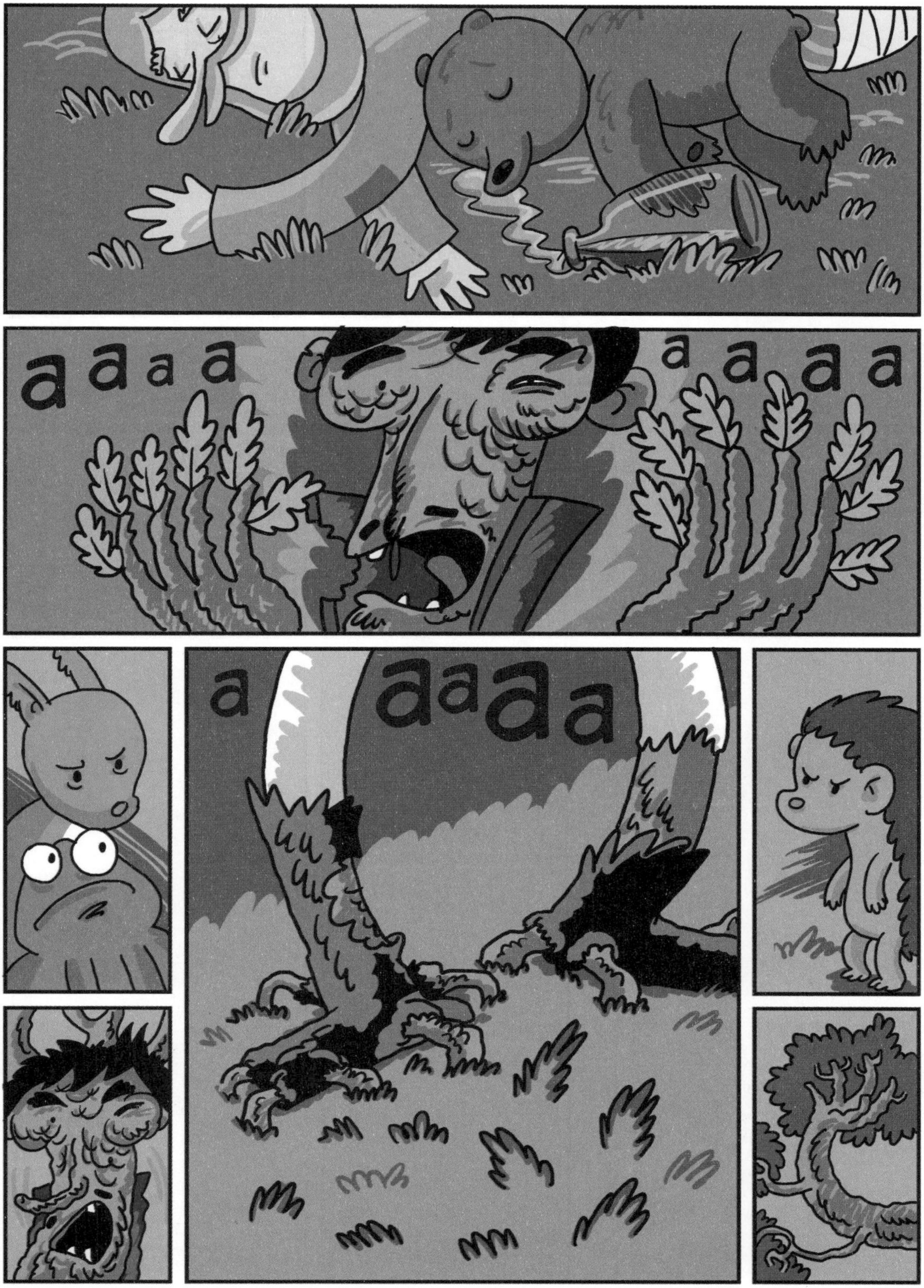
a a a a
a a a a a
a
a a a a

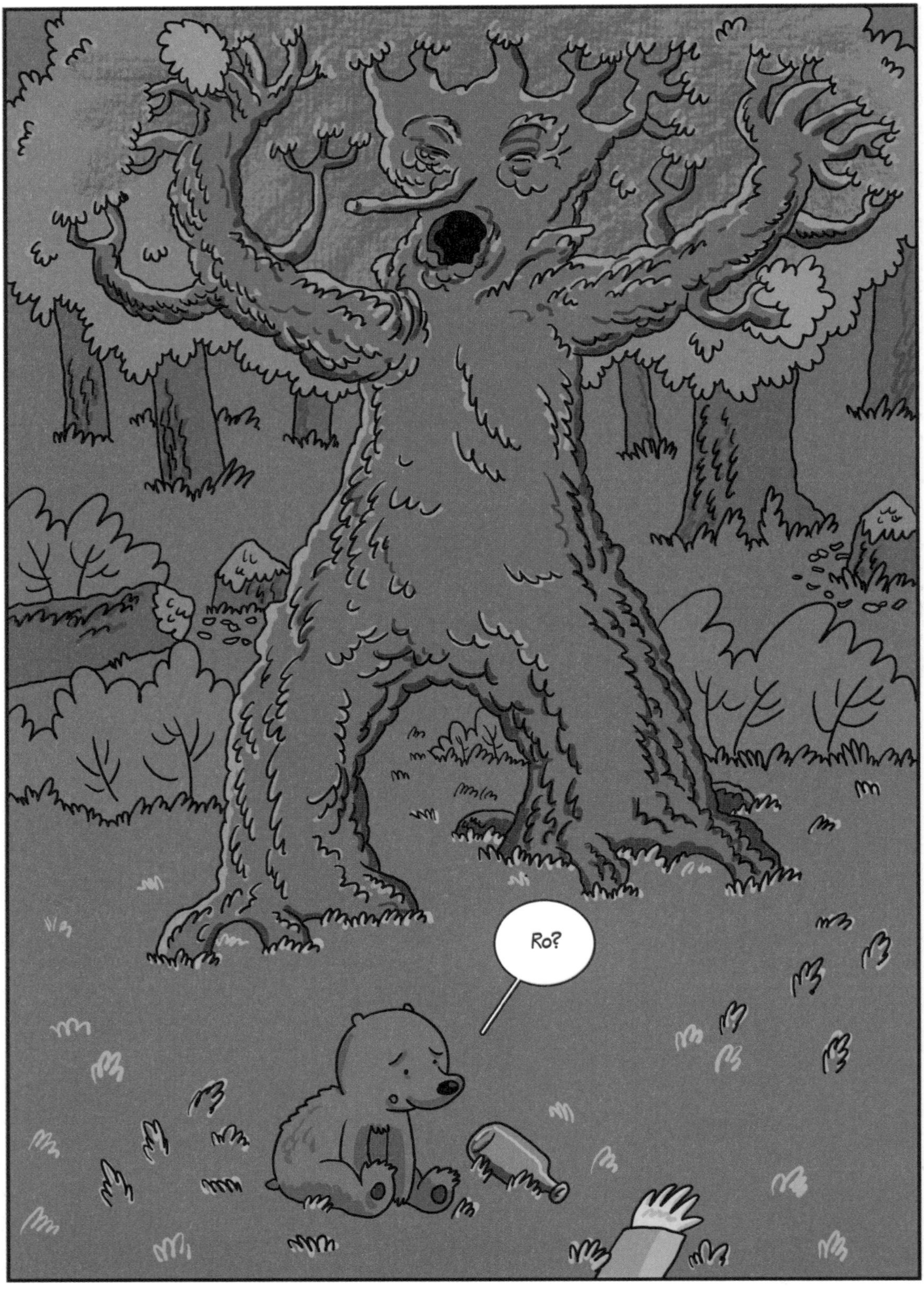
Ro?

Bear! You are alive! It's the water!

Oh no! Only a drop left!

Grandpa! Grandpa!

Please! Please! Please!

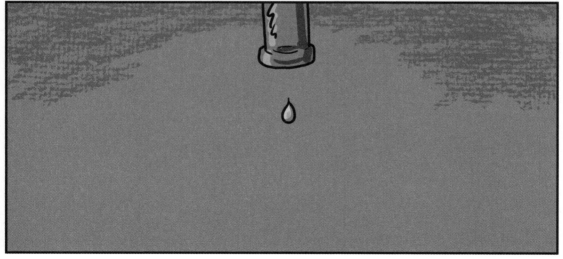

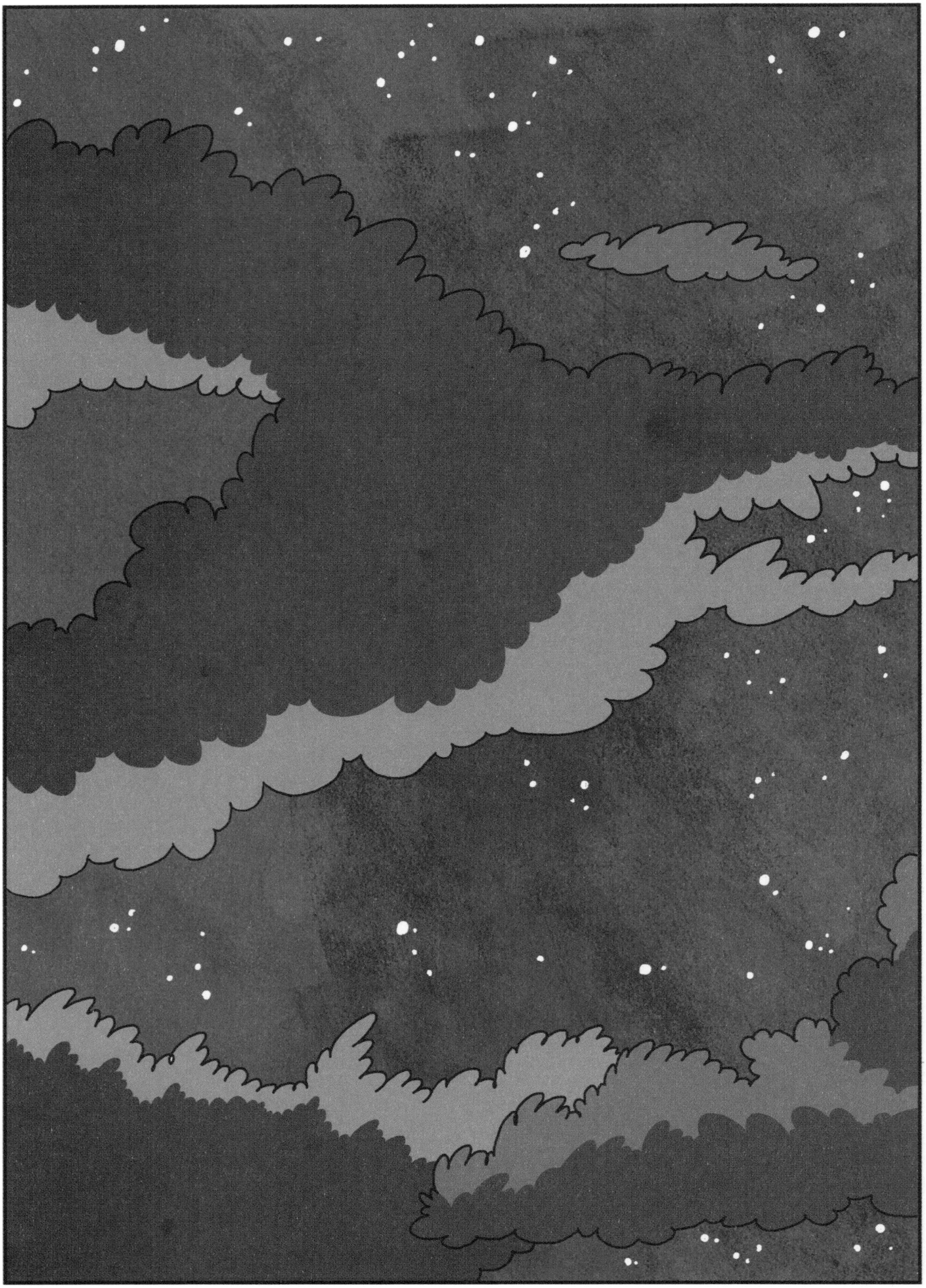

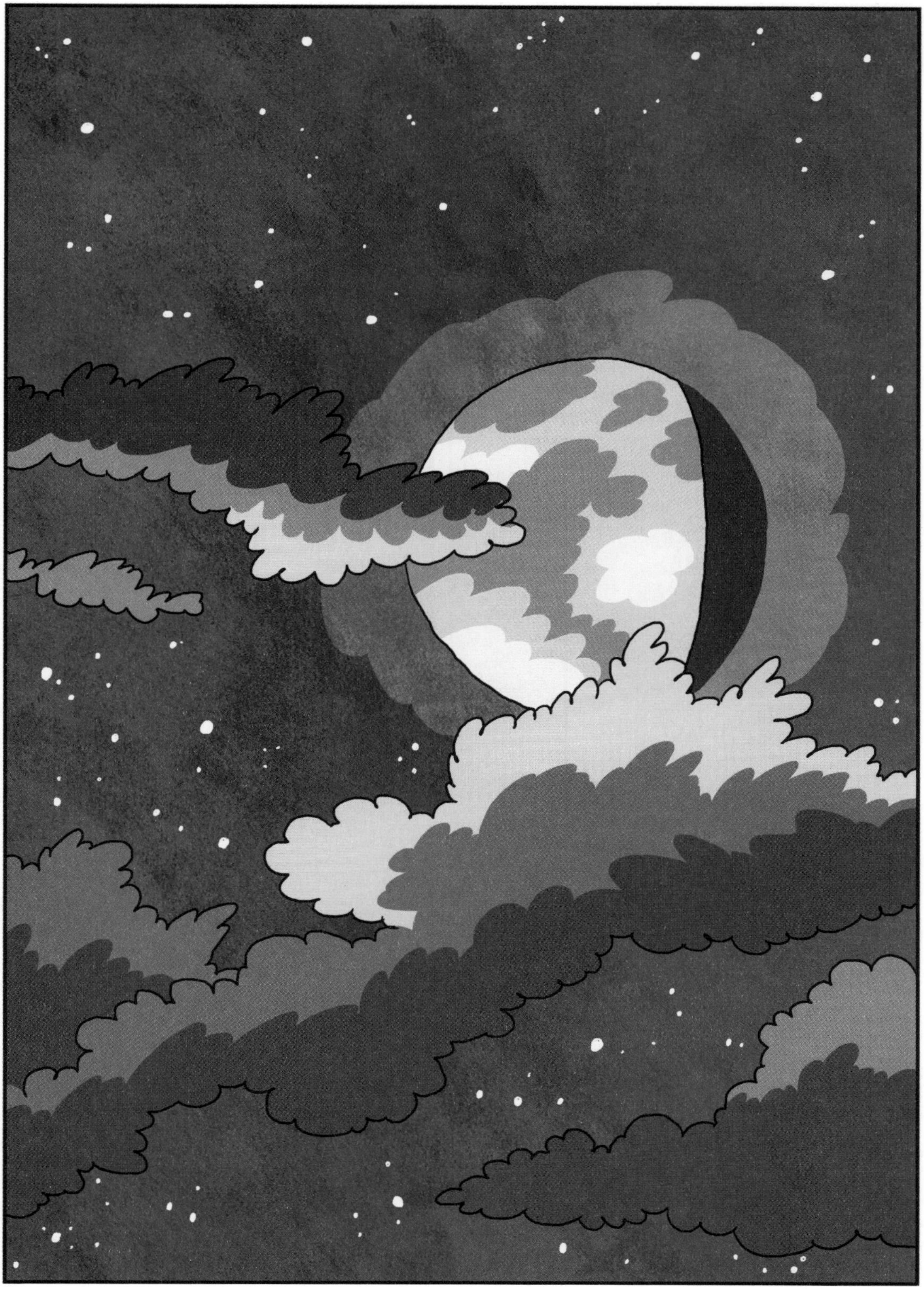

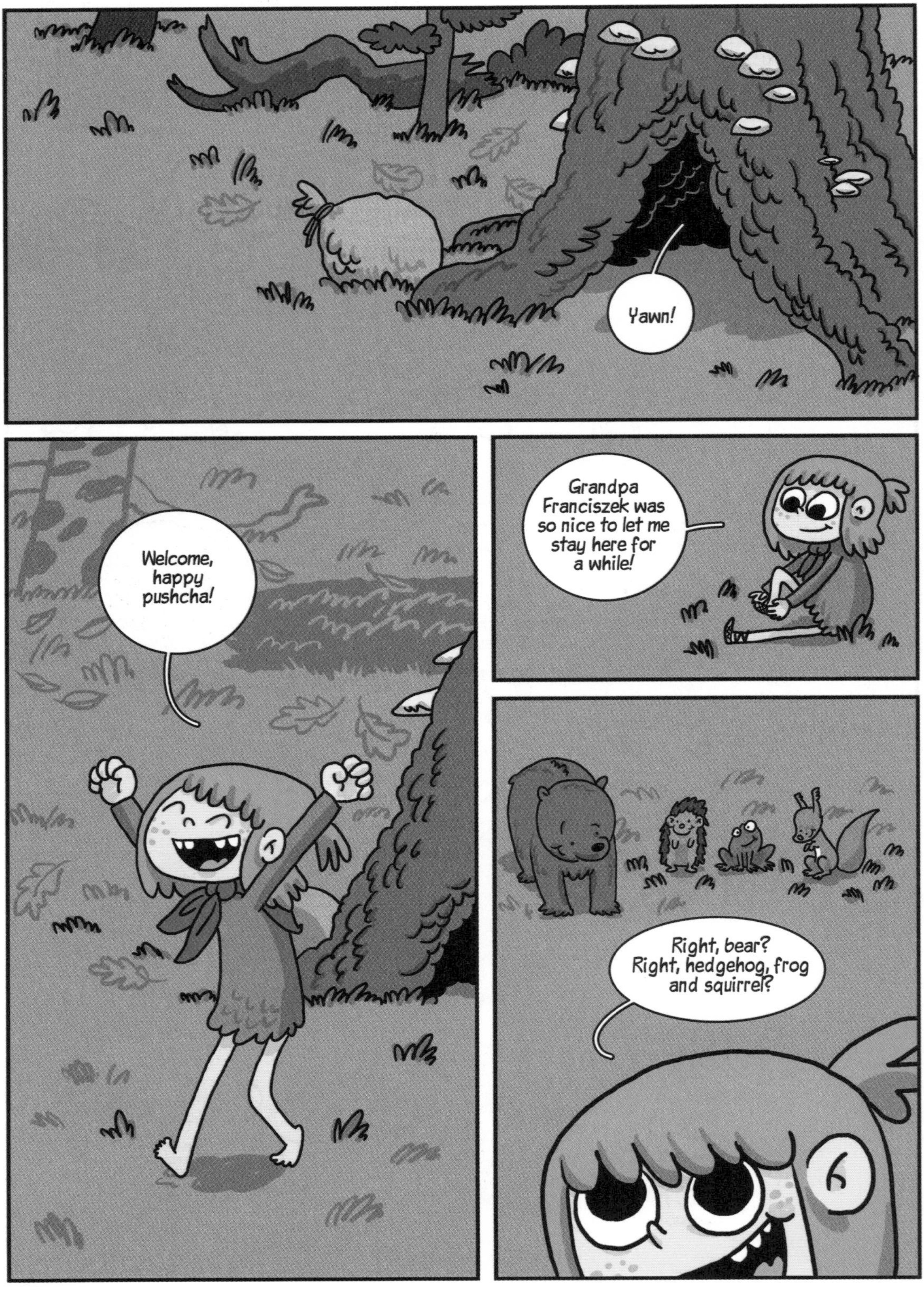
Yawn!
Welcome, happy pushcha!
Grandpa Franciszek was so nice to let me stay here for a while!
Right, bear? Right, hedgehog, frog and squirrel?

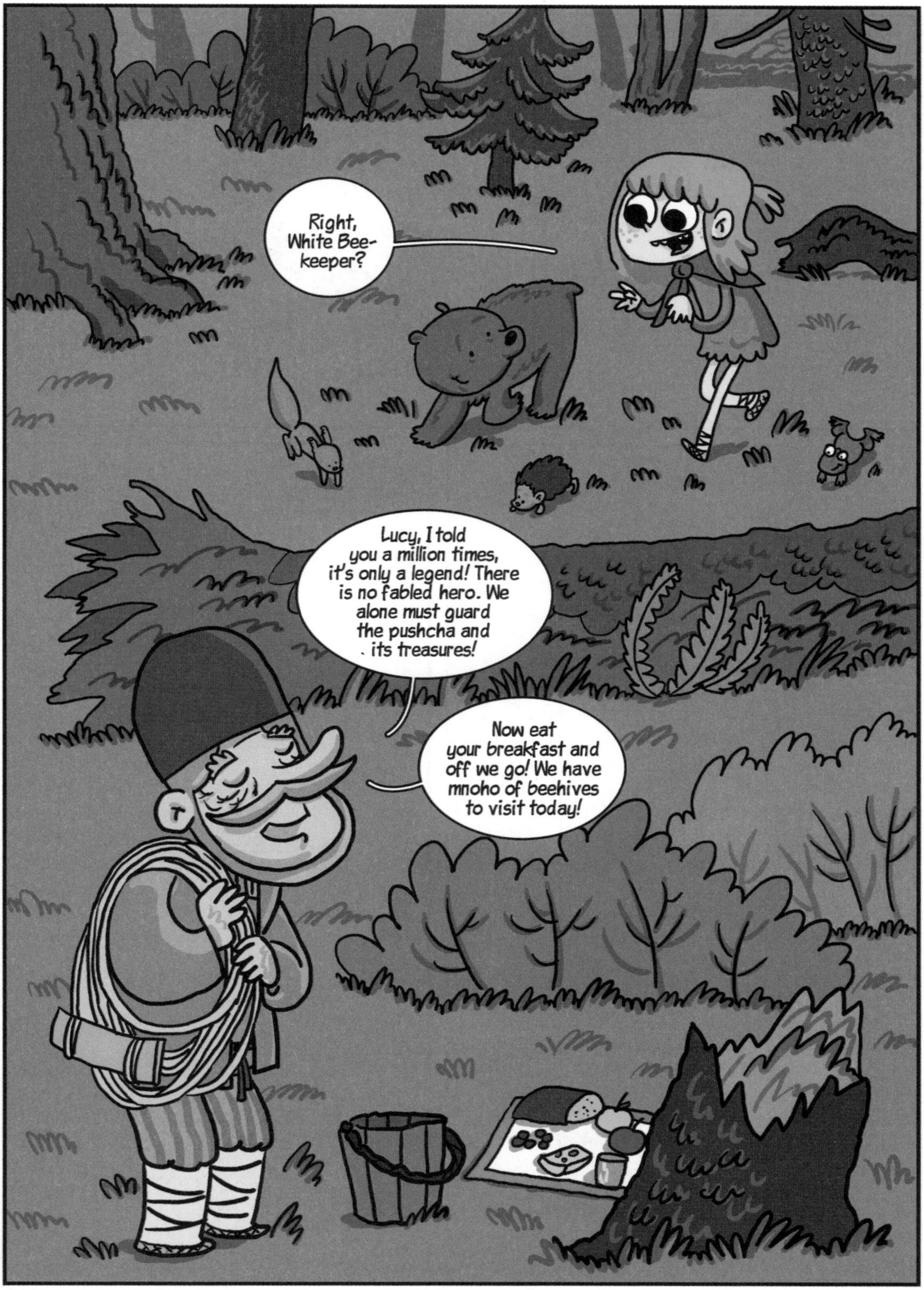
Right, White Bee-keeper?
Lucy, I told you a million times, it's only a legend! There is no fabled hero. We alone must guard the pushcha and its treasures!
Now eat your breakfast and off we go! We have mnoho of beehives to visit today!

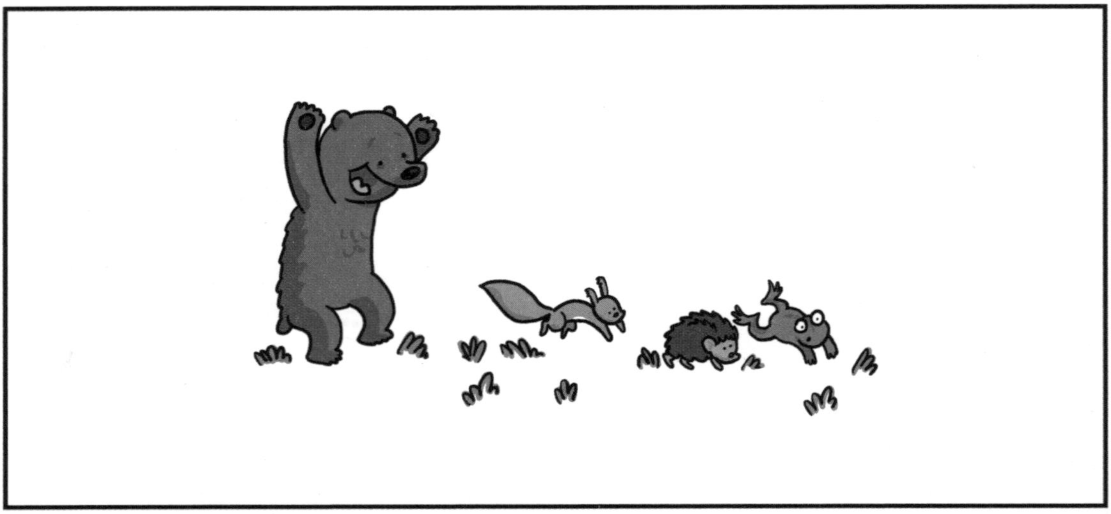

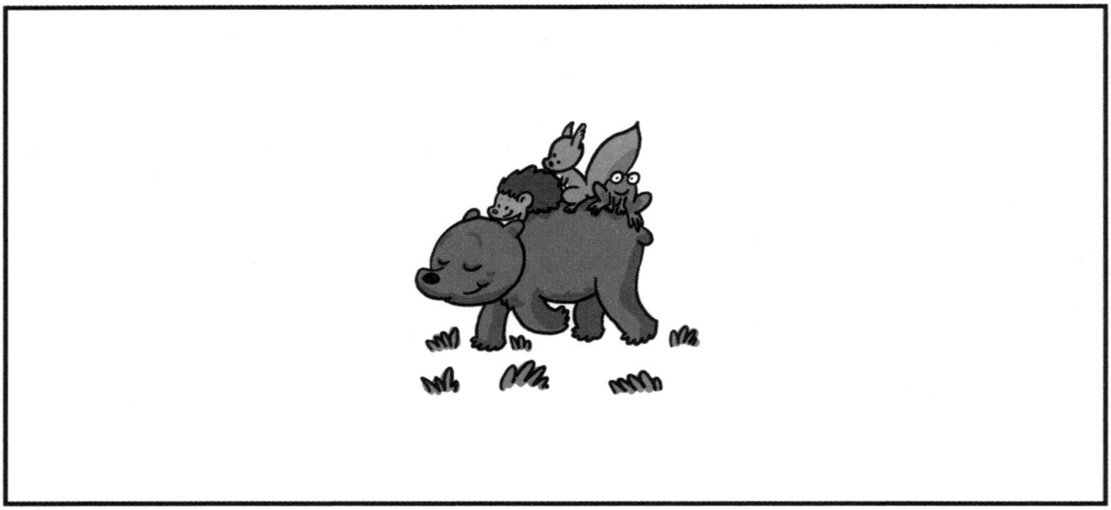

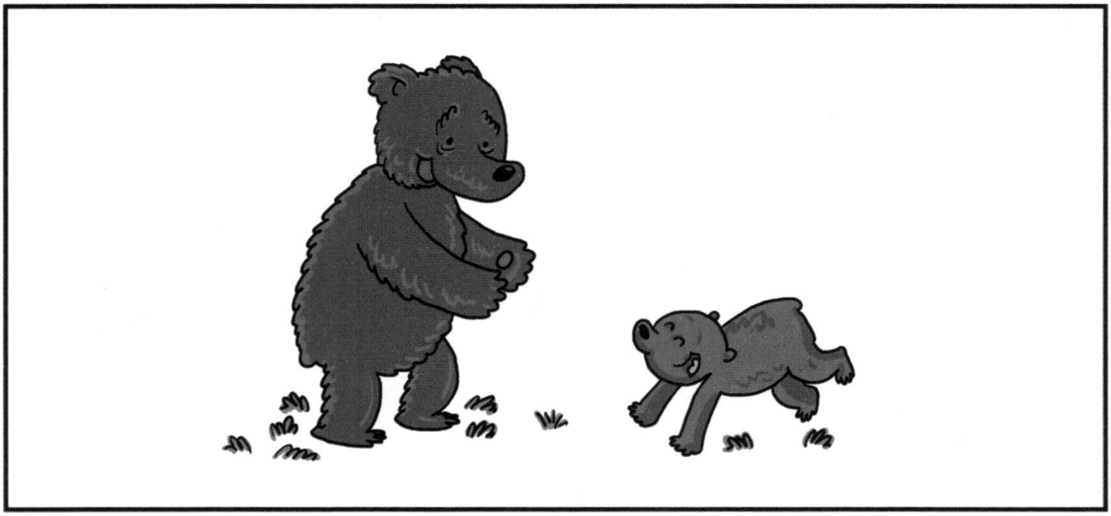

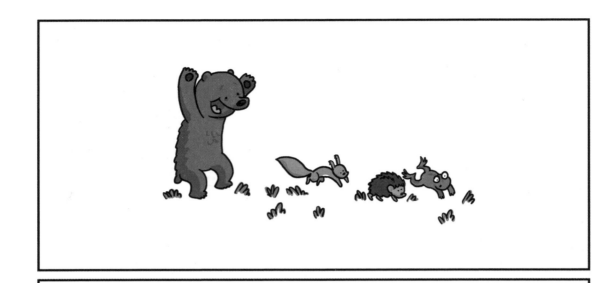

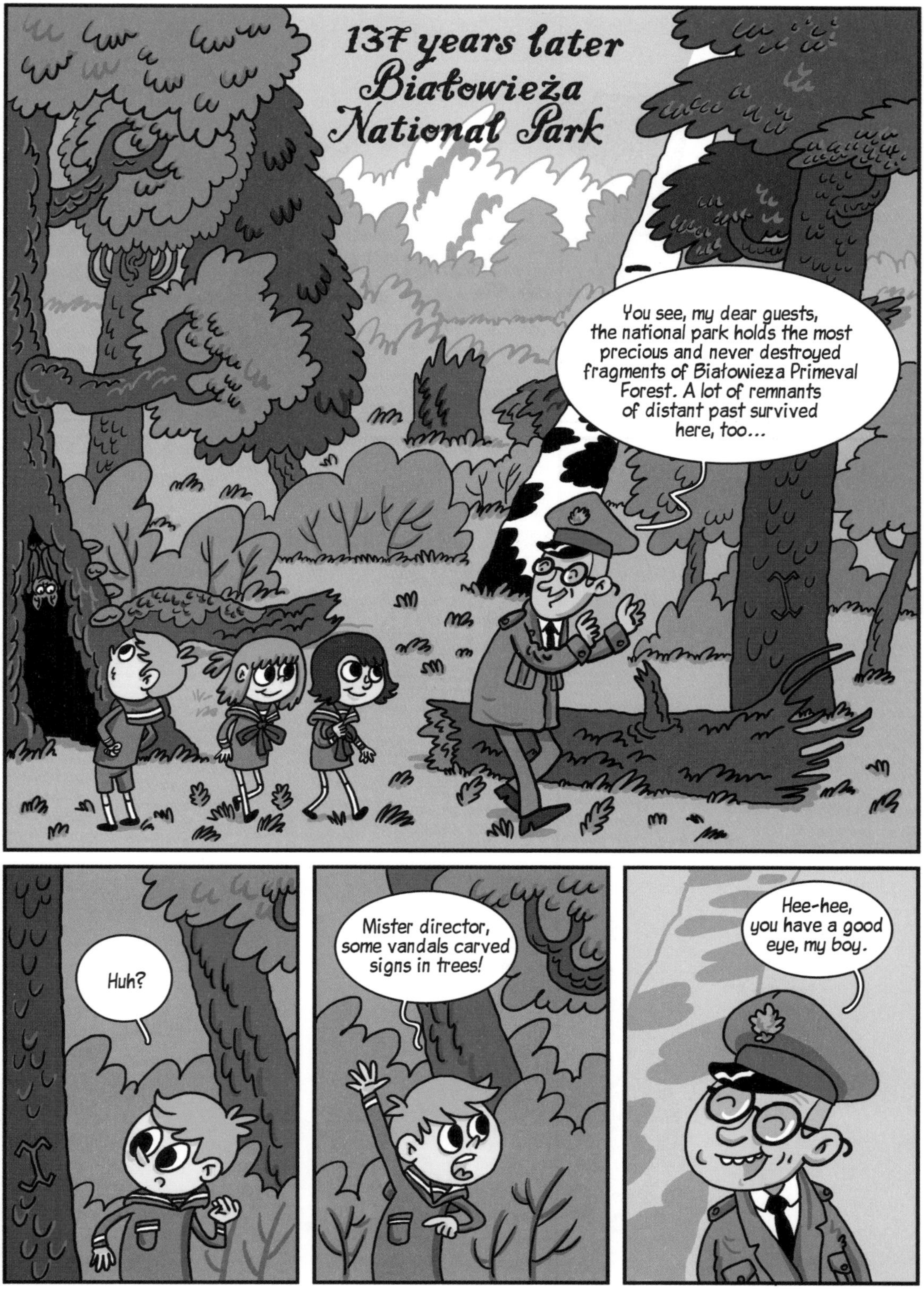

137 years later
Białowieża National Park
You see, my dear guests, the national park holds the most precious and never destroyed fragments of Białowieża Primeval Forest. A lot of remnants of distant past survived here, too...
Huh?
Mister director, some vandals carved signs in trees!
Hee-hee, you have a good eye, my boy.

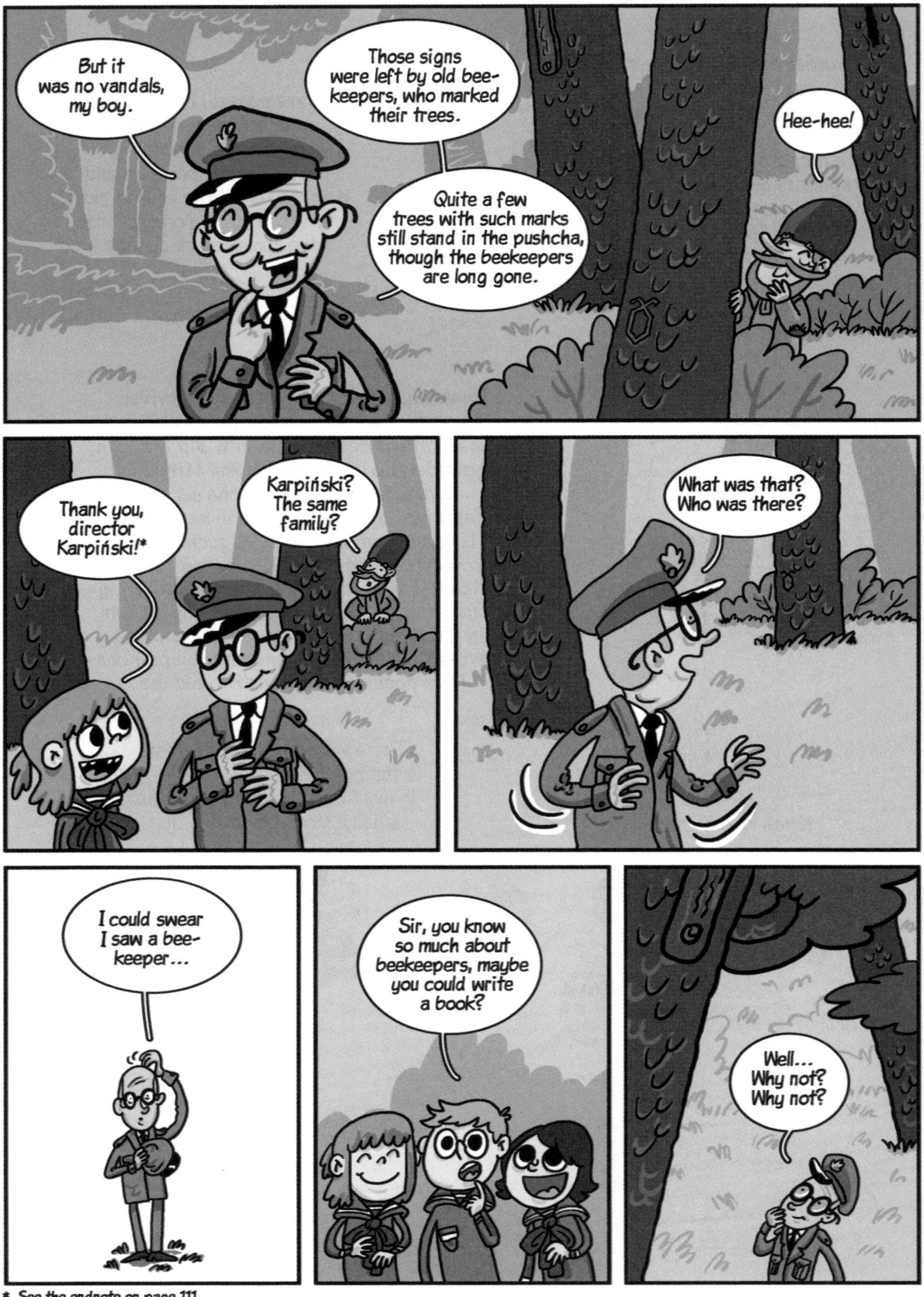
But it was no vandals, my boy.
Those signs were left by old bee-keepers, who marked their trees.
Quite a few trees with such marks still stand in the pushcha, though the beekeepers are long gone.
Hee-hee!
Thank you, director Karpiński!*
Karpiński? The same family?
What was that? Who was there?
I could swear I saw a bee-keeper...
Sir, you know so much about beekeepers, maybe you could write a book?
Well... Why not? Why not?

* See the endnote on page 111.

Notes

Białowieza Primeval Forest, located in the central Europe and straddling border between Poland and Belarus, is not a regular wood. It incorporates the last preserved fragments of primeval forests that once covered the vast lowlands of Europe. Those ancient forests - pushchas - were regulated by natural processes, and were enormously rich in plant and animal species.

As time passed, humans began to interfere with natural processes. Eventually, the settlement pressure and demand for timber erased most of those virgin forests from the European landscape.

Białowieza Primeval Forest has survived until now thanks to centuries-old conservation. Between the 14th and the 18th centuries, during the Polish and Lithuanian Commonwealth, the pushcha served as a hunting ground of Polish kings and Lithuanian grand dukes. As such, it was protected by beaters, riflemen and guards. Originally, their main duty was to help during royal hunts, yet those happened only seldom - in the time between hunts royal people fully devoted themselves to guarding the pushcha from poaching and unauthorized use.

There were more royal forests in the Polish-Lithuanian state, yet in most cases nothing more than a name survived to this day.

Kings who hunted here:

Władysław Jagiełło

Zygmunt Stary

Zygmunt August

Stefan Batory

Zygmunt III Waza

Władysław IV Waza

Jan Kazimierz Waza

August III Sas

Stanisław August Poniatowski

Samojlik T. (ed.) 2005. Conservation and hunting. Białowieza Forest in the time of kings. Mammal Research Institute PAS, Białowieza.

Notes

Even though Białowieża Primeval Forest was protected for centuries as a royal property, it was not closed for the public.

On the basis of special royal permissions, so called "access rights", or for a fee, the riches of the pushcha were available to royal forest servants, kings' lieges from villages on the border of the forest, local nobility, townspeople and clergy. They were allowed to use the forest in traditional ways, excluding timber felling but fulfilling a variety of people's needs at the time (therefore this utilisation is called "multifunctional").

Brushwood collecting.

Mushroom, herbs and forest fruits gathering.

Tearing strips of lime bark (bast) used by locals to produce bast shoes (called here "lapcie"), baskets, trugs, twines...

Torch wood collection. Singeing caused impregnation of pine trunks with resin. Wood chipped from such pines was used to kindle fire and as a source of light.

Livestock pasturing in the forest near villages and in the outer border of pushcha.

Additionally, lime was important in herbal medicine, its soft wood was used to produce vessels and furniture; also, bees used the nectar from its flowers to produce an excellent type of honey.

Samojlik T., Rotherham I., Jędrzejewska B. 2013. Quantifying historic human impacts on forest environments: a case study in Białowieża Forest, Poland. Environmental History 18(3): 576-602.

Notes

Utilisation of Białowieża Primeval Forest
on the basis of access rights
in the royal period encompassed mainly:

Haymaking, scything forest meadows, usually in river valleys. Hay was stored in huge haystacks and later transported to villages outside of the forest.

Fishing in forest rivers accompanied by the permission to erect small river dams.

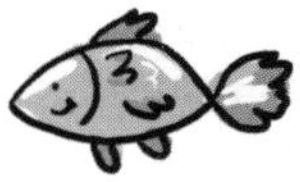

Sometimes such haystacks would stay in the pushcha for the entire year, serving as a perfect additional fodder for European bison!

Traditional beekeeping

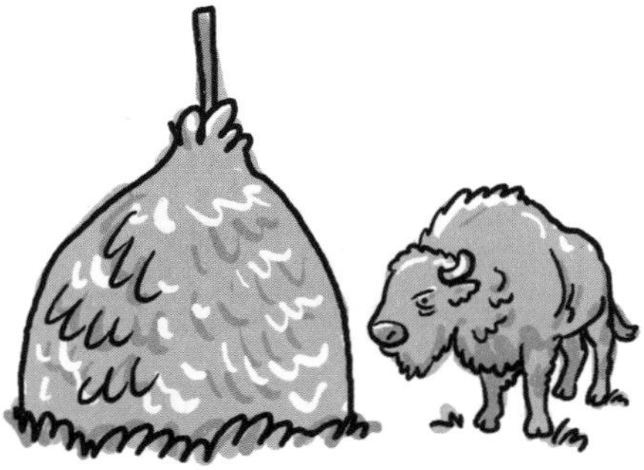

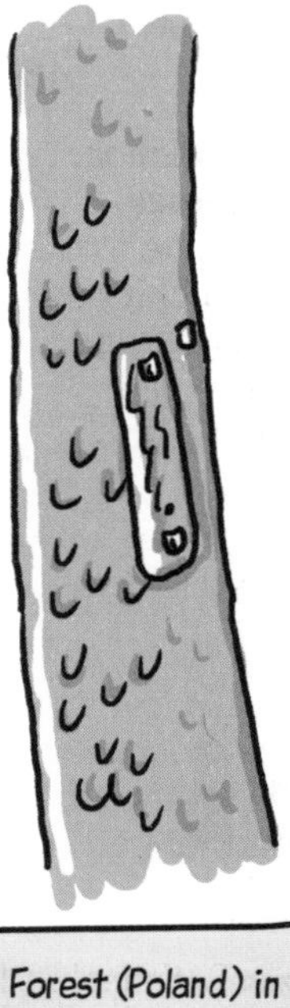

Regular scything enlarged the area of riverside meadows and created the specific landscape of wide river valleys.

Samojlik T. 2010. Traditional utilisation of Białowieża Primeval Forest (Poland) in the 15th to 18th centuries. Landscape Archaeology and Ecology 8: 150-164.

Notes

Traditional beekeeping involved carving beehives (artificial hollows) in trees, mainly pine, less often in lime or oak. Special herbal mixtures were then applied to beehives which attracted wild bees to settle there and produce honey and wax.

Beekeepers tended to bees and collected honey and wax using traditional equipment and complicated climbing techniques. Secrets of the beekeeping craft were passed from generation to generation.

Those were one of the most sought after and expensive forest products.

Beekeepers needed to protect beehives and apiaries on platforms in tree crowns from honey and bee larvae enthusiasts: brown bears, pine martens, forest dormice, woodpeckers, wasps and ants.

Apart from trees with beehives, other forms of traditional beekeeping were present in the pushcha: wooden platforms with hives on tree branches or beehives attached to tree trunks.

Like other traditional uses of the forest, beekeeping involved handling fire. According to research, small fires occurred very often in the pushcha in the 16th-18th centuries. Interestingly, they did not lead to destruction of the forest, quite the opposite - they contributed to the creation of a unique landscape of so called "lado forest", in which frequent burning left only old, thick barked pine trees. Nowadays, such landscapes do not exist.

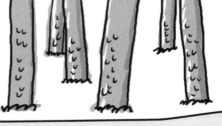

Traditional beekeeping persisted in Białowieża Primeval Forest until the second half of the 19th century.

Niklasson M. et al. 2010. A 350-year tree-ring fire record from Białowieża Primeval Forest, Poland: implications for Central European lowland fire history. Journal of Ecology 98(6): 1319-1329.

Notes

More destructive types of forest use - burning of wood and birch tar, potash and charcoal, or commercial timber felling - were introduced in Białowieża Primeval Forest in the second half of the 17th and in the 18th century, much later compared to adjacent forests.

Potash, produced from ash of deciduous trees, was an expensive commodity used for bleaching fabric and in glass, ceramics and soap production.

Wood tar was produced from pine wood, especially lower parts of trunks, and from roots. It was used as a grease (e.g. for wooden axles of carts), all-purpose glue, insulation (for barrels, boxes and boat hulls), leather and wood preservative, and also as a medicine.

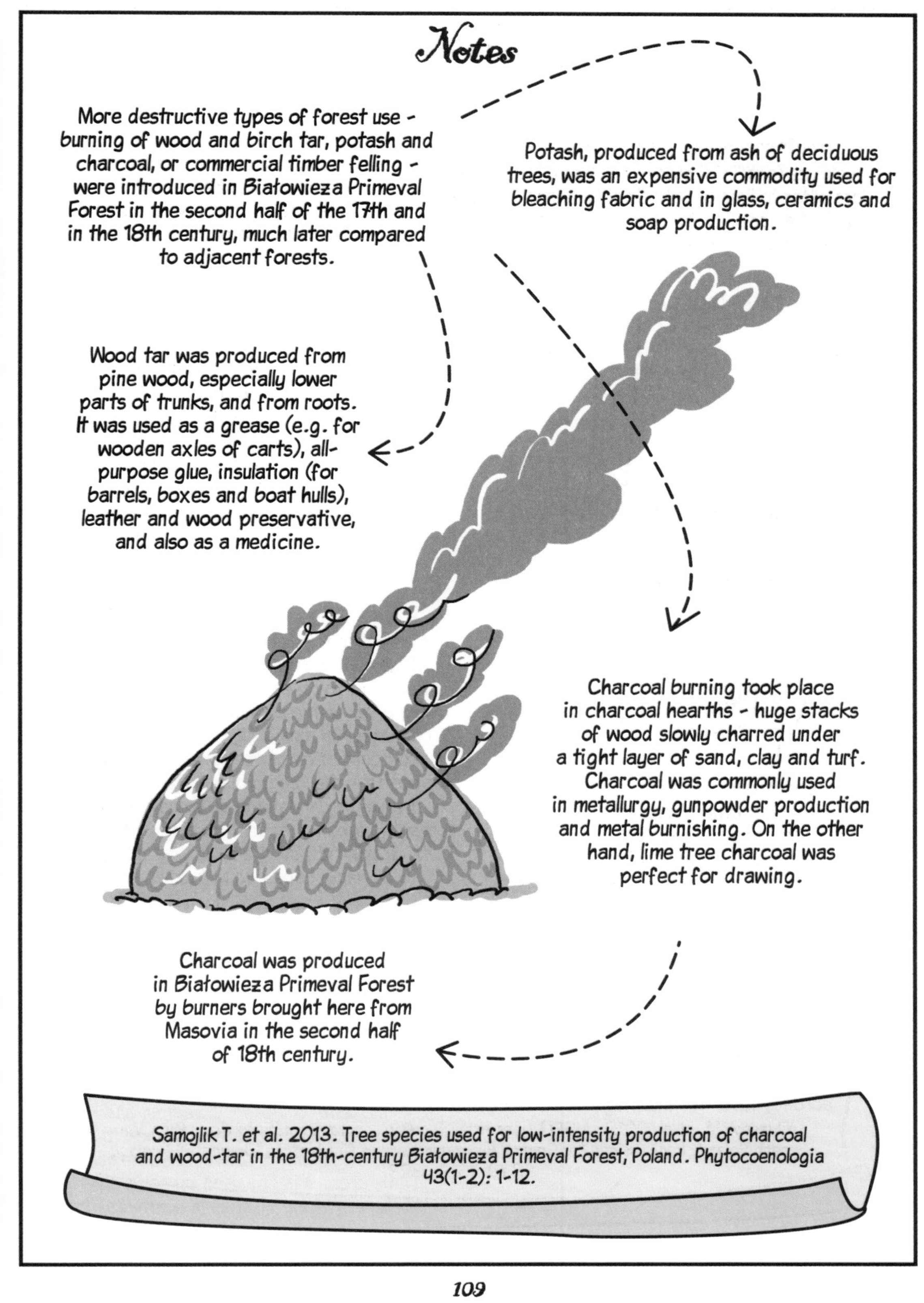

Charcoal burning took place in charcoal hearths - huge stacks of wood slowly charred under a tight layer of sand, clay and turf. Charcoal was commonly used in metallurgy, gunpowder production and metal burnishing. On the other hand, lime tree charcoal was perfect for drawing.

Charcoal was produced in Białowieża Primeval Forest by burners brought here from Masovia in the second half of 18th century.

Samojlik T. et al. 2013. Tree species used for low-intensity production of charcoal and wood-tar in the 18th-century Białowieża Primeval Forest, Poland. Phytocoenologia 43(1-2): 1-12.

Notes

In the years 1772-1795, Polish-Lithuanian state was gradually taken over by neighbouring countries (the so called partitions of Poland): Habsburg Austria, the Kingdom of Prussia, and the Russian Empire. At the end, the entire Białowieza Primeval Forest fell under the rule of the latter, causing a grave danger for the forest. All the kings' people - for generations engaged in protection of the forest - were suddenly deprived of their function and turned to serfs.

Additionally, Empress Catherine (Yekaterina) the Great gave one of the 13 forest districts to her favourite, count Pyotr Alexandrovich Rumyantsev (1725-1796), one of the most famous Russian generals.
In a matter of years, this part of the pushcha was completely deforested.

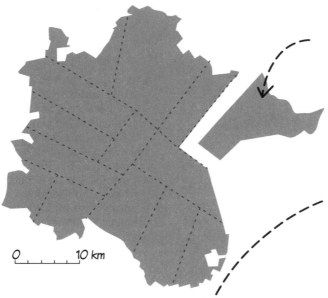

0 ⊢—⊢—⊢—⊢—⊢ 10 km

Fortunately, not everything was lost. In 1802, the new tsar - Alexander I - ordered to reinstate a part of the old forest personnel to their previous duties to protect the European bison, since Białowieza Primeval Forest was the last place where this animal still lived.

Traditional forms of forest use and conservation were nevertheless vanishing, especially after the fall of the Polish national uprising in 1831. Almost all guards and riflemen that took part in the uprising were killed or forced to flee abroad, never to return again.

What has not vanished, though, was the specific local culture, visible in the wooden architecture, embroidery, paper cutting, and language. Ignat the beekeeper sometimes uses single words or phrases taken directly from the local dialect of Białowieza Primeval Forest. The origins of this dialect, combining elements of Polish, Ukrainian and Belarussian languages, reach back to the very beginning of Slavonic settlement in this area. It is still used by some elderly dwellers of many villages in north-eastern Poland.

Notes

On the edge of the forest district given to count Rumyantsev, in a little village Kraśnik (nowadays in Belarus), lived one of the foremost Polish poets of the Enlightenment period: Franciszek Karpiński (1741-1825).

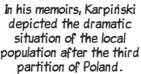

He is remembered for his sentimental and patriotic poems, as well as religious works (including the Christmas carol "God is born", sung to this day).

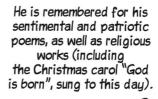

In his memoirs, Karpiński depicted the dramatic situation of the local population after the third partition of Poland.

After over a hundred years another member of the Karpiński family became prominent in the history of Białowieza Primeval Forest. Professor Jan Jerzy Karpiński (1896-1965) was a naturalist and an expert on pushcha's secrets, including traditional beekeeping. For many years, Karpiński served as the director of the Białowieza National Park.

Franciszek Karpiński was influenced by Jean-Jacques Rousseau's ideas of primacy of nature and freedom. Rousseau wrote a treatise on education, according to which a child should be raised in a close bond with nature, without disastrous effects of laws, orders and other strict rules imposed by society.

In Jean-Jacques Rousseau's biography, there is indeed a mention of his plans to move to Białowieza. In 1778, in return for his essay "Considerations on the Government of Poland" Antoni Tyzenhaus, the treasurer of the Grand Duchy of Lithuania, invited him to move to Białowieza Primeval Forest. Tyzenhaus promised to build a house according to Rousseau's wishes and to provide him with all the comforts. Everything was on the right track until some Polish troublemaker swindled money out of Rousseau. The angry philosopher abandoned the thought of moving to Białowieza.

Lucy, a granddaughter of Karpiński's sister, is mentioned in his memoirs, yet nothing is known about her possible stay in Białowieza Primeval Forest.

CENTRALA BOOKS

Adventures on a Desert Island by Maciej Sieńczyk

Blacky. Four of Us by Mateusz Skutnik

www.centrala.org.uk

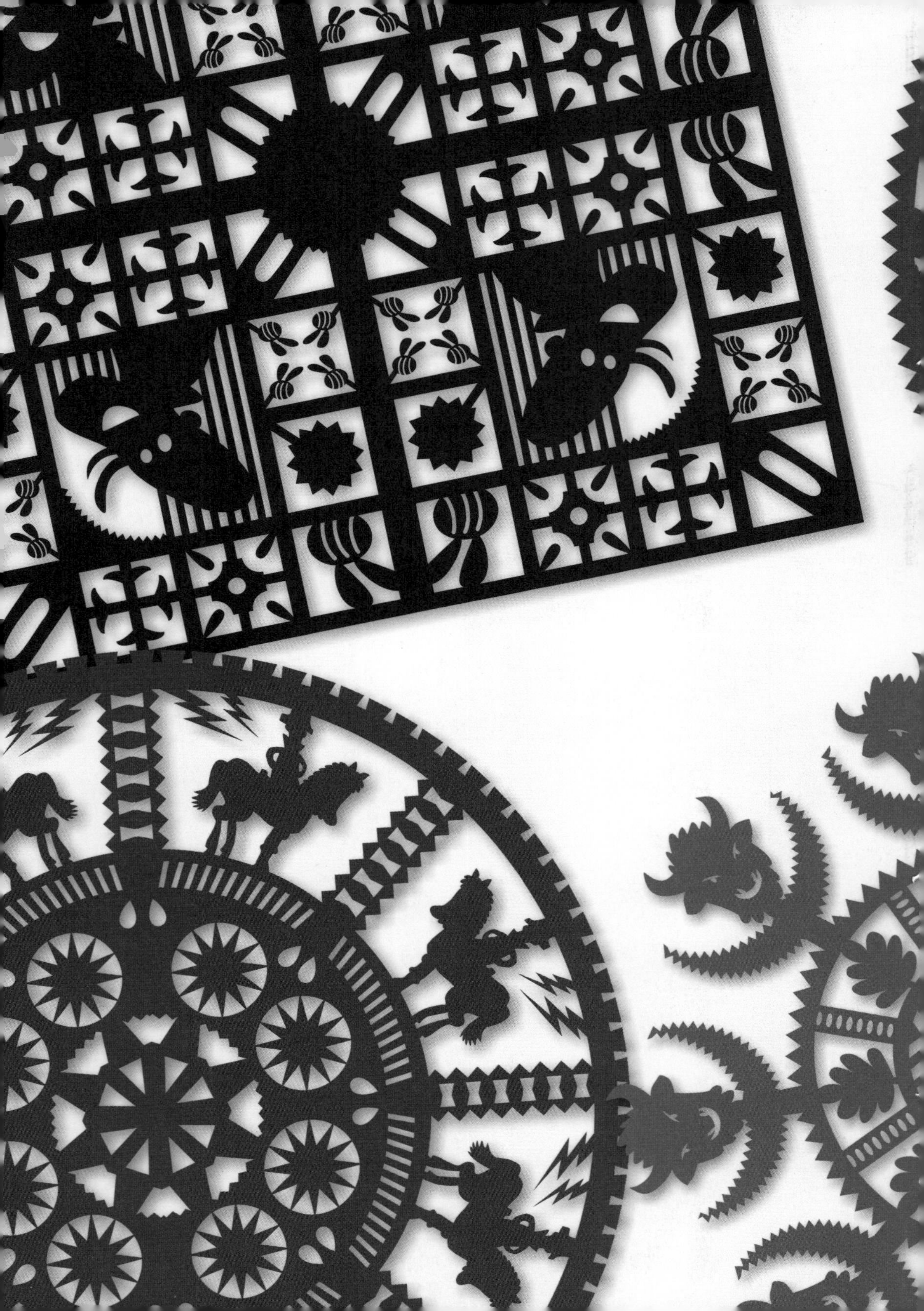